# 'I am twenty-nine years old, Sir Remy, and I have never been kissed…'

Remy squinted a look at Beatrice, the light slowly dawning.

'I can expect to live twenty, maybe thirty years as a nun. Alone. Unloved. I would like to know…that is…will you kiss me?'

He stared at her, silent.

'So that I may know what it is like,' she continued. 'And take that memory with me.'

He shook his head. 'I cannot oblige you. 'Twould be more than my life is worth. Your father—'

'He will never know! I promise. No one will know.'

'Nay.' He turned to go.

'Wait! Please. Just a kiss. 'Tis all I ask. I hear most men are willing to kiss maids...'

**Catherine March** was born in Zimbabwe. Her love of the written word began when she was ten years old and her English teacher gave her *Lorna Doone* to read. Encouraged by her mother, Catherine began writing stories as a teenager. Over the years her employment has varied from barmaid to bank clerk to legal secretary. Her favourite hobbies are watching rugby, walking by the sea, exploring castles and reading. She lives near to the site of the Battle of Hastings.

**Recent titles by the same author:**

MY LADY ENGLISH

# THE KNIGHT'S VOW

Catherine March

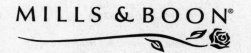

**MILLS & BOON**®

*First published in Great Britain 2004*
*Paperback edition 2005*
*Harlequin Mills & Boon Limited,*
*Eton House, 18-24 Paradise Road, Richmond, Surrey TW9 1SR*

© Catherine March 2004

ISBN 0 263 84352 1

*Set in Times Roman 10½ on 12½ pt.*
*04-0105-77171*

*Printed and bound in Spain*
*by Litografía Rosés S.A., Barcelona*

For Calvin, Bruce and David
With love

# Chapter One

*April 1277*

The wind howled and the rain drummed a steady beat against the shutters of Castle Ashton. In the great hall the most privileged knights of the household sat close to a fire glowing in the hearth, wide enough to burn logs the length of a man.

Some of the knights threw dice upon a game of chance, several talked earnestly about past heroics upon the battlefield, two played chess and one tried his luck with a pretty serf who had, thus far, eluded his pursuit.

A door banged above and the wooden stairs creaked as footsteps pounded down from the lord's solar on the first floor. The knights looked up, expectant, wary.

Lord Thurstan exuded a vibrant energy as he strode across the hall, despite his years of some two score and six. There was a touch of grey at his temples and threading through his thick brown beard, but his heavy body was still that of a warrior—in King Edward's army he held a high rank.

'Radley!'

'My lord?' Sir Giles Radley, second-in-command, leapt to his feet, his game of chess forgotten.

'On the morrow you will escort Lady Beatrice to the convent at Glastonbury. Take forty men-at-arms and,' he paused and looked around, eyes narrowed as he considered his twelve knights, 'take Grenville, Montgomery, Woodford, Fitzpons, and...Baldslow. Oh, and take young St Leger as well. 'Tis high time the boy earned his keep. And make haste, for we leave for Wales at the end of this week.'

The knights broke away from their idle pastimes and now crowded around Lord Thurstan, questions tripping eagerly over one another as they begged for news of the Welsh campaign.

'So Edward is determined to conquer Llewelyn ap Gruffydd, and make him rue the day he ever refused to pay homage?' asked Sir Hugh Montgomery.

'Aye.' Lord Thurstan accepted a goblet of wine, 'The king has set his sights on Gwynedd and naught, neither reason nor argument, will deter him.'

Their discussion upon the merits and means of forcing the Welsh into submission went on well into the night. Those who had an early start on the morrow drifted away to bedrolls before the warm hearth. One hovered at Lord Thurstan's elbow—Cedric Baldslow, a man who matched his lord in age, his square, solid frame not yet running to fat, his face well worn and tanned to the hue and texture of saddle leather, his greying head shaved. His thin mouth and narrow eyes reflected the portrait of a hard man, a man Lord Thurstan valued only as a knight who could, and would, fight hard in any battle.

'My lord,' said Sir Cedric softly, 'the Lady Beatrice…' he hesitated and Lord Thurstan looked painfully away, knowing full well what was to come next '…she is determined to take holy vows?'

'Aye. That she is. The girl would be a nun and there is no one who can change her mind.'

Cedric clutched urgently at his lord's sleeve, almost desperate, as he pleaded, 'You cannot sanction it, for the love of God! Persuade her, my lord, to accept me and I will make her a fine husband.'

Thurstan snorted and took a deep gulp of his wine, before slamming down the cup in a way that brooked no further argument. He could not tell Cedric that not only did he neither like nor trust him and would not give his only daughter in marriage to such a man, but that Beatrice herself had made it clear that she neither liked nor trusted not only Cedric, but any man.

'The girl is twenty-nine years old,' said Thurstan gruffly. ''Tis her own decision. Now, I am off to bed. Fare thee well, Cedric, and I entrust you to deliver Beatrice safely to the Abbess at Glastonbury.'

In her chamber Beatrice knelt upon the floor and carefully folded her garments into a coffer made of oak and bound with strips of iron. Between the layers she slid in her personal possessions: Bible, hairbrush, sewing kit, a brooch, shoes, soap, writing paper, quills and ink.

A soft tap upon the door made her pause, and look up, as her father came in. He folded his arms over his broad chest and surveyed the stripped room and the open coffer, now almost full to the brim.

'It is done,' he said, abruptly. 'Radley will escort you on the morrow to Glastonbury.'

'Thank you, Father.' Beatrice lowered her eyes, hands clasped, searching for words.

'Come here, girl.' Her father opened his arms and she ran to him, laying her head upon the barrel of his chest, her small hands clutching at his tunic. He stroked her hair, noting that its honey colour was so like her mother's. 'I have no argument with your decision. My only disappointment is that you will never know the joy of being a wife and a mother—' he held up a hand, hushing her protest '—but as I am away to Wales, to march with your brothers and the king's army, 'tis just as well you go now to the nuns. God alone knows if I shall return, and I would have not a moment's peace to think of you here alone at Ashton.'

'Oh, Father, you will return safely! I shall pray every day for you, for Hal and Osmond, and for all our knights who go to Wales.'

With a smile her father smoothed the soft golden-brown head laid against his chest, his other hand patting her shoulder. 'You are a good girl, Beatrice. Just like your mother, God rest her soul.' And with that he set her aside and left her alone to finish her packing.

It was her thoughts that occupied Beatrice, more than her packing. She could not deny that she was filled with sadness at the prospect of leaving her home, yet since her mother had died two months ago the empty space she had left only reminded Beatrice more acutely that her life had little meaning and no purpose.

How hard it had become to rise each day and trudge through her dreary routine of chores! To deal with petty domestic problems and conflicts between the serfs, when inside of her there ached a loneliness that could never be fulfilled. At least in the convent she would have the company of the nuns, and a tranquil life spent in prayer and devotion to a being whom she loved more dearly than any man.

The morning dawned cold, pearl-white with mist, a soft rain dripping from the trees and rooftops. Beatrice broke her fast early, alone in her room, having first attended mass in the castle chapel. Finishing her last crust of bread and cheese, Beatrice summoned her maid, Elwyn, who came at once and began to brush her mistress's hair with long, slow strokes, her face glistening with silent tears.

'Come now, Elwyn,' chided Beatrice gently, taking away the brush and laying it back in her coffer, ''tis not the end of the world.'

'Oh, my lady,' Elwyn sobbed, 'do not go! 'Tis not right, for one so young and lovely to shut herself away with those old crones.'

Beatrice clucked her tongue in disapproval, 'I am neither young, nor lovely, nor the nuns of St Jude "old crones". Be happy for me, Elwyn, for 'tis a great honour to be accepted and I go to live a life of tranquillity, devoted to our Lord in prayer.' With a smile she wiped Elwyn's cheeks with her sleeve, 'You have been looking after me since I was twelve years old, and well you have done it. But shall you not be glad now for the respite? Mayhap you should marry. Goodness knows Big Al the blacksmith has asked you enough times.'

'Oh, I am too old for all that nonsense.' Elwyn sniffed, and with a valiant effort set about braiding Beatrice's hair, fastening on her cloak and lacing her boots. Reluctantly, she accepted a final embrace, helped Beatrice lock her coffer and accompanied her downstairs to the hall.

The serfs were lined up, waiting, and Beatrice clasped hands with each one, with a murmur of thanks and best wishes for the future, until she came at last to her father. He tucked her arm in his and led her out of the wide main door and on to the steps. Beatrice resisted the temptation to look back, blinking away the sudden and unexpected tears. She had not thought to be so anguished at this final parting; indeed, she had imagined it would be a relief to be leaving after all the long, lonely years, but at this moment she only felt awash with sadness.

In the bailey horses champed on their bits, stamped and snorted, tails swishing as girths were tightened. The air rang with clanking swords, jingling spurs, and the deep voices of men as they made final preparations for an important task—to protect their baron's daughter from all harm.

For the knights a journey to Glastonbury would take scarce a day, but to accommodate Lady Beatrice they would ride at a more leisurely pace, and spend the night at an inn along the way. Nothing would be left to chance and the knights, well trained and well prepared, took seriously the task entrusted to them.

A groom led Beatrice's horse forward, a pretty

chestnut mare of mature years, dependable if not swift. Beatrice stroked Willow's soft pink nose, delaying the moment when she must make her final farewell to her father. His hand laid upon her shoulder and she looked up with a wan smile.

'I can come with you,' he offered, hopefully.

Beatrice shook her head, flung her arms around his waist and hugged him tight. Tears crowded her throat, but she shook her head again. 'Nay, Father. 'Tis far better if I go alone. Otherwise I might never have the courage to leave you.'

'One way or another,' he whispered against her temple, 'you will always be with me. Here.' His meaty fist struck his heart.

They hugged one another for some long moments, and then Lord Thurstan broke away, cleared his throat with a gruff cough, and boosted Beatrice up into the saddle of her mare. She reached down and clasped his fingers.

'Farewell, Father. May God be with you.'

'Farewell, my little Beatrice. Remember, if all is not well, you have only to send word.'

Beatrice smiled softly. 'I will not forget, Father. And give my love to Hal and Osmond when you see them.'

With raised hands they saluted one another and then Beatrice turned her horse about and followed the seven knights, who rode close about her. Their hoofbeats drummed loudly across the wooden drawbridge, followed by the forty men-at-arms, all mounted and well armoured with swords, bows, spears and shields.

The day brightened and the sun peeped through the

clouds, lifting Beatrice out of her sombre mood. She could not recall ever hearing birdsong so sweet, as it came now from the larks and starlings, nor seen elder and hawthorn trees blossom so prettily. The hedgerows were full of yellow pepper saxifrage and evening primrose, interspersed with the bright blue of periwinkle and the ramblings of pink-and-white wild dogroses. The slope of the land appeared magnificent to her eye as hill and dale spread about her in a great vista.

Amidst the constant creak and rattle of leather and armour, the talk of men all around her, there was little peace to enjoy the beauty of this, her last day of freedom. She admonished herself inwardly, trying to uphold the view that she should not consider her commitment to the church to be an end, but a new and wonderful beginning.

And yet...

Cedric Baldslow nudged his destrier alongside Willow and persisted in his attempts to engage Beatrice in conversation. If her smile seemed more aloof than the smile she gave to others, he did not appear to notice. Arrogantly he was confident of his charms, convinced that the lass needed only persuasion to accept his troth. The fact that she had rejected him three times already seemed not to trouble him at all.

At last Sir Giles Radley, seeing her predicament, sent Baldslow away on an errand to the rear of the column, to check on the cart bearing Beatrice's coffer. She smiled her thanks as Sir Giles rode alongside, and to fill an awkward moment, she asked him, 'Who is the tall young man with the ash-blond hair?'

'That is Remy St Leger, my lady, son of an old friend of your father's who married a countess of Aquitaine. Both his parents have died recently and his elder brother holds the family estate. He has a reputation in France for being one of the finest swordsmen and has done well, very well, in tournaments.'

'I cannot say I have ever noticed him at Ashton.'

'He has been at Hepple Hill, your father's estate in Wessex, training the new men-at-arms who will go with us to Wales. He arrived at Ashton but two days ago. Besides, with the death of your lady mother only two months past—' they both crossed themselves '—I am sure your father has taken great pains to keep a hot young blood like Remy St Leger far distant from his pretty, virg…um…virtuous daughter.'

A flush of pink stained Beatrice's cheeks, but still she laughed, softly. 'Oh come, Sir Giles, I am an old maid. A "hot young blood" would certainly have no time to waste on me!'

Sir Giles looked at her, with a frown, once again amazed that she did not know her own worth. 'My lady, neither beauty nor love knows the limit of age.'

For a moment he surveyed her heart-shaped face, dainty upturned nose, dark brown eyes with thick, long lashes, soft pink mouth and buttermilk skin. ''Tis the church's gain and our great loss tomorrow, my lady.'

Beatrice stiffened in the saddle and looked away. She could not bear any more arguments against the path she had chosen, for she feared that far too easily she could be persuaded to return home. Quickly she searched for another topic. 'Sir Giles, why has my father taken this Remy St Leger into our household?'

'Because he is a fighter, my lady, a warrior, and we have need of such men, going into Wales.'

'I see.' Beatrice surveyed the broad shoulders of the young man they discussed, a frown creasing her brow, 'He can surely not be very old.'

'He is four and twenty and was knighted in his first battle at the age of sixteen. From a distance he may not seem very old, but if you look into his eyes, you will see a man full grown and wise with experience. They say he has killed over two hundred men.'

Beatrice shuddered. 'I think it is very sad, Sir Giles, that young men have become old before their time because of war.'

''Tis the way of the world, my lady.' Lest her curiosity about the Aquitaine become too avid, Sir Giles steered the conversation elsewhere and made comment upon the weather.

Later that afternoon Woodford and a party of ten men-at-arms were sent on ahead, with a pouch of silver coins, to secure a room for Lady Beatrice at the Red Lion inn. The men would sleep in tents in a nearby field, whilst the seven knights—Radley, Grenville, Montgomery, Woodford, Fitzpons, Baldslow and St Leger—would sleep in the common room and take turns to guard Lady Beatrice's door throughout the night. Not for one moment would she ever be undefended.

Storm clouds broke towards dusk and it rained heavily. By the time Beatrice reached the Red Lion she was soaked through to the skin. The downpour was so heavy that the yard of the inn was transformed into a quagmire and the men trudged ankle-deep in mud. There was much shouting as Radley, Baldslow and Montgomery steered the men-at-arms into their makeshift field quarters, Grenville and Fitzpons took charge of her coffer and Beatrice looked helplessly about for assistance. Her eyes encountered a fiercely blue male gaze and, instinctively, her own dropped. But Remy St Leger dismounted and was striding through the mud to Willow. He reached up, seized Beatrice about the waist and hauled her down from the saddle, carrying her easily across the yard to the inn. He slipped once, and with a small cry Beatrice clutched at his shoulders, feeling beneath her fingers the bulk of his muscular frame. His eyes flashed at her, with a mocking smile. He jiggled her weight closer against his chest and held her more tightly as they continued their precarious journey.

Within the flagstoned doorway of the inn he set her down upon her feet and Beatrice had to tilt her head back to look up at him, for he was very tall.

'Thank you,' she murmured and, remembering her conversation with Sir Giles, looked into his eyes. And backed away. His features were indeed handsome and pleasing, but Remy St Leger was not the sort of man that a maiden would trifle with.

Despite several attempts by the landlord to ingratiate himself with Lady Beatrice of Ashton, he saw nothing more than the top of her head, as she was swept upstairs to the finest chamber in the house, surrounded by five knights who seemed gigantic and armed to the teeth.

Beatrice breathed a sigh of relief as she was shown

into her chamber for the night. It was small, compared to her own room at home, but more than adequate for one night. There was a four-poster bed hung with dark blue damask, a roaring fire, two chairs placed before the hearth, a table set with plates of food and a flagon of wine. The windows were well shuttered and Beatrice flung off her sodden cloak, draping it over the back of a chair. A tap at the door made her pause as she reached to pull off her boots.

'Come in.'

Sir Giles entered, bearing a large pitcher of steaming water, followed closely by Sir Hugh carrying a bowl. They placed both on the hearth before the fire, checked the supply of logs, food and wine, and then turned to Beatrice with a deep bow.

'Is there anything else my lady requires?' asked Sir Giles.

'Nay, thank you. I have everything I need.' Rubbing her aching backside, with a rueful grin, she added, 'I will sleep like a babe this night.'

'You will not be disturbed, my lady.'

They left her then and Beatrice knew there was no need to bar the door, for there would be a guard all night long. Returning to the hearth, she stripped off her clothes and boots and stood naked to wash. The water was deliciously hot, but the room wasn't and Beatrice finished quickly, reaching to wrap a blanket around her while she fumbled in her saddlebag and drew out her nightshift. Long-sleeved and tied about the neck with a silk ribbon, she warmed the garment before the fire flames, then slid it quickly on. Sitting in a chair, feet curled beneath her, Beatrice took her time unbraiding her hair and smoothing it out with her fingers.

Then she ate some of the hearty fare laid out for her—chicken and ham pie, roasted capon, fresh white bread and crumbly Leicester cheese, plum cake and spiced apples—but, inevitably, there came a time when she could no longer busy herself. She sat idly, staring at the fire, alone with her thoughts. Very alone. The reality of tomorrow suddenly came upon her and she was swamped with fear and doubt.

Her father's words echoed again and again within the confines of her mind—'...you will never know the joy of being a wife and a mother.' With a sigh Beatrice rose from the chair and padded barefoot across the wooden floor to the bed, pulling back the covers.

For a moment she surveyed the broad expanse of mattress, set with two pillows. A bed made to accommodate two people. Husband and wife. Lovers. Tears pricked her eyes. She climbed in and lay down, drawing up her knees into the warmth of her own body and away from the cold linen. After a while she turned on to her back, staring up at the ruched canopy.

Why? she wondered. Twenty-nine years old and she could find no man worthy enough to claim her love, loyalty and respect. Always she found fault with the men who pursued her hand, for there had been no shortage of offers. Of course, now she was too old. Except for obnoxious Baldslow the offers had dwindled away to nothing.

When she had been sixteen she had been betrothed to a young man that Beatrice had found acceptable in every way, but William de Warenne, a respected

knight, handsome and brave, had been killed. The pain
of his death still ached in her breast and she wondered
if she had truly ever recovered from his loss. Her
mother had warned her against holding on to a love
that was long gone, that its grip would become so
fierce that she would never be able to love again.

Many years had passed since that anguished time,
but time had not erased the pain completely. It was
dull, but not gone. Mayhap she should reconsider
Baldslow. He was old, but experience and wisdom
were not to be scorned. Beatrice cringed, however, at
the thought of his rough, scarred hands touching her,
and here she came to the crux of the matter. She could
not give her body to a man she did not love. The mere
thought made goosebumps rise upon her flesh.

She had raged furiously over William's death and
laid the blame at only one door—God's. After a time
she had been ashamed and guilt-ridden, taking as penance a pious devotion to God and the church that her
parents had questioned and misliked, but had been unable to alter.

Beatrice turned over onto her side, a dozen thoughts
jostling for favour. With a low, frustrated moan she
flung back the covers and sat up. If only she had
thought to pack her Bible close to hand, instead of in
her coffer, then she would be able to read, until her
mind was soothed and she fell asleep.

She left the bed and poured a goblet of wine, taking
it and a wedge of plum cake to sit before the fire. She
wondered what her father would be doing now; no
doubt dining, as she was, and packing his gear for the

venture to Wales. And tomorrow, tomorrow she would be at the convent.

The fire warmed her and Beatrice glanced down at her feet, peeping out beneath the long hem of her nightshift. William had said she had pretty feet, on that one occasion by the river when he had found her paddling in the cool water, and had almost kissed her. Almost. Within a few days he had ridden off to war, and within a few weeks more he was dead.

Beatrice wondered, as she munched on the sweet crumbly cake, what it would be like to be kissed by a man. Her mother had always complained that her father's beard tickled and Beatrice thought she would prefer a face cleanshaven. Into her thoughts intruded the image of a handsome male face, with bright blue eyes and dark blond hair long at the neck. Remy St Leger. She could not recall how his mouth had been, but she was certain he had no beard.

Eventually Beatrice went back to bed and, at last, fell asleep. But it was not for long. She woke again, and the night was dark and still. The logs had burned down to ruby embers. She lay for a long while, listening to the sigh of the wind rustling in the treetops, the creak of roof beams, an owl hooting. She snuggled down deeper into the warmth of the bed, meagre as it was, and then she thought it might be wise to pile on a few more logs to keep the fire going until morning.

She padded silently across the floor, lit a candle and reached for a log, laying it carefully in the grate, and then another. She found a poker and stirred up the embers, and then jumped back with an exclamation as the topmost log rolled and scattered tiny burning coals upon the hearth. One hit her foot and she yelped with pain.

At once the door flung open. A knight charged into the room, his sword half-drawn, looking about him with eyes narrowed in question.

'Be at ease, sir,' Beatrice called, and then gasped as she turned and faced Remy St Leger, her voice sinking to an uncertain whisper. 'There is no one here who does me harm, except my own foolish self.'

His glance took in the fallen log and the poker in her hand, but not before he noticed how the firelight silhouetted her slender body through the fine white linen of her nightshift. He noticed, too, that her hair fell unbound in a ripple of glorious honey to her hips. With a hiss his sword was rammed home in its scabbard and he strode across the room, knelt to retrieve the log smouldering on the hearth and to place it back in the grate. Looking up at her, he held out his hand until she relinquished the poker.

Beatrice stepped to one side, watching his broad back, the taut line of muscular thigh and buttocks as he knelt to tend the fire. She felt a heat of colour sweep over her cheeks. Then he turned and, taking her elbow, indicated that she should sit down.

A man of few words, thought Beatrice, complying, mystified at his intention. She flinched as his fingers touched her, and he lifted her foot into the palm of his hand. As he examined it carefully, his action caused her nightshift to slide up to her knees. Quickly Beatrice snatched at the hem and pulled it down to cover her legs. By the flick of his eyes she knew that he had noticed her reaction; then she was startled by the sound of his voice when he spoke, in clear English charmingly accented by his native French, the timbre of it finding a place deep within her soul.

'I will fetch a little goose-grease and a bandage.'

'There is no need!' Beatrice leapt quickly from the chair. Too quickly. Her knee connected with his chin and a resounding crack echoed about the room, 'Oh, I am sorry! Are you all right?'

He regained his balance by grasping the chair, trapping Beatrice between his spread knees and arms. She looked down at his ash-blond head, breath tensely held, for she had never been so close to a man, and was acutely aware that she wore nothing but her nightshift. He rubbed his chin, and then rose slowly, his full height dwarfing Beatrice, who barely reached to his collarbone.

'I have taken worse than a tap from a maiden's knee,' he said, hands on hips, smiling down at her in a way that was almost insolent.

Beatrice had nowhere to retreat, standing so close to him and with the chair against the back of her knees. She sensed the impropriety of their position and would have been further outraged if she had known that from his vantage-point of greater height he could see down through the open neck of her shift, and his eyes fell upon the soft swell of her breasts.

Beatrice found it hard to believe that this man was a full five years younger than she. It was she who felt the awkward youth. She glanced up at him, and in that moment saw for herself where his eyes lingered. Quickly, with a clumsy trip, she stepped over his boots and presented him with her back as she clutched at one ornately carved bedpost, suddenly feeling a little dizzy. In a voice cool as ice, she said, 'You may go.'

His footsteps thumped across the floor, and then she heard the snap of the door as it shut. Whirling round, Beatrice let out a gasp and stared at the dark planks of the solid oak door. How dared he! The insolent knave! Her father would most certainly hear of this!

Then Beatrice remembered that she would not see her father come morning, that mayhap she would not see him for many months, and that she would soon be committing herself to life as a nun. Remy St Leger would be the last man ever to look upon her in such a way, as a man looks upon a woman.

*Did he like what he had seen?* Her hands flew to both hot cheeks, horrified at the sinfulness of her thoughts. His mouth had been wellshaped and not too wide, his jaw cleanshaven…

No! No! Beatrice ran to the bed and dived beneath the covers, pulling them over her head. In the muffling darkness her gasps for breath sounded like the panting of a wild animal. Her body felt different—her breasts ached, her legs felt weak. The male smell of him was still in her nose. He seemed to have invaded her every sense, every pore… One part of her sternly berated Beatrice for being a weak human being, another cajoled that she was only as God had made her—a woman.

*What would it feel like to lie in his arms? To feel his hard, muscular body moving against her softness?* Heat flooded her and through all her thoughts pounded one drumbeat—tomorrow, tomorrow, tomorrow.

Beatrice was certain that she would have only this

one night to learn of things that would never be a part of her life. Why, she had never been kissed, let alone bedded! What harm would it do? She would still go to the nunnery a chaste virgin, except for one kiss. That was all she wanted. All she asked. And Remy St Leger would be the one to kiss her, Beatrice decided impulsively. No doubt the 'hot young blood' would not cavil, and even if he did she would remind him of his sworn duty to Lord Thurstan and his family to do as he was told!

Throwing back the covers, Beatrice leapt out of bed and hurried to the door. Her hand reached out to open it, and then drew back, checked by her natural sense of caution. She turned away, chewing on her knuckles, pacing, darting many glances at the impervious door, a frown creasing her brows.

*Tomorrow, tomorrow, tomorrow…* Resolutely, she turned back and quickly jerked open the door, before she could change her mind again.

He sat opposite upon a three-legged stool, leaning his back and broad shoulders against the wall. In one hand he held a dagger, in the other a whetstone. Looking up, pausing in his task, he eyed her with one brow raised in question, before bending once again to sharpen the dangerous blade.

'I wish to speak with you.'

He looked up. 'My lady?'

'Privately. In my chamber.'

Again the stone rasped along the gleaming steel. 'I think not.'

'At once, Sir Remy!' Beatrice resisted the temptation to stamp her foot. She had no wish to appear any more of a child that she already did.

'Very well. 'Tis late and I would not wish your voice to waken the entire inn.'

Beatrice flushed painfully at his censure and then stepped back as he rose from the stool and came into her chamber. She closed the door and moved past him, to stand before the fire, with her back to him.

'My lady?' prompted Remy, hands on hips, enjoying her silhouette and knowing full well that he should not be here alone with her.

'As you know, I am on my way to join the nuns of St Jude.'

'Aye.'

'I will dedicate my life to God.'

He bowed, in silent acknowledgement of her great sacrifice.

'I…' she hesitated '…of course I am…' again she could not say the words '…I go…chaste. Untouched.'

Remy St Leger shifted uncomfortably, staring at his boots, wondering where this strange conversation was leading. He took a step backwards, to the door.

'I am twenty-nine years old, Sir Remy, and I have never been kissed. Properly. By a man. Not a relative. If you know what I mean.'

He squinted a look at her, the light suddenly dawning.

'I can expect to live twenty, maybe thirty, years as a nun. Alone. Unloved. I would like to know…that is…will you kiss me?'

He stared at her, silent.

'So that I may know what it is like. And take that memory with me.'

He shook his head. 'I cannot oblige you. 'Twould be more than my life is worth. Your father—'

'He will never know! I promise. No one will know.'

'Nay.' He turned to go.

'Wait! Please. I will grant you any favour in the future, and use what influence I have with my father in granting such favour, should needs be. Please. Just a kiss, 'tis all I ask. I hear men are most willing to kiss maids.'

With his back to her he smiled, and then wiped that smile from his face before turning round to face her, looking her up and down with a penetrating stare that made her heart beat faster. He walked slowly across the room and stopped when he was but a sword's length away from her.

'Mayhap you are not aware that a kiss can lead to other things. Things which you know nought of.'

'I am aware of what a kiss can lead to.'

He controlled his surprise and met her eyes stare for stare. Of course, even though she was so small and looked so young, she was not. No shrinking violet, this maiden. Was she even truly a maiden? he wondered.

Beatrice dropped her gaze to her fingers, twisted one around to the other against her chest. 'I shall rely upon your honour as a knight to make sure that…we… you…shall refrain from… that.'

He laughed then and closed the space between them. Boldly he laid his hands about her waist. 'There is no need to be coy. We both know what it is you want. One last tumble before donning your habit?'

'What!' His hands upon her were a new experience, yet his blunt words astonished her even more.

'Surely you do not expect me to believe that a woman of your age has never been bedded?'

'Nay! I have not.'

His eyes challenged her, and she glared back.

'Very well. My lady commands a kiss, so a kiss my lady shall receive.' He closed the space between them and she gasped as his hands slid up along the curve of her ribs, slowly traced the outline of her breasts and then travelled over her delicate shoulders. His fingers lingered on the line of her collarbone, so fragile, and then he slid his hands up into her hair and cradled her head.

Beatrice felt her breath stop in her throat and she stared up at him, wide eyed. His shoulders stooped, his body solid and warm against her, and then his head descended and she closed her eyes, waiting. She felt the warmth of his breath and then the cool touch of his lips on her lips. Her hands slid between them, resting on his chest, leaning on him for support. He held her gently while his mouth moved on hers and he persuaded her lips to part for him.

A shock of surprise shivered through her body as his tongue slid into her mouth, moist and hot. He tasted her, savoured, and his jaw moved more quickly. He lifted his head and slanted his mouth the other way over hers, his kiss driving harder and deeper. Their mingled breath came in pants and Beatrice felt sheer excitement flood through her body.

With a whimper her hands moved up his chest and slid around his neck. He groaned, his own hands sliding down to her buttocks and grinding her into the hard bulk of his arousal. They kissed, again and again, and then, without releasing her mouth from the possession of his, he picked her up, swinging her feet off the floor and carrying her to the bed. He laid her down, and himself alongside her. For a long while he did nothing more than continue to kiss her, with hungry urgency.

Beatrice surrendered herself to the most wonderful sensations she had ever felt. The feel of his mouth, the taste of him, the male aroma of him, the heavy muscles of his body, all were new to her. Exciting. Intoxicating. The flood of excitement had welled up so deep within her, and expanded, straining for release in some strange way that she could not fathom, that she made a small noise in her throat, turning to him for guidance.

Hearing this familiar female sound of melting, he smiled to himself and he became bolder. His thigh slid between her knees and his hand found her nipple.

Beatrice opened her eyes and stared at him. She knew that she should not let him touch her in such a way, but it felt so glorious, and her lashes fluttered down with a strangled moan.

Then suddenly his hand moved away from her breast and she felt a sense of loss. Her eyes snapped open again and she looked up at him, and then gasped as he found the hem of her gown and lifted it up to expose her lower body, naked to his touch.

Her cry was lost inside his mouth. She did not dare

to move and held herself tensely still, but as his hand slid between her knees and travelled along the silken warmth of her slender legs she shook her head, broke their kiss, and she cried out, 'Nay! You must stop!'

'Why?' he asked, in a hoarse whisper. 'No one will know whether you are a virgin or not.'

'I will know! God will know!'

His thumb stroked the soft curve of her outer thigh and he gazed at her with lazy amusement, his voice husky as he stated, 'I want you.'

'Nay, it cannot be!'

'You could not stop me, if I wanted to take you now.' He squeezed her thigh with his fingers, demonstrating to her his strength as the hard muscles of his arms flexed and rippled.

'Please,' she gasped, 'please do not shame me.'

Suddenly he released her, withdrew, and she felt cold air as he levered himself up off the bed, the four-poster creaking at his sudden movement. Beatrice sat up, quickly pulling down the hem of her nightshift to cover her nakedness, and leapt to her feet. She rushed at him and made a move to strike his face, but he was too tall and too quick, and checked her, grabbing her wrist in mid-air.

'You have broken your oath of honour,' she accused in an agonised whisper.

He blinked, with surprise, 'I have done naught, except kiss you. At your request. I see nothing dishonourable in that.'

Every line of her body was taut with tension. 'You should not have touched me...there.'

He laughed then. 'If I had touched you "there",

instead of just upon your lovely little thighs, you would not now be making protest but crying out your joy as I possessed you.'

Beatrice gasped and flushed scarlet at his explicit words. 'Go, for I was vastly mistaken to believe that you are a chivalrous knight.'

The light in his eyes flared with anger at her accusation. He stooped and covered her mouth with a kiss so sweet and tender that it left her reeling as he released her wrist and strode to the door. He turned and looked back at her for a moment before issuing his dark warning, 'Kittens should not play with lions.'

# Chapter Two

The convent of St Jude was situated in Northload Street and backed onto the manor house of the Abbot of Glastonbury. The nuns leased ten acres from Abbot John, and from this small parcel of land eked out sufficient food so as to provide enough for their community to live upon, rarely having to resort to buying anything from the market. There were three cows to be milked, a half-dozen sheep for mutton and wool, twenty chickens for eggs and meat, fish ponds and a thriving vegetable garden that yielded carrots, turnips, swedes, onions and herbs. There were apple and pear trees and also two acres of vines. The convent buildings themselves consisted of a hall, known as the refectory, where the nuns ate; a parlour, where Sister Huberta had her desk and went about the business of correspondence and discipline; a large kitchen, which faced on to the vegetable gardens to the rear, adjoined by the buttery. Below stairs there was a cellar, and eight sleeping chambers above stairs. Central to all, of course, was the chapel, ensconced within the body of the convent, so that there was easy access at all hours of the day and night.

A great deal of hard work was required by all to keep this little farm going, and Sister Huberta, Abbess, made sure that she wrung every last ounce out of every last nun, twenty-five in all, excluding the Abbess and the novices.

It was Tuesday, market day, and so large a party as the Ashton cavalcade attracted some attention as they entered the town from the south, along Chilkwell Street, and then turned to clatter up the High Street. Beatrice glanced at the market stalls as they passed by and noted a variety of interesting goods—cheeses, wooden spoons and rowan besoms, silks and ribbons, delicious-smelling pasties, leather boots and copper pots.

All too quickly they left the market behind and wheeled into Northload Street. Just before the end they came to a high brick wall that ran for some distance and abutted the solid posts of a wide, wooden double gate. The gate was barred from the inside and visitors were required to ring a wrought-iron bell set high up in the wall—high enough to discourage small children from tormenting the nuns and the neighbourhood with silly games of ring-and-run.

Sir Giles leaned over in his saddle and tugged on the rope. They could not hear its jangle, but it was not long before a small trapdoor opened and a wimpled face peeped out.

'Good morning, Sister,' greeted Sir Giles politely, 'Lady Beatrice of Ashton has arrived.'

The door slammed shut. They glanced at one another and Beatrice smiled with a small shrug. After some moments the trapdoor opened again and another nun peered at them with hard eyes. She was older than the first one, and had sharp features that reminded Beatrice of a ferret. She looked directly at Beatrice and spoke to her in a tone that well matched her features.

'I am the Abbess here, Sister Huberta. What do you mean by bringing all these men to my door? Look how you have blocked the road and created unseemly interest.'

Beatrice felt a small shock of surprise at this abrupt greeting, and she glanced over her shoulder, surveying the men-at-arms who did indeed block the road and had attracted a small crowd of onlookers. Even now Sir Hugh was shouting and pushing his horse through in an attempt to get her coffer to the convent's door. Beatrice turned to make her apology, but was forestalled.

'They may go. At once. You may step down from your horse and I will admit you to St Jude's. If that is still your wish.' Sister Huberta stared straight at her.

'Indeed,' replied Beatrice slowly, her voice naturally soft and now scarcely audible above the stamp and snort of horses, the jingle of harness, the shouts of men down the road, 'I have a coffer, if you would be so kind as to open the gate.'

'Are you not aware that this is an enclosed order? I had thought I'd made it quite clear in my letters. We have not opened the gates in thirty years and will surely not do so now. We take you as you are, Mistress Beatrice—' her name was pronounced almost with a sneer '—besides, I cannot allow one nun to own more than any other. You will be provided with what you *need*, even if it may not be what you *want*.'

'But, my Bible—'

'We have one.'

'My hairbrush.'

'You will not need it. Your hair will be shorn.'

The knights and men-at-arms nearby gasped. Beatrice closed her mouth upon her protests to salvage her soap and sewing kit and other possessions. She turned then to Sir Giles and said in a quiet voice, 'Would you help me down, please?'

'My lady.' Sir Giles dismounted, and all the knights dismounted at once, with an audible creak of leather, clank of swords and ringing of spurs that made Beatrice cringe.

As Sir Giles set her down upon the ground Beatrice stroked Willow's nose in farewell, let go of the reins and took a step towards the gates of St Jude. Then she stopped and turned around again, her eyes flitting from one knight to another.

'Fare thee well,' she whispered. 'My thanks and may God go with you all.'

As one body they came and knelt in a semi-circle before her. She went to each one and kissed him upon the cheek. They remained silent and kept their gazes upon the ground, although every one of them longed to shout their protest and sweep her up on to her horse, to gallop away home.

When she came to Remy St Leger, last in line and furthest away from the gate, it was he, and he alone, who raised his eyes and looked upon her. He reached for her hand and kissed it.

'Your father said to remind you that if all is not well, to send word.' His voice was very low, not to be heard by the Abbess.

'I know. But tell my father that I will not shame him by my lack of courage.'

''Tis not courage you need now, but common sense. Come away from this place.'

'Let go of my hand!' Beatrice said through clenched teeth.

'Come along, young lady, I do not have time to waste idly waiting upon your pleasure.'

Remy cast the Abbess a look of sour contempt. Still clasping Beatrice's small hand between the rough palms of his own much larger hands, he looked up at her, as he knelt in the mud on one bended knee. 'You do not belong here.'

Beatrice leaned forwards and kissed his cheek. 'Fare thee well, Sir Remy.' She spoke sadly but firmly, and resisted the temptation to brush aside the lock of ash-blond hair that fell across his forehead. She tugged her hand free and stepped back.

The knights rose to their feet, and watched, many with hands on hips or the hilt of their swords, as Beatrice stooped through the small door, set in the gate, that closed almost at once behind her, revealing nothing of the convent or its inhabitants to the outside world.

For a long moment the knights stood there, staring, and then Sir Giles roused them and vaulted upon his horse. 'To Ashton!' he cried.

It was scarce midday and with hard riding they would make the castle by nightfall, forgoing the temptations the taverns of Glastonbury had to offer, in their haste to return to Lord Thurstan and impress upon him his duty to rescue Lady Beatrice from her own folly.

As the door slammed shut behind her Beatrice blinked in the gloom of the gatehouse. Then the Abbess swept past her and marched across the yard to the main building of the convent.

'I have never seen such a carry on,' Sister Huberta complained. 'If I had known that your father intended to send you to us with such—such pomp, then I would most certainly have written and persuaded him otherwise.'

Beatrice stopped in her tracks, brows raised in a challenging way and she faced the Abbess. 'I believe my father paid you a substantial dowry to accept me as a novice.'

Sister Huberta stood with hands tucked into her voluminous sleeves, back ramrod straight and looking down her nose at Beatrice from a greater height. Inclining her head slightly, she agreed, 'Indeed, he did.'

'I assume that, if I should not be happy here, and decide to leave, my dowry goes with me.'

A slow smile spread across the sharp features, and the Abbess took a step closer to Beatrice, her voice very soft, yet lethal as a blade. 'I know your game, *my lady*. Don't think I haven't come across your sort before. Too old to wed, too young to cast off. Families have many ways of getting rid of the burden of trying daughters—' She stepped back, turned and carried on into the building.

'But—' Beatrice protested in her own defence, hurrying after her.

'Silence! You will not interrupt. Let me tell you one thing only. If you stay or if you go, it is your own choice. But you leave as you came. With nothing. Your dowry belongs to St Jude. Now, 'tis the dinner hour and the sisters will be waiting to eat. Come along, and I will introduce you to everyone.' She turned to Beatrice with a wide smile that showed yellow, pointy teeth, her voice over-sweet. 'Now, we shall pray long and hard, to make amends for our poor beginning. I am sure, *dear child*—' this as they entered the refectory room set with two long trestle tables, and bustling with black-garbed nuns as they laid out the noonday meal '—that you will be very happy here.'

Lord Thurstan had been drinking heavily since the moment Beatrice had left. In the space of two months he had lost both a wife and a daughter, and both of his sons—Lord Henry, his heir and affectionately known as Hal, and young Osmond—might well be dead as they rode on campaign with the Earl of Chester in Wales. No word had been heard from them for many months. In an attempt to dull the pain their absence had inflicted, he consumed as much red Burgundy wine as his stomach and his head could tolerate.

By the time Sir Giles and his knights reached the castle it was dark, and they dismounted and entered the hall, guided by the light of pitch flares, their mood tired and sombre.

'What ho!' exclaimed Lord Thurstan from his chair upon the dais, wiping a hand across his mouth and wagging a lamb chop at his men. ''Tis a sorry lot I take with me to Wales. Mayhap I would be better off taking the kitchen wenches.'

The men allowed their squires to come in and disarm them, to wash their hands in bowls of hot water brought from the kitchen, before finding their places at the table and helping themselves to food and wine, all in gloomy silence.

Lord Thurstan sat up as Sir Giles took his place nearby. 'What of Beatrice?' he asked, with considerable restraint. 'Was she well? Did she seem happy? And the Abbess? Was she a good woman?'

'Aye, my lord,' replied Sir Giles tersely, 'Lady Beatrice was well when we left, although the Abbess refused to accept her coffer and she went in with nothing more than the clothes upon her back.'

Lord Thurstan grunted, not pleased with this news. The men chewed upon their meat and bread, gulped deep draughts of wine and eyed one another warily, the truth an unpalatable dish.

It was Remy St Leger who rose from his place and approached their lord seated upon his dais. Some admired him for his courage and others shook their heads over his foolhardiness.

Remy bowed deeply. 'My lord, I would speak with you. In private.'

Lord Thurstan's shaggy brows climbed to his forehead and he flicked his eyes about the hall. 'We are all family here. I have no secrets in my own hall. If you wish to speak, then speak.'

Remy cleared his throat, but to his credit did not shrink. 'I would ask you for your daughter's hand.'

The hall went silent. All movement ceased. All eyes were agog.

'What did you say?' Lord Thurstan asked quietly, slowly setting aside his meat.

'Lady Beatrice does not belong in a convent. I ask that you would give her in marriage to me.'

A wordless roar burst from Lord Thurstan as he leapt to his feet, and then one large fist swung through the air and Remy St Leger went crashing to the floor. For a moment the blow stunned him, but none went to his aid. Lord Thurstan stepped down from the dais and knelt at the young man's side, his eyes cold with fury. He watched while Remy sat up, shook his head and wiped the blood from his mouth.

'What do you know,' asked Lord Thurstan quietly, 'of my daughter?'

Remy did not falter. 'I know that God did not make her to be a nun.'

'Is that so? And you know her so well, then?'

Remy was silent, uncertain of the correct answer.

Lord Thurstan stabbed a finger in his chest. 'My daughter is not for the likes of you!'

He turned away then and went back to his chair, refilling his goblet with wine and chewing fiercely upon his food. Everyone watched as Remy picked himself up off the floor, expecting him to slink away to lick his wounds, and vastly entertained to find that the Aquitaine was willing to provide them with more sport.

Remy strode to the dais and shouted, 'What sort of man sends his daughter to a convent to rot?'

Lord Thurstan rose menacingly to his feet, quickly

followed by Sir Giles and Sir Hugh, who anticipated a brawl. 'I did not send her. She went of her own choice.'

'You could have said nay!'

'Who, I? Say nay to Beatrice when she will say aye?' Lord Thurstan put his head back and laughed. 'Indeed, you do *not* know my daughter very well.'

'I had thought my pledge was given to the king's commander in honour, but now I see I serve a man who is no more than a coward!' Remy leaned forwards and jabbed his finger in Lord Thurstan's face. 'I will prove to you, my lord, that I *am* worthy of your daughter!'

'Take him away,' growled Lord Thurstan, 'before I rip his head off.'

Slumping down in his chair, he watched as Sir Giles and Sir Hugh persuaded Remy to go outside and cool off. The young man reluctantly allowed himself to be escorted from the hall, and Thurstan stroked his beard thoughtfully, a tiny glint of admiration in his eyes as he watched the tall, muscular figure of Remy St Leger retreat.

The bell for Compline rang and Beatrice struggled to extricate herself from the warm cot she had been given in the dormitory set aside for novices. There were only four of them, and most of the time they were too tired and bewildered to talk to each other. The hated bell rang again, and again, until Beatrice wanted to scream.

Throwing back the thin blankets, she fumbled about for her shoes, pulled them on and a plain wool cloak over the grey linen kirtle that was the uniform for novices. She was sure that she had hardly slept in the two days she had been here, and certainly had not changed her clothes nor bathed, apart from washing her face and hands in a bowl of cold water.

It was the middle of the night, and cold, and she found her way out into the passage by running her hand along the wall. They were not allowed a light, an extravagance that was reserved for the chapel only. Fortunately it was not far, and she could see the soft glow spilling out from the open chapel door.

Shuffling in, half-asleep, she knelt down beside Emeline, a novice from Somerton, a simple-minded young girl afflicted with skin so badly pock-marked that no man would look upon her favourably, nor treat her respectably. The church had been her only option. Beatrice glanced at the girl and gave her a kind smile, her knees aching upon the cold stone floor. Indeed, every part of her body ached, her hands were raw with blisters and her face burnished from the sun.

On her first day she had been sent to the vegetable garden to help Sister Joan and she had spent many hours hoeing and weeding and watering turnips, carrots and onions. Today she had been sent to the fish ponds and her arms ached from the tasks she had been set. Never in her life had she been required to work and it was rapidly becoming apparent to Beatrice that her vision of a tranquil life spent praying and gazing sweetly upon the Lord and the Virgin Mary was only a myth. Abbess Huberta would make certain of that.

At last the mass came to an end and they shuffled off to bed. The hard, uncomfortable cot now felt like a bed of swan feathers and Beatrice fell gratefully into it, asleep at once. But not for long. Before she had time to dream the bell was ringing for Prime; afterwards, she was taken out into the cold, dark morning by Sister Audrey to help her milk the cows.

Once a year Lord Thurstan owed the king thirty days' service. This year his thirty days, probably more, would be spent in assisting Edward wrest control of Brecon and Gwynedd from the Welsh. He set off on Friday. The dawn muffled the ringing cavalcade of twelve mounted knights and a hundred men-at-arms. It was intended that they would march north to Evesham and join forces with the Earl of Hereford.

Two weeks later, having enjoyed several small skirmishes against the Welsh, they camped against the walls of Carmarthen Castle, while the Marcher lords met in council with Edward's commanders and decisions were made upon deployment.

Seated in a tent round a small fire circled with stones were Radley and Montgomery. These two had become the best of friends and close comrades over the years, and with them sat Woodford, Baldslow and Remy St Leger. They huddled into their cloaks and passed a flask of brandy from man to man, while the wind and the rain lashed outside upon the wild hills of Wales. The remains of a meagre supper of rabbit stew congealed in a three-legged iron pot and their squires sat in corners carefully polishing the rust from swords and armour.

The conversation was largely centred on the coming

fight with Welshmen, whom they judged to be short and wild, but courageous in battle.

'The only problem is drawing them down from their mountain lairs and out into the open,' commented Radley.

The others nodded in agreement, and after a long moment of silence Radley mused, 'I wonder how fares Lady Beatrice.'

Remy squinted at him with narrowed eyes, his mouth tightening, wondering if it was a deliberate ploy to draw him into an argument, or whether the good knight was genuinely expressing his concern. Remy decided upon the latter, and took a swig of brandy before passing on the flask to Baldslow.

'I think Lord Thurstan misses her sorely, although he would be the last to admit so,' said Montgomery.

'Aye, more fool him,' Woodford said, poking a stick into the embers of the fire, ''Tis no easy life for a nun, not at St Jude's. They provide for themselves, with no help from any man, and Lady Beatrice is not accustomed to hard manual labour.'

Remy felt a burning sensation tighten in the pit of his stomach, not caused by the fiery brandy. His fists clenched, and he hid them beneath the folds of his cloak. He could not bear to think of Lady Beatrice with her back aching and her hands chafed by labour fit only for peasants.

''Tis certain even the angels wept when they cut her hair.'

There was a loud chorus of agreement and Remy murmured, staring at the fire flames, 'Aye, her hair was indeed beautiful. Like honey. It fell in waves to her hips.'

Silence fell over the men, all movement stilled as they stared at him. Remy looked up quickly, suddenly realising his error and making quick amends as he stammered, 'So I hear. Or was told.'

'Indeed?' Cedric Baldslow stared hard at the younger man, his suspicions aroused and spoiling for a fight with this pretty face. 'Methinks you speak in a manner too familiar. I wondered, that night at the Red Lion…' He let his words dangle while the others, except Remy, who remained silently staring at the fire, prompted Baldslow to continue. He shrugged, pouting somewhat belligerently, 'I came up to check that St Leger had not fallen asleep at his post, and he was not there. I thought I heard a sound from my lady's room.'

At that implication Remy leapt to his feet, 'What are you accusing me of? What sort of sound?'

Baldslow rose slowly, and sneered, 'The sound a woman makes when she lies beneath a man.'

Remy swore and swung his fist, but not before the tide of red that stained his face had been noticed by one and all. ''Tis a lie, Baldslow! You besmirch the honour of a lady!'

'An honour you have already taken?' shouted Baldslow, neatly side-stepping the blow. 'Come now, Sir Remy, you are sworn by knighthood to always tell the truth!'

'Have no fear,' snarled Remy, glaring at his tormentor, 'Lady Beatrice is still a virgin.'

'Is she, *still,* by God? I think I greatly mislike the sound of that!'

There were mutters from Radley and Montgomery, and even Woodford had one or two well-chosen epithets to throw at Remy. Now they all turned to stare at him, as they stood about the fire, and Radley demanded in a voice that was used to obedience, 'Have you had intimate knowledge of the Lady Beatrice, Sir Remy?'

'Nay!' Remy hung his head, hands on hips, staring at his feet, his voice very quiet, 'I...but kissed her. 'Tis all. No more, I swear.'

'You fool!'

'Idiot!'

Baldslow erupted, but not with words. Roaring like an enraged beast, he charged at Remy, head down, and cannoned into him with his shoulder. His momentum thrust them both through the tent flap and out into the night.

It took only a moment for Remy to recover his wits and he punched back at Baldslow, thrusting his knee into his stomach until the grip that threatened to break his ribs loosened. With snarls and shouts the two men engaged in a fierce fight, smashing one another about the head and body with both fists, slipping and falling in the mud, soaked by the rain, but neither willing to give any quarter.

The fracas attracted attention, and some came out of their tents to stare, to cheer, to exclaim, and one of them was Lord Thurstan. At his furious command it took half a dozen men more than a few moments to tear the two combatants apart, and drag them before their lord for accounting.

'We are here to fight the Welsh, not each other! What goes on? Baldslow? St Leger? Answer me!'

Both men remained silent, uncertain of the wisdom of truth now, when the punishment could be far greater than the reward. After a few moments, in which Lord Thurstan harangued them with dire threats if they did not speak, Baldslow decided to take the risk—after all, he had nothing to lose.

'My lord, it came to my attention that St Leger has taken liberties about the person of my Lady Beatrice.'

'Indeed?' Lord Thurstan was inclined to be sceptical of any accusation uttered by Baldslow, a man whose own suit had been thoroughly thwarted and mayhap would stoop at nothing when presented with so threatening a rival for his daughter's affections as the handsome young Remy St Leger. Seeing that this was not a matter to be aired in public, he summoned both men to his pavilion.

Lord Thurstan dismissed his squire, who reluctantly went out into the cold wet night and found himself lodgings with Fitzpons and Grenville. With arms akimbo, Lord Thurstan turned to face his knights and silently demanded their explanation. Baldslow was the first to speak.

'My lord, I have reason to believe that St Leger entered the bedchamber of Lady Beatrice, when we lodged for the night at the Red Lion inn. There, I believe, he became intimate with her.'

Lord Thurstan controlled his instinctive rage at this accusation. 'St Leger? What say you?'

'My lord, I did nought. She asked me for one kiss, as she had never been kissed before. I swear on the

Holy Bible and on my oath as a knight that nothing else happened.'

'She is still a virgin?'

'Aye, my lord.'

'Baldslow, you may go. And I trust you will keep your tongue between your teeth.'

'Of course, my lord.' Baldslow bowed deeply and departed, throwing St Leger a triumphant look that was yet tinged with wary jealousy at Lord Thurstan's lack of reaction.

'I have half a mind,' said Lord Thurstan quietly, 'to thrash you within an inch of your life, St Leger. How you even dared to lay one finger on my daughter, I do not know. But…' here he stroked his beard thoughtfully, eyeing the tall young man who stood silently before him, 'I know my Beatrice, and she is no wanton. Long ago, when she was but sixteen, she was betrothed to a young knight whom she greatly admired—mayhap loved, such as a girl so young can love, knowing little of it. He was killed, and since then she has felt no fondness for any man. Many times I had hoped to have my hand forced, but none had the courage. My wife often chastised me for this view, saying it was barbaric, but I think a forced wedding is better than no wedding. Do you not agree?'

Remy looked awkwardly at his boots, 'I…well… sir…it depends.'

'On what?'

'From what side of the bed the wedding is viewed. For the groom a moment of pleasure may be rewarded with a lifetime of misery.'

Despite the seriousness of the situation Thurstan

laughed and clapped Remy upon the shoulder. 'Is it your view that a life spent wedded to Beatrice would be one of misery?'

'Nay. She is beautiful, sweet, kind.'

'She is older than you. By five years.'

Remy shrugged. 'Her innocence is her youth.'

'As your experience is your maturity?'

'Aye, my lord. Do not doubt that I am man enough for Beatrice.'

Blue eyes met Lord Thurstan's dark brown, with unrelenting challenge. Nodding, as if suddenly coming to a decision, Lord Thurstan moved to his saddlebags and extricated a folded, stained parchment. He waved it at Remy. 'I have this evening received a letter from the Abbess of St Jude. I had planned to send Woodford back, but I think it will be you, Sir Remy, who goes to fetch my daughter home.'

'Sir?' Remy stood up straight, a bolt of surprise shooting through him.

'It seems the Abbess is not as enamoured of my Beatrice as you are.'

Several times in the past few days Beatrice had managed to sneak away to the barn. At mid-morning the hayloft was flooded with sunlight and here she made for herself a warm nest and managed an hour of blissful sleep. It seemed her entire life revolved around this desperate need for sleep, and food.

Although the food was well cooked and tasty there was little of it, and the Abbess would not spend her coin on purchasing flour. There was no bread, no pies, no tarts or cakes. Breakfast consisted of stewed fruit or a thin, coarse gruel made from oats grown on the holding; the midday meal was vegetable soup; supper was a meat or fish stew, sometimes followed by cheese or fruit. The gnawing ache of hunger clawed constantly at her belly and even her dreams were rampant with images of food. She longed to taste just a crust of bread, let alone the sweet curd tarts, game pies and spiced apple cake that Cook at Ashton was so good at making.

Waking from her nap, Beatrice hurried down the rickety ladder from the hayloft, the bell for the noon Angelus ringing like an alarm. She knew that she must hurry and, brushing the stalks of dusty hay from her skirts, Beatrice ran along the path that threaded between the vegetables and herbs. She had been sent to collect eggs and realised, with a small gasp of fear, that she had failed to do so.

When she reached the kitchen door, hoping to slip in and make her way through the convent to the chapel, she was stopped by the large bulk of Sister Una, assigned to the kitchen as cook. She paused as she wielded a massive knife through a pile of turnips and swedes.

'Sister Huberta said to tell you not to go to the chapel, but to her parlour. At once.'

Biting her lips, Beatrice nodded and smiled her thanks for the message. The first time she had been summoned to Sister Huberta's study, and severely reprimanded for some misdemeanour or another, Beatrice had shook with terror. But now, it was a regular occurrence and she visited the Abbess on a daily basis.

Her footsteps tapped on the flagstones of the passage and from the chapel she could hear the uneven tones of discordant singing. Beatrice knocked on the door.

'Enter.'

She opened the door and came in to find Sister Huberta at her usual place behind her desk. The Abbess sat back in her chair, fingers steepled before her, and smiled unpleasantly.

'Ah. Beatrice. How nice to see you. Again.'

'Abbess.' Beatrice dipped a small curtsy.

'Come closer, girl. I do not wish to shout at you across the room.'

Beatrice took three paces forward.

'I would ask you to do me a favour.'

'Of course.'

'Take off your wimple.'

Beatrice gasped, her hand flying defensively to the linen wrapped around her head and neck. 'I…I must…protest, Sister.'

'Indeed, you must. But I am afraid that I must insist. You see, dear Beatrice, it has come to my attention that once again you have breached our covenants. This time, 'tis most serious. Now, remove your wimple, or I will fetch Sister Una and have her do it for you.'

Beatrice sighed, admitting defeat and too tired, hungry and dispirited to raise further protest. Slowly her small, pale hands unwound the linen wimple and her glorious mane of honey-brown hair spilled about her shoulders, slithering down like silk to curl about her hips.

'I—I am not, by law, required to cut it, Sister Huberta, until my second year. When I am certain of my vocation.'

'I see. And you have doubts about your, um, *vocation*?'

'Nay, Sister. I wish to praise and honour our Lord and devote my life to Him in prayer.'

'But?'

'Well…' brightening suddenly at this invitation to unburden herself and disguising her surprise at Sister Huberta's willingness to listen, Beatrice hurried on '…life is harsh here, for everyone. I am sure that if our bodies were not troubling us so much from lack of sleep and constant hunger, we would be able to devote ourselves more entirely to God.'

'Indeed!' Sister Huberta now rose from her chair, and scraped it back. 'Thank you for that advice, Beatrice. Now, I have some for you.' She opened the door of her study. 'Go home.'

'Sister?'

'I am sending you away. Back to your father.'

'But—'

'I have written to him once already, but received no reply. Unfortunately, St Jude cannot afford the burden of a lazy, useless chit!' She rang a bell and Sister Emily, the gatekeeper, came. 'Mistress Beatrice will be leaving us. Kindly escort her to the novice dormitory. She will remove these garments and dress in her own. Then take her to the gate and show her out.' Sister Huberta gained immense satisfaction from every word she spoke.

'But—' Beatrice, struggling to comprehend the situation, pointed out '—I have no horse, no escort, no money! How can you—?'

'Silence!' Sister Huberta held up her hand. 'Collect your bundle from the dormitory. I have given you two pennies to help you on your way.'

Utterly bewildered, Beatrice followed Sister Emily to the novices' dormitory, where upon her cot sat a bundle. It was her cloak, her own dark blue fustian, that had been used to tie up her shoes and clothes.

'I have put in some cheese and two apples,' whispered Sister Emily. 'Come now, do not look so distraught. You are lucky indeed to be escaping.' Glancing over her shoulder, she added in a conspiratorial whisper, 'Do not change your clothes, for your habit will lend you some protection on the outside.' With nimble hands she fastened Beatrice's wimple on, tucking away the glorious hair and assuring her, 'There are few who would dare to accost a nun.'

Beatrice was numb with shock. She followed Sister Emily across the yard, and clutched at her bundle as if to a lifeline while the large key attached to a leather thong at Sister Emily's waist clanked and scraped in the lock. The nun stepped to one side, and held the door open. Reluctantly, she stooped through the doorway, as she had only three weeks before.

'Fare thee well, sweet Beatrice. God will go with you.'

Beatrice could do no more than smile weakly, and then she was standing alone in the dusty road, she, who had never stood alone and unprotected in her life.

## Chapter Three

For a long while Beatrice simply stood there, unaware of the passers-by who glanced at her. Then a hand touched her sleeve and she looked down into the plump, tanned face of an old woman, a basket of eggs over her arm.

'Are you all right, my dear?' she asked, in the broad country accent of a farmer's wife.

Beatrice blinked, and then smiled, her smile growing wide as it reached her eyes and suddenly she laughed 'Aye, I am, mistress.'

'Chucked you out, has she?'

'What?'

The old woman laughed. 'No need to be shamed.' Jerking her head at the convent, she added, 'She don't like the pretty ones. Sent you on your way?'

'Aye. It is so.'

'Well, never you mind, dearie. Come along, now, I'll walk with you to market. Have you far to reach your home?'

'Indeed. I am from Castle Ashton.'

The old woman frowned, 'I've not heard of it. Must be a long ways off.'

Beatrice fell into step, and half-listened in a daze as the woman chatted in a friendly manner. They came to the market and Beatrice felt quite overwhelmed by the noise and bustle. She parted from the farmer's wife and wandered amongst the stalls, pausing to gaze upon the wares displayed as though she had never seen before such simple things as leather boots, wooden spoons, bolts of cloth in lovely colours of mulberry and emerald and saffron. The most fascinating was the pieman's stall and Beatrice stood gazing hungrily upon the golden pastry, filled with meat and vegetables, whose savoury aroma hung deliciously on the air. Succumbing to temptation, Beatrice felt for the two coins the Abbess had thrust into her kirtle pocket, and offered one to the pie seller.

'What will it be, mistress? Cornish, ham and chicken, or apple?

Beatrice pointed to a Cornish pasty, and accepted it into her hand as though it were Crusade treasure, pocketing her change and scarce knowing whether she had enough money left to find her way home. She had never had to deal with money before and had little knowledge of its value.

Taking her pie and her bundle, she went and sat down upon the steps of the stone cross that marked the place for trade. She savoured every last mouthful, and then sat back and turned her face up to the sun. Before she realised it she was praying, and felt the sweet presence of her God return to her. Remy St

Leger had been right. She did not belong in the convent.

For these long weeks past she had forced his memory from her mind, although sometimes he invaded her dreams. Now, knowing that he existed, that even at this moment he too felt the sun upon his face, filled her with a happiness that she had not felt for a very long time. Yet the moment she felt that little burn of pleasure she immediately quelled it, for it was her experience that pain usually followed swiftly and she was not eager to feel such an emotion again. It spurred her to rise and turn her mind to the task of reaching home, rather than idly mulling, and she set out upon the road that led her from the town centre and into Chilkwell Street.

Her surroundings looked somewhat different from afoot than on horseback, but Beatrice was sure that this was the way to Ashton. She thought that if she walked quickly she would make the Red Lion by dusk and there take shelter for the night.

The road was not deserted, as at first she had feared, and these were friendly country folk who offered her no harm. Sometimes there were curious glances, and greetings of, 'Bless us, Sister!' called out as they passed her by. Children often turned to stare at her, and she would smile and wink at them.

As the afternoon faded, and clouds gathered on the horizon, Beatrice began to tire. Her feet ached and the thin soles of her shoes afforded little protection from the sharp stones and twigs of the track she followed. She stopped to rest several times, and took solace from the peaceful shade of great oak trees, leaning back to listen to the song of birds, and watch clouds scudding across the sky. There was contentment in gazing upon the green countryside, ripening now with spring foliage into summer. It was the end of May and soon the fields would be golden with crops of wheat and oats and barley.

She was acutely aware of being alone, and was both cautious and watchful of the road ahead and behind her. If she spied the advancement of a group of men more than two in number, or a party of soldiers, she ran and hid in the trees and bushes crowding thickly on either side of the track. Only when they had passed by did she emerge, like a little rabbit, and hurry on her way.

The light faded quickly and Beatrice began to fear that she would not make the Red Lion before nightfall. Behind her she could hear the rumbling of a cart and her hopes picked up. She glanced carefully over one shoulder, and saw that the cart carried only two men, one quite old and one very young, father and son mayhap, and she paused, the countryside about her no longer peaceful and welcoming but vaguely threatening and hostile.

The cart rumbled closer and the two men caught sight of her and called their mule to a halt. The men doffed their hats and Beatrice eyed them warily.

'Good day to you, Sister. 'Tis far you be out on your own.'

Beatrice smiled coolly. 'Good day. Am I on the right track for the Red Lion at Littleton?'

'Aye, but it be a good three mile down the road.

You'll not make it on foot afore dark. Hop on t'back, mistress, and we'll see you right.'

'Thank you for your kindness, sir.'

Beatrice walked around to the back of the cart and jumped up, settling herself amongst the sacks of grain and vegetables, her legs dangling. With a lurch they set off, and the swaying motion and low-toned, sober conversation of the men, probably farmers, lulled her. She took her wimple off as exhaustion swept over her and she soon fell into a doze.

The soft pink evening sky had long since been swallowed up by inky night when they trundled into the yard of the Red Lion. Beatrice roused herself, with some difficulty, and jumped down from the cart, thanking her escorts, who watched as she went inside.

A warm, smoky fug greeted Beatrice as she stepped over the threshold, holding her cloak tight about her as several leery-looking men glanced her way. She recognised the innkeeper from her previous visit, and approached him.

'Good evening, sir. I am Lady Beatrice of Ashton. I require a room for the night and supper.'

To her surprise he laughed, and turned from wiping a table and flung a damp cloth over his shoulder. 'Oh, aye? And I'll be the King of Spain!'

Several nearby laughed heartily into their tankards of ale, and speculative stares were turned upon Beatrice. She drew herself up, brows arched and a frosty glint in her brown eyes.

'You will recall that I stayed here some three weeks ago, when I was escorted by seven knights, and forty men-at-arms. My father, Lord Thurstan, will be most displeased to hear of your reluctance to accommodate me.'

At that, and hearing the haughty culture of her voice, the innkeeper was taken aback and he paused, looking her over thoroughly and a vague memory stirring in his dim mind. He had not actually seen the Lady Beatrice face to face—the knights had made damn sure of that—but he recalled that she had been a small woman, such as the one before him now, and her hair had been golden-brown, such as the one before him now. Clearing his throat and quickly wiping his hands upon the stained apron about his waist, he hedged, 'Well, now, I am happy to be of service to Lady Beatrice any day, but how do I know that this dusty little nun standing before me is she?'

Beatrice smiled, acknowledging his caution. 'I am not a liar, sir. I *am* Lady Beatrice and to show good faith I shall write you a promissory note, if you would be so kind as to bring quill and parchment.'

Greatly impressed, for few except the clergy and nobility could write, the innkeeper shouted for his wife, who came shuffling along with a small square of coarse parchment and a bedraggled quill. The inkpot was old and a drop of acquavit was used to swill up some ink. Then, leaning on a scarred table, Beatrice wrote a note promising to pay the bearer the cost of one night's lodging and two meals, plus an extra reward for the loan of a saddled riding-horse, which would be returned by Cas-tle Ashton once Lady Beatrice had arrived safely home. The innkeeper blus-

tered a bit over the last part, but she managed to persuade him that her father was good for any debt.

Finally, after adding her signature with a flourish,
the innkeeper accepted her note and his wife showed
Beatrice to a room upstairs. Not the grand one she had
enjoyed before, for that was already taken, but one
smaller, at the back. Nevertheless, after the dormitory
at St Jude it seemed like heaven to Beatrice.

'I'll bring you up some hot water, and a bite to eat.
You don't want to be sitting downstairs on your own
with that mob of roughnecks.'

'You are most kind. Thank you.' Beatrice smiled,
and set her bundle down on the bed. As soon as the
door closed and she was alone, she opened it up and
shook out her cloak, her dark-green wool gown and
her fine linen shift, laying these across a chair to warm
before the fire.

Tomorrow she would wear her own clothes, but for
tonight Beatrice gloried in the luxury of good food,
hot water and a comfortable bed. Before going to sleep
she said her prayers with heartfelt and earnest thanks.

Remy St Leger had ridden hard from Wales to reach
the town of Glastonbury by mid-week, the urgency of
his mission being impressed upon him by an anxious
Lord Thurstan.

'I'll not be surprised if Beatrice has been put out in
the cold, without so much as a by your leave.'

'The Abbess would surely not leave a woman alone
and de-fenceless in the street?' questioned Remy, with
a frown.

Lord Thurstan shook his head, tugging nervously at

his beard. 'I cannot spare even one man to go with you, St Leger. But I trust you are more than capable of dealing with the Abbess alone. And she'll not be keeping the dowry either,' he huffed. 'Four hundred marks that will be, not a penny less.'

Remy bowed. 'I understand. Fear not, my lord, I will make certain that the Abbess keeps nothing that belongs to Ashton.'

He left at first light, armed with his sword, a dagger to be used in his left hand, a crossbow and thirty feather-tipped bolts. He was bulky indeed kitted out in a leather jack and chainmail hauberk with articulated shoulder plates. He refused a helm in favour of a chainmail coif, beneath which he wore a lambrequin, a cloth hood that protected his head and neck from the rain, both of which he felt allowed him more ease of movement in close-quarter combat.

Remy stopped only briefly along the way to rest, feed and water his horse, feeding himself standing by the road and aware that with every passing moment Beatrice might be vulnerable. The thought of her being at the mercy of any common serf in the street spurred him on. The time spent in the saddle gave him a chance to think upon his strategy, for he was certain that he would gain nothing if he meekly rang the bell at St Jude's gate and asked for admittance. Nay, the circumstances called for more cunning than that.

He reached Glastonbury as the afternoon waned on the third day, and went at once to the convent, stinking of sweat and dirt and wiping his brow with one sleeve. For a long while he sat upon his horse behind the shelter of some mulberry bushes and gazed at the impervious walls, more than two ells high. He squinted at the sun and guessed at the hour, and when his judgement was confirmed by the thin sound of female singing, he swung down from his horse. He tied the reins to the branch of a yew tree, confident that his destrier, a finely trained warhorse of Hanoverian breed, would not allow himself to be stolen. From his saddlebag he took a rope and attached it to a grapnel—a three-pronged iron hook and a useful item in times of siege.

Remy tossed the grapnel over the wall, jerked it back until it locked against the brickwork, and then hauled himself up and over the top, no mean feat for a big man heavily armoured. Lightly he dropped down, cast a quick glance about and then, crouched low, ran soundlessly through the garden. He peered through the small-paned windows, tried a door, which proved to be locked, and then skirted around until he gained entrance by the refectory, deserted while the nuns attended mass.

After a brief, furtive exploration he let himself into a parlour, and there sat himself down to wait, with his booted feet up on a cluttered writing table. From its scabbard he drew his sword, an immense weapon of gleaming Toledo steel that had served him well, and laid it down across his knees.

Sister Huberta clanked with keys as she walked along the passage, her shadow thrown gigantically across the walls by the bright rays of the lowering sun. As she let herself into her parlour and closed the door she noticed at once a male odour, one that she had not known for many years, not since she had been widowed. She whirled quickly, and let out a frightened gasp as she spied the man lounging with casual grace in her chair, behind her desk.

'What are you doing here?' she spluttered. 'Who are you? How dare you—'

'Be quiet, woman,' said Remy softly, rising to his feet and filling the small room with his broad bulk. 'I am here for Lady Beatrice.'

The Abbess relaxed a little, with relief, and was able to tell him truthfully, 'Well, be on your way, for you are too late. She is gone.'

'Indeed?'

She didn't like the soft menace of his tone, nor the way he was staring at her. 'Tell me at once, sir, who you are.'

'I am Lord Thurstan's man. Where is she?'

Sister Huberta eyed him impassively, for the first time swallowing a little nervously. 'She left this morning. Gone home. The girl was quite unsuitable.'

'How did she go?'

'How?'

'By horse, cart. On foot?'

'On foot, of course.'

'So, I should tell Lord Thurstan that you set his daughter outside the gate, in the street, alone, and told her to go home? On foot?'

'She is no child. She can well find her own way.'

'You had better hope so. Now, there is one other matter. The dowry.'

'What of it?'

'Lord Thurstan wants it back. 'Tis a tidy sum and he is not of a mind to let you keep it.'

Sister Huberta laughed harshly, 'Well, I care not a fig what Lord Thurstan wants! His daughter has caused us enough trouble these weeks past and we require compensation.'

Silver flashed through the shadows and the Abbess gave a small shriek, as she felt the cold point of steel at her throat.

'I am averse to killing holy nuns,' snarled Remy, 'but I have no aversion to killing a witch! Now, give me the money!'

Under the circumstances, she was obliged to reach for a key at her waist and hurry to an iron-bound, padlocked oak chest that was tucked away in a corner. She opened it and scrabbled about inside for a moment, before drawing out a soft leather pouch that contained four hundred marks. Her mouth a tight thin line, she rose and handed the pouch to her visitor.

Taking it with his left hand, he made a deep bow to her and departed with a final promise. 'Pray, sister, that I find Lady Beatrice, and that she is safe and well. Or I will be back, and next time I will come with a hundred men and burn this foul place to the ground!'

The Abbess stepped back with a gasp, clutching at her racing heart as the young man left as silently as he had arrived.

Remy found his way back over the wall, vaulted on to his horse and packed away both grapnel and the four hundred marks. Then with a shout and swift kick he galloped through Glastonbury and set off on the road to Ashton. He was anxious to make the Red Lion that night, and urged his horse onwards.

He came upon half a dozen soldiers and joined them

to hear what news of Wales. But they were mercenaries, Flemings, and their English was neither good nor pleasant. Dissatisfied with their paymaster, King Edward, they were on their way to Dover and home. Remy felt his nerves twinge and mistrusted the way they looked him over and eyed his saddlebags. He soon parted company with them and galloped on.

The morning was bright and sunny as Beatrice, sitting neatly side-saddle, arranged her dark blue cloak over the folds of her green kirtle. She called out her thanks to the innkeeper and his wife before setting off on the road that would, she hoped, lead her home before the day was out.

She felt refreshed after her night of blissful sleep and two good meals, and she had washed thoroughly in a bowl of hot water before the fire. She was grateful to acknowledge that at least her experience at St Jude had taught her to appreciate even the most basic pleasures of everyday life. With a light heart, humming a tune, she set her horse into a smart trot.

It was a sunny day, but not a market day. There were few people on the road, especially as she was going further and further away from Glastonbury. By mid-morning she paused to water her horse—a fat, unwilling creature—and to eat the cold chicken and bread the innkeeper's wife had wrapped for her.

Setting off again, they came to a section of woodland and the road was soft with pine needles. The trees crowded in thickly on either side, dark and dense, a blanket of tall bracken spread between them. Beatrice felt a moment of doubt, as she peered fearfully about, unnerved by the sudden lack of birdsong and sunlight. She clicked her tongue to her horse and urged him on, hoping to pass through the woods quickly.

Then she heard a shout, muffled cries, and as she rounded a sharp bend in the track she came upon the two farmers who had helped her yesterday. Their cart was surrounded by a group of men, soldiers by the looks of them, and they were busy ransacking the goods on the back of the cart. Beatrice gave a small cry, shocked at such outrageous behaviour, and would have urged her horse forwards, intending to deal with them in no uncertain manner, when one of the farmers gave a scream and gurgled. His throat was cut and Beatrice halted, her eyes wide with horror. The younger one, perhaps the farmer's son, turned and saw her, waved his arms and shouted for her to go back, before he too was slashed without mercy.

Beatrice wasted no time in wheeling her horse about, but already two or three of the soldiers had leapt astride their own horses and were after her.

'Come on!' shouted Beatrice, kicking furiously at the barrel of the fat gelding's ribs. He lumbered into a reluctant canter and, whipping him with the reins, Beatrice leaned over his withers as he stretched into a gallop, her cloak flying out behind her.

She heard the pounding of hooves fast approaching and with urgent shouts tried to force a little more speed from her horse. But it was too late, the three soldiers gained ground and soon they surrounded her. They reached over and snatched the reins from her grasp and Beatrice, heart pounding, screamed as leather-gloved hands seized her about the waist and dragged her down. One of them hit her in the face, and she gasped with shock, head reeling. The three soldiers had dismounted and loomed over her. Quickly they searched her saddlebags and finding nothing of interest turned to her with eyes that left her in no doubt as to what they wanted.

They spoke in a foreign language—Dutch, she thought—and she realised they were mercenaries. They jostled her, fingering her fine clothes, her hair. She screamed again as one of them grasped the neck of her kirtle, and ripped it, exposing the soft white skin of her chest. The other two argued over who would go first and fumbled with the fastenings of their braies, shoving one another aside in their eagerness.

She remembered a move she had seen her brothers use when fighting and locked her two hands together, into a fist. She jerked it up, delivering a sharp blow to underneath the chin of the man who held her. His teeth snapped on his tongue and he yelped. She quickly followed this with a vicious kick to the shins. He was so surprised that a small noblewoman was willing to fight, for one moment his hold on her slackened and Beatrice jerked away. In that instant she took to her heels, running as fast as she could up the track, back the way she had come, hoping to find help.

She saw a horseman approaching in the distance and screamed, waving her arms to attract his attention. The mercenaries were quickly gaining on her as their booted feet pounded hard behind her. She had no doubt that it was their intention to catch her, drag her off into the bushes and hold her quiet, until the lone horseman had been dealt with.

With her bodice torn, holding up her skirts as she ran, and her mouth wide open in a scream, she made for a wild sight. Suddenly something whooshed past her and the man nearest made a strange sound. Blood sprayed across her arm and, glancing back, she saw that a small arrow protruded from his neck. He fell instantly.

The horseman galloping towards them lowered a crossbow and, as he had not the time to reload, drew his sword with a ringing hiss of steel. Roaring a war-cry that echoed around the woods, he charged down on the other two men. Beatrice dived into the bracken lining the side of the road, out of the way. She fell to her knees, panting, gasping for breath, and pulling together the torn edges of her kirtle. She looked up, peering through the bushes, and then quickly away, one hand smothering a cry as the horseman slashed with his sword and one of the mercenaries lost his head. She did not look to see how he dealt with the other, but the noise was ferocious, as steel rang on steel, and both men profaned loudly with each blow.

At last, after what seemed like an eternity to Beatrice, all went quiet, except for the snorting pants of his horse and her own harsh breathing that was laboured more from terror than anything else. She rose cautiously, and then remembered that there had been others. The horseman had dismounted and was inspecting the men he had slain, but he turned quickly at her warning shout and had a moment to collect himself before the other three mercenaries ran at him with swords drawn.

With a despairing cry Beatrice covered her face. He

would surely not win against these three and suddenly she thought it best to flee, whilst the mercenaries' attention was elsewhere. With the clash of steel, the grunts and shouts of the fighting men echoing in her ears, Beatrice turned and began to run into the shelter of the woods.

She was hampered by the fact that she could not catch her breath, and her ribs and heart ached painfully as terror took its toll. She stopped and leaned against a tree, gasping for air. Then she heard the drumming of a horse cantering, and she looked back, her eyes wide with terror. At first she could not see anyone and cautiously she began to move, stumbling backwards as the thunder of hooves came louder and closer. Then he emerged through the trees, and the lone horseman called to her.

The big black destrier was vaguely familiar and Beatrice stared as he came to a shuddering halt and his rider pushed back his chainmail coif with one hand. 'Remy St Leger!'

He smiled, and leapt down from his horse. Without thinking of propriety or anything else, Beatrice ran to him and flung her arms about his waist. He held her, and let her sob against his blood-spattered chest.

'Shh,' he said softly, calmly, 'you are safe, my lady.' He wanted to touch her, to stroke her hair, but his hands were not clean.

Gulping, wiping her wet face with her hand, she tipped back her head and looked up at him, asking with a wobbling smile, 'What on earth are you doing here?'

'Your father sent me to escort you home. But it appears I was too late.'

Her eyes lowered and she hung her head, ashamed that the convent had rejected her. 'It seems I am not fit to be a nun.'

At her sorrowful tone he smiled, gave her shoulders a quick hug with his arm and then stepped back, peering down to look into her face. He asked carefully, 'You are not hurt, my lady? Those men, they did not…touch you?'

She understood his meaning at once and with a blush she shook her head. She noticed that his gaze fell upon her torn kirtle and the glimpse of bare white flesh. Dragging her cloak tightly over her bosom, she met his eyes warily, afraid of what she would find there.

'Do not look at me so, my lady. I am not the kind of beast that rapes women.' His voice was angry, his eyes a very bright blue as they flashed at her.

'Of course not, Sir Remy,' she murmured, unable to meet his glare, 'Come, let us not tarry here, for I feel sure 'tis an evil place.'

She fell into step at his side as they walked back to the road, her eyes avoiding the gruesome sight of bloodied bodies lying there. They spent some while calling and searching for her horse, but it soon became apparent that he had taken to his heels and returned to the Red Lion.

'Walther will carry us both,' said Remy indicating the massive Hanoverian, who stood patiently, unfazed by the smell of fresh blood and seeming to relish the conflict as much as his master.

As he put his hands on her waist, and made to toss her up on to Walther, Remy suddenly grunted and stooped, clutching at his ribs. Beatrice looked up quickly, catching her breath in alarm. 'Are you hurt, Sir Remy?'

He shook his head, and valiantly grasped her about the waist again, but again he was seized with pain and doubled over. Then, to her amazement, he gave a command to Walther and before her wide eyes the horse knelt down on his two front legs, and Remy mounted him, indicating that Beatrice should climb up behind.

'I have never seen such a thing!' she exclaimed, as she settled herself pillion on Walther's broad back, her arms fastening about Remy's waist.

'You have never been in battle. If you had, then you would know 'tis quite a common trick. A man in full armour, maybe injured, can sometimes find it difficult to mount a tall warhorse quickly.'

They set off, and Beatrice was aware that she had never felt so safe in her life. What bliss it was just to sit back and let someone else make all the decisions. Remy set a fast pace and it was certainly not comfortable bouncing around on the back of Walther, the chainmail links of Remy's hauberk pressing painfully into her cheek and bosom as she clung to him to keep herself from falling off.

The clouds gathered darkly overhead and thunder grumbled. Even with the first spit of rain Remy did not stop. They came to a small stream and here they paused to let Walther rest and drink some water. They dismounted and Remy went to the bank, where he knelt and washed the blood from his face and hands.

Beatrice was sitting quietly on a rock, looking up at the sky and wondering if it would rain hard, when suddenly she saw Remy slump and heard his low moan. He tried to straighten up and take a deep breath, only to moan and slump again.

Frightened, Beatrice jumped up and ran to him, kneeling at his side and exclaiming, 'You are hurt, Sir Remy! Take off your hauberk and let me look.'

Reluctantly, for he was anxious to make Castle Ashton before nightfall, he agreed. Remy groaned, as he lifted his arms. 'You will have to help me.'

With a struggle Beatrice dragged off first his coif, revealing lank blond hair dark with sweat, and then his hauberk. She staggered beneath its slithering weight and dropped it in the grass. Turning back, she unlaced his leather jack, pulling it off over broad shoulders and arms thick with the bulge of hard muscle. His linen tunic was wet with sweat, but she did not remove it, only lifted the hem up to his armpits and peered at the offending area he held his hand to. His ribs on the left side were stained purple with dark bruises, but she was thankful to see no open wounds or bleeding.

'I think you may have broken a rib, or at the very least taken a nasty bruising.'

'They are not broken,' he assured her, for he knew what that felt like. He clasped her wrist and pulled away her exploring fingertips, a shiver of ecstasy, which was agony too, running down his back. Dropping down his tunic, he made to stand up. 'I will be fine. Let us be on our way.'

'Nay,' said Beatrice firmly, her hand on his shoulder

forcing him to stay on his knees, 'let me make a cold compress and bind your ribs. That may afford you some comfort.'

He looked quickly away as she lifted the hem of her skirt, and ripped several strips from her shift. These she knotted together, until she had a serviceable bandage. Then she tore another piece off and wadded it into a square. She leaned down to the stream and soaked it in cold water, squeezing the excess out and laying the makeshift compress against his ribs. He flinched, with a low, throaty groan and her eyes lifted to his.

'You torture me.' His gaze fell on her soft cheeks, the curve of her pink mouth. 'I see you still have your hair.'

Beatrice found she could not look away from him, as his eyes explored her face, and her breath came quickly from between parted lips. She could feel the heat of his body, and beneath her fingers his flesh was solid, his sun-gold skin smooth along his ribs. She noticed that his chest was dusted with dark-gold hair, a thin dark line arrowing along the flat planes of his stomach to his navel, and beyond. Quickly she tore her eyes away. His male smell, mixed with sweat and dirt, was heady indeed and not repugnant. Her senses seemed to float, a spark lighting inside her.

She lifted the compress away and began binding his ribs with her handmade bandage. Remy held himself tensely as she leaned against him, her bosom brushing his midriff and he swallowed, fists clenched hard.

'There,' she said, surveying her efforts, 'does that feel better?'

To please her he said aye, although in truth it made little difference. What he needed was a bed for the night. In more ways than one, he thought ruefully, as she helped him don his armour and they remounted Walther. They set off again, this time with her arms about his hips.

Beatrice was silent for a long while. Her thoughts returned again and again to the sight of his bare chest and the feel of his smooth skin beneath her fingers. He stirred up powerful emotions within her, which she had never felt before.

'My lady?' said Remy.

'Aye?'

'Could you—' his voice was curt and rough '—move your arms, please?'

'I'm sorry,' said Beatrice quickly. 'Am I hurting you?'

'Nay.' His reply was somewhat strangled, but he was relieved when her arms shifted to his waist. She could not know, through his armour, that her slender forearm had rested on his shaft, and that the bold creature, never long dormant, had been roused by the contact as they jogged along.

Beatrice was puzzled by his request, thinking that she would hurt his ribs less if she gripped him about the hips. Apparently it was not so, but she thought no more of it and asked him, 'Will we make Castle Ashton this day, Sir Remy?'

'Aye. I hope so, my lady.'

'Please, do not call me *my lady* all the time. My name is Beatrice.'

'Only if you do not call me *Sir* Remy.'

She laughed, 'Agreed. Should we not stop along the way and tell someone about...' she hesitated '...the bodies?'

'Aye. I had planned to stop in Somerton and report to the sheriff.'

'Is it far?'

'About five miles down the road.'

She fell silent and they rode along in companionable ease. Then Beatrice asked, 'How is my father? Did he meet with my brothers, Hal and Osmond?'

'He is well and, nay, we have not yet met up with your brothers.' He did not want to upset her by repeating the fears Lord Thurstan had harboured that his sons were both dead.

'I see. Does it seem likely that my father will return after his thirty days' service?'

'Nay, my la— Beatrice. The king is determined to drive the Welsh into the mountains and starve them into surrender. There are thousands of more troops on their way from Cheshire and Lancashire and there is talk that Edward has raised the largest army since William the Conqueror.'

'Indeed? And do you have a great love for war?'

Her question took him by surprise, and he floundered with the answer. 'I have neither love nor hate for war. 'Tis as much a part of life as eating and breathing.'

'Ah, but there I cannot agree with you. If Edward was content to sit at home with Eleanor, there would be no war now in Wales.'

Remy snorted. 'What man is content to sit at home twiddling his thumbs and pestering his wife?'

'Mayhap…' she smiled '…a wife would prefer to be pestered than widowed.'

''Tis a woman's view,' he said sharply.

Beatrice abandoned the subject and yet she was eager to keep up their conversation, to hold at bay from her mind the horrors of the day. She searched for a topic that would not lead to argument and thought it safe to ask, 'Do you play chess?'

'Aye. Do you?'

'Indeed. Mayhap one day we might have a game.'

He grinned at her over his shoulder, looking down into her brown eyes as she clung trustingly to him. 'Only on one condition.'

'What is that?'

'You promise not to *let* me win.'

'Why would I?' she asked with genuine surprise.

'Some men do not like a clever woman, but I am not one of them.'

'I am far from being clever. Why, even the convent would not have me!'

Remy remembered his visit of the day before with the Abbess of St Jude. 'I fear 'twas your dowry that was the greatest attraction.'

Beatrice pouted. 'I am sorry to say that my father has lost all of it.' With a little laugh she jested, 'He will have the devil's own job in getting rid of me in wedlock now, without a dowry, for she would not give it back to me.'

They both knew who *she* was and Remy was about to reveal the contents of his saddlebags, when he hesitated. If he chose to ask Beatrice for her hand in marriage, he did not want her to think that it was because he lusted after her dowry.

During the course of their conversations, as they jogged along through the countryside, they discovered they had both slept at the Red Lion last night, and they chafed over the fact they had been so close.

''Tis my fault,' said Remy, with a frown. 'I should have thought to ask.'

'But 'twas late,' she soothed, 'no doubt you were tired.'

'A knight must never be tired.'

'You are only human.' Quickly she thought to distract him from his supposed failings. 'It seems to me that a knight must be many things. Warrior, horseman, swordsman, courtier, accomplished at singing and dancing. Do you like to dance?'

'Nay.' He scowled, unwilling to admit to her that his preference for dainty females often left him without a partner, for little women were mostly intimidated by his great size.

'I love to dance,' she said, aware that she had touched a sore spot and wondered at the reason, her guess fairly shrewd. 'Couples are my favourite, but of course my father will allow me to dance couples only with my brothers, and they are very tall. How tall are you, Remy?'

'I am six foot two.'

'Oh, I would say Hal is at least two inches taller than you, and he is a wonderful dancer.'

'Is that so?' replied Remy sourly, still scowling.

Undaunted by his reticence, Beatrice plunged on and discovered they shared a love for archery; laughingly she challenged him to a contest. Then, wisely, she fell silent, for her mother had oft warned that a man did not like a chatterbox. Tired, she laid her cheek against Remy's back and leaned against him. He made no objection.

It was dark when Walther plodded wearily over the drawbridge of Castle Ashton. Beatrice was half-asleep, her head pillowed against Remy's back. Pitch lights flared and dazzled them with brightness, and grooms came running to assist them. There were hearty welcome cries from the serfs as they recognised Beatrice and quickly she was swept inside, while Remy went to make sure that Walther was properly taken care of and bedded down for the night with a good feed.

As she stepped into the hall, Beatrice was flooded with a warm feeling of joy to be back in her own home. She wondered what fever of the mind had persuaded her to abandon it in the first place, and put it down to the shock and grief of losing her mother only a short while ago. But now, some devilish little voice chirped inside her, she had found Remy.

From the chairs beside the fireplace several figures rose and Beatrice turned towards them, exclaiming with surprise, 'Aunt Margaret! How came you to be here?'

'My dearest Beatrice—' her aunt, who was her father's youngest sister, came to her with hands outstretched, kissing her on both cheeks '—your father sent word to me about your...' she hesitated '...change of plans, and that he did not wish you to be alone while he is away. So, here we are.'

'We?'

'Of course.' Her aunt turned and Beatrice felt her heart sink, felt hopes that had not even had the chance to become dreams evaporate. 'Joanna, come and greet your cousin.'

Remy entered the hall just as Joanna rose from her seat and came towards them. Beatrice had no need to turn and see if he stared, for any man would stare at Joanna. A tall, slender girl, she had wheat-blonde hair and blue eyes, a lovely face and a full-bosomed graceful figure. But worse, far worse than any of that, she was eight years younger than Beatrice.

# Chapter Four

Stricken as she was, Beatrice composed herself quickly. Her aunt had brought with her several knights as escort from her home in Oxford, as well as two of her ladies. Beatrice made the introductions.

'Sir Humphrey Stanhope…Sir Kendall Mortimer… and Sir Richard Blackthorn.'

The knights bowed to one another, each taking their measure. Remy, although undoubtedly the youngest in years, had the advantage in stature and towered over them all. Beatrice watched him carefully as she introduced him to her cousin. He bowed over Joanna's hand and kissed it, but she could not see his expression as he glanced at Joanna's lovely face.

'My aunt, Lady Margaret of Birchlea, and her companions, Lady Constance and Lady Germaine.' Beatrice made haste to bring forth the older ladies, being matronly of both figure and face, manoeuvring Joanna away from Remy.

'Why, Beatrice, whatever have you done?' Aunt Margaret touched her fingertips to the faint swelling and bruise on her niece's cheek.

Beatrice launched into an explanation of their journey, and there was much exclaiming, fussing and gallant praise for Remy's swift and bold action. Then her aunt took charge and ordered a tub of hot water to be drawn and for someone to fetch her medicine chest from her chamber.

'Beatrice, you go first, while I tend to Sir Remy, there's a good girl.'

Seeing that Elwyn hovered nearby and was anxious to greet her, Beatrice left the hall to make her way to the curtained-off alcove beside the great hearth in the kitchen. She embraced Elwyn and they exchanged murmurs of heartfelt enquiry and affection.

A large wooden tub stood ready and waiting, steam rising from the water tipped in by the bucketful. With the kitchen fire going day and night it was a warm corner and, once Elwyn had drawn the curtain, Beatrice looked forward to bathing in the hot water, fragrant with her favourite infusion of vanilla, lavender and rose petals. She stripped off her clothes and stepped into the tub, unbraiding her hair as she sank with a soft sigh into the water.

'Oh, my lady,' moaned Elwyn, 'look how thin you are! Why, one gust of wind and you'll blow away.'

'Nonsense.' Beatrice smiled, leaning back and submitting to the soothing motion of Elwyn's fingers as she washed her hair with camomile and rosemary scented soap. 'Have you been well, Elwyn? Has all been quiet here at Ashton?'

'Oh, aye, very quiet. What with my lady gone, and then the master and all our knights, why, 'tis been like a grave round here. Glad we are to have you home, and with Sir Remy.'

Elwyn chuckled. Beatrice opened her eyes and looked up at her maid, with a little frown creasing her delicate brows. 'Now what is that supposed to mean?'

'Well, my lady,' said Elwyn slowly, with great importance and vastly pleased to have a tale to tell, 'the first night you were gone and the men came home, very late, mind, tired and hungry, well, Sir Remy, he goes and asks your father, in front of everyone, for your hand.'

'My hand?'

'In marriage!'

'What!' Beatrice sat up, slopping water on the floor with her sudden movement. 'My father, what did he say?'

'Not a lot. But he sent Sir Remy flying across the room. Knocked him out for a moment or two, he did. They was shouting at each other and then my lord had Sir Remy thrown out of the hall to cool him off.'

At the sound of footsteps and voices Beatrice cautioned Elwyn to silence. Beyond the curtained sanctuary they could hear several people, the scrape of chairs, a low laugh. Then suddenly the curtain swished back and Aunt Margaret exclaimed, 'Come now, Beatrice! Sir Remy waits for his turn. 'Tis the least you can do considering how well he saved your life.'

Her aunt had always been lax about privacy and Beatrice started, hunching her shoulders and crossing her arms over her bosom, as half a dozen interested faces caught a glimpse before the curtain was jerked shut again. Among them had been Joanna, and Remy, sitting at the table and stripped to the waist while Sir Kendall's squire shaved him. Beatrice gave her aunt a scowl as she snatched at the soap and washed. She stood up so that Elwyn could rinse her with a bucketful of warm water.

'Beatrice,' said Aunt Margaret slowly, stooping to pick up her discarded kirtle from the floor, 'there is blood upon your gown.'

''Tis a common fact, Aunt Margaret, that men bleed when they are killed by an arrow. Or a sword. And a spurt of blood can travel surprisingly far.'

'Nay. I see that upon your sleeve, but here…' she held up the seat of her skirt '…there is a patch.' Her aunt speared her with a sharp glance. 'What have you been up to, girl?'

Beatrice blushed fiercely, both angry and embarrassed. She realised that the headache and belly-cramps plaguing her all day heralded the start of her monthly flux, and she wondered how to explain that to her aunt, without everyone else overhearing. Beckoning to her aunt to come closer, she whispered in her ear.

'Ah. I see. Elwyn, fetch your mistress a clean robe. And her monthly linens. Quickly now.'

Beatrice stepped quickly from the tub and wrapped herself in a large linen cloth, before Elwyn slipped through the curtain.

Mortified, Beatrice submitted to her aunt's ministrations. She briskly rubbed at Beatrice's hair with a linen towel and suggested a little arnica cream for the bruise on her face.

'I thank you, Aunt, but I am perfectly well. It will be gone in a day or two.'

Her aunt sniffed. 'A lady should take care of her beauty.'

'Indeed?'

'Beatrice, is something wrong?'

'Nay, dear Aunt, nought is wrong.' But that she had lost all hope of getting to know Remy, for he would surely not notice her with Joanna radiating her youthful loveliness like a beacon.

'Mayhap I could make you a tisane to soothe your mood and your cramps. I know they have always been bad. I told your mother that regular intercourse and a babe or two would soon cure you of your affliction but—'

'Aunt Margaret, leave me, please!'

'I am only trying to—'

'I am not a child. I can well manage to dry and dress myself. Please!'

As soon as Elwyn returned, with her nightshift and a robe of soft rose brocade, Beatrice dressed and steeled herself for the moment when she must draw back the curtain. In the kitchen Remy moved aside to let her pass. Her cheeks flagged red, as from the corner of her eye she noticed his broad chest, sun-bronzed and bulging with hard muscle, that only served to remind her of her own femaleness. With head ducked down, she all but ran as she fled to her chamber.

Remy hid a smile, intrigued by the revealing female intimacies that so obviously caused Beatrice deep embarrassment. He thought that someone should take her aunt to task, but that 'someone' would certainly not be him. In his pursuit of Beatrice he could not afford to make enemies of any member of her family, not even a meddlesome aunt whose tongue needed curbing!

Any hopes Beatrice had of solitude to console herself in vanished as Joanna followed her up the stairwell. They had always been close as children, despite the fact that they were not true blood cousins. Joanna had been adopted as a newborn babe when her own mother, a lady-in-waiting to Lady Margaret, had taken a fever and died. Often Beatrice had carried the baby Joanna on her hip and as they grew up it was only natural that the younger cousin should idolise the elder. Beatrice had been flattered, patiently accepting the incessant questions and constant shadowing that accompanies adulation.

Joanna put her arm about her cousin's waist as they entered her bedchamber, which was warm and cosy, lit by a fire that Elwyn had carefully tended. The bedcovers were turned down and warmed by a hot stone that Elwyn pressed back and forth, her hands protected by linen wraps.

'Forgive her, coz. She means well, but she does not hear the sound of her own voice.'

Beatrice smiled, turning to give her cousin an affectionate hug, ashamed of her own jealousy, that seemed so cruel in the face of Joanna's gentle spirit. She sat down in a chair beside the fire and began to comb and dry her hair, gratefully accepting the mug of hot milk spiced with cinnamon and sweetened with honey that Elwyn had ready for her. Joanna was inclined to chat and she listened patiently, but saying little, too exhausted and disheartened to do more than nod and smile at the appropriate place. Elwyn, who had been maid to Beatrice since her mistress was twelve years old, was long familiar with her monthly woes, and massaged her back with firm hands while the cousins talked and the evening waned.

When her hair was completely dry Beatrice climbed into bed, snuggling down into the warm covers of the familiar and much missed four-poster bed. Joanna scrambled in on the other side and turned to face her cousin.

'I have something to tell you, Bee,' whispered Joanna, glancing cautiously over one shoulder as Elwyn tidied things away and made ready to sleep in her own truckle bed at the foot of the four-poster, 'but tomorrow. I'm too tired now…' her eyelids drooped and she wriggled closer to Beatrice's warmth '…only to say, I have lost my heart.'

Beatrice felt her own heart plummet. No doubt on the morrow Joanna would tell her how she had lost her heart to Sir Remy. He was so handsome that anyone would fall in love with him on first sight. Beatrice turned her face into her pillow and sniffed back silent tears.

It was late when Beatrice awoke in the morning. For some moments she lay still, listening. The household seemed strangely quiet. In the distance she heard the low blast of a hunting horn, and guessed, with the sunny weather, those who could and would had taken the advantage to go hunting.

'Elwyn?' called Beatrice. Hungry and thirsty, she called for her maid, but when there was no response she climbed out of bed and padded across the wooden floor.

She opened the door and called again for her maid, her voice echoing on the stone walls of the stairwell. But there came in response only silence. With a sigh Beatrice closed the door and crossed the room to open the shutters. Sunlight streamed in bright and warm and she basked in it for a moment. Then quickly she set to bathing, in water that was cold, and changing her shift and linens.

The second day of the curse was always the worst, but if she lay quietly in bed it would ease. Gratefully she climbed back up into the big bed and lay down again, feeling nauseous and a little dizzy. She called again for Elwyn, but obviously the maid had gone on an errand beyond the hall.

The sound of a knock on the door attracted her attention. Relieved that at last someone had responded, Beatrice called, 'Come in.'

The door creaked back. It was not a servant who stood in the passageway, but Remy St Leger. She gasped, and pulled the bedcovers up to her chin, wide-eyed at his temerity.

'I heard you call,' he said, his glance direct, but he did not cross the threshold. 'There is no one here, I'm afraid. They have all either gone hunting or to the fair in the village.'

'Well,' said Beatrice, 'it was nice of them to wake me.'

'Your aunt said to let you sleep. Is there something you want from Elwyn?' he asked carefully, uncertain of the delicate needs of a woman and fearing lest they should both be embarrassed.

'Only that I am parched from thirst and Elwyn has left me nothing to drink.'

'Do you want to go downstairs? I can carry you, if—'

'Nay! I am not crippled and could walk the distance, but if there is no one here…' she shrugged pointedly '…well, then, I will wait. When Elwyn returns, be so kind as to send her to me. Please.'

He bowed and with a small smile withdrew, closing the door behind him. Beatrice sighed, tingling with pleasure from their encounter and somehow bereft at his departure. She closed her eyes and settled down to sleep, but soon she was staring wide-eyed at the sunshine slanting across the oak floorboards, her thoughts galloping one after the other. Restlessly she tossed and turned, moaning now and then at the pain gripping vicelike in her lower belly. Then came another knock and again she called, with expectant hope, 'Come in.'

Remy opened the door and this time he came into her chamber, closing the door carefully behind him and bearing a tray. 'I have brought you wine and some food. It may be some while before Elwyn returns.'

'Thank you,' murmured Beatrice, glancing shyly up at him as he set the tray down on a coffer beside her bed. 'Were you not in the mood for hunting or fairs, Sir Remy?'

He was quick to note her formality. 'Nay, I too am tired. 'Tis a long trek from Wales.'

'Forgive me, I had forgotten that you had ridden so far. Did you volunteer, or was it drawn by lots?'

'Your father sent me.' He smiled, but avoiding her eye, and turned to leave, aware that he would be severely reprimanded, if not worse, if he was found in her bedchamber.

Anxious to detain him for just a moment longer, Beatrice called out, 'Would you be so kind as to close the shutters? The breeze has cooled.'

Obligingly he strode to the window embrasure and did as she asked. His glance fell upon the unfinished game of chess, set up on a small rosewood table inlaid with mother-of-pearl and flanked by two small stools, items that her father had brought home from his Crusade to the Holy Land when he was a youth. Seeing where he looked, Beatrice explained, ''Tis a game my father and I have yet to finish.'

'We…' he hesitated '…we could…' He waved his hand invitingly.

She smiled. 'Have you not better things to do, Sir Knight? No doubt you have a sword that needs sharpening, or your horse to exercise.'

''Tis a day of rest. Come, 'twill help pass the time.'

'Very well. I am white, so you will have to be black.'

Picking up the small table, chessboard and all, Remy carried them over to the bed, and then returned for a stool, placing this on the far side of the table, opposite to Beatrice, who lay upon her side in the bed. He sat down, his great size dwarfing the table and leaving Beatrice acutely aware of his masculine form and presence, the warmth of his body emanating to her across the space that divided them. Thoughtfully he considered the board for some long moments.

'I believe it was my turn next,' said Beatrice and reached out one pale hand to move her Bishop.

'If you do that,' he warned, 'my rook will move, so, and then my Queen can take you.'

'Indeed?' Beatrice considered her options, frowning, and then glanced up at his face, admonishing him, 'You must not make it easy for me.'

'I'm not!'

'You are. My father gives me no warning if I make a bad move.'

'I am not your father.'

'I know.' She smiled. 'You are a knight and you feel 'tis chivalrous to guide me. Not so?'

Remy flushed beneath his tan, his handsome mouth thinning to a grim line.

'Then, my lady, I will be utterly ruthless and give you no quarter.'

She laughed. 'Engage, Sir Knight!'

They paid no heed to the passing of time as they fought their battle of wits upon the small wooden checkerboard. Triumphantly Beatrice seized his last remaining knight and lined it up with the other black pieces she had won. All that remained were a Bishop, two pawns, his Queen and his King. She watched with interest to see what his next move would be, and then gave a low moan as pain knifed through her belly. She stifled the sound quickly in the palm of her hand, aware that he had looked up from the gameboard and was staring at her.

'Are you all right?'

'Aye,' she whispered, flushing. She longed to rub her hand over the ache in her belly, but was too embarrassed.

'Is there anything I can do?' he asked softly, hating to see the pain that shadowed her soft brown eyes and made them sharp, bruised beneath by shadows. He reached for the cup of wine and handed it to her, 'Here, drink this. It may help.'

She knew it would not but reached out and took it, sipping slowly before placing it back on the coffer.

'In Aquitaine,' he said softly, 'I have two sisters, both younger than me. Mathilde and Pierette. My mother often used to rub their backs and…' he hesitated '…their…' he cleared his throat and muttered '…fronts.' Then he smiled at her, 'Now I understand why. Not that I do not know,' he rushed to clarify, 'about how a woman's body works.'

Beatrice folded her lips upon a smile, uncomfortable at the intimacy of his words, her eyes lowered, and yet amused at his endearing concern. By rights she should have long ago banished him from her chamber, but she found that she wanted his company. Wanted to look upon his handsome face and hear his husky voice, and breathe in his delicious male smell. Her cheeks grew hot as he rose from his stool and knelt beside the bed.

Greatly daring, aware that at any moment she could censure him, he leaned over and laid his hand in the small of her back. He began moving it in slow, small circles. His hand was much larger, stronger, and seemingly even warmer, than Elwyn's and Beatrice closed her eyes. A soft sigh of pleasure escaped from her parted lips, as the motion of his hand helped to ease the pain that gripped her insides.

They neither spoke nor looked at each other as he performed this service for her. She seemed to be under his spell, mesmerised by the heat and pressure of his hand. Her body felt like it was floating on a cloud. She wanted him never to stop. And yet, in the same instant, she wanted more.

Beatrice made no protest when his other arm slipped beneath her ribs, and she kept her eyes tightly shut as he pulled her closer. She gave a low murmur of exquisite pleasure as his right hand continued its circling in the small of her back, softly, slowly, with a delicate touch that astounded her, from so big and powerfully built a man. Yet she shivered as his left hand worked independently, his fingers gently tracing her spine and then back again, moving between her shoulder blades until he found the tender nape of her neck, warm and soft beneath the swathe of her hair.

Watching her, as she lay with eyes closed, Remy drank in the vision of her loveliness. His eyes roamed over the pale white skin of her throat, where two thin blue veins forked at the hollow. Her lips were soft and darkly pink, the curve of her cheeks so smooth he imagined them to be like peaches if he touched them. Her hair was unbound and waved about her shoulders and arms in a wanton mass of honey brown. Slowly, so very slowly, he leaned closer, until his face hovered just an inch above her own.

Beatrice felt his warmth, and his bulk, as he leaned down. She felt the pressure of his hand behind her neck as he urged her to lift her head. She opened her eyes and looked up at him. She read in his face the desire he felt, and she smiled. Taking this for consent, he laid his mouth on hers and kissed her.

His kiss was soft and sweet. His circling hand stilled. She felt his stubble scrape her chin, and shivered again with pleasure. With a soft sound her arms lifted from her side, and her fingers found the hard, smooth column of his neck. Her fingertips explored his skin, his hair, his ears, his rough jaw. With a growl Remy gathered her closer, his arms sliding around her slender body and pressing her to him. His mouth opened hers and his tongue skimmed her teeth, the cavern of her moist sweetness, before finding her own tongue and delightfully playing with it.

Their pulses raced, and their skin flushed with hot damp sweat as passion soared between them. His fingers found her breast, the sensitive bud of her nipple quickly taut beneath his teasing. He sent stabs of excitement shooting through her body and Beatrice gasped, moving against him, soft moans vibrating in her throat.

Realising that he was too close to the threshold of no retreat, Remy forced himself to lift his head, staring at her. He whispered, 'Be thankful you have your flux, for if you did not I would take you now.'

Abruptly he let her go, and stood up. She tried to stop him, fingers clutching at his sleeve, his tunic, but he tore away and strode from the room, banging the door shut.

Beatrice listened to his footsteps as he ran down the

stairs, berating herself for putting temptation in both
their paths. She must never be alone with him again!
It could not be, between them. Her father would not
sanction their marriage, for though he came from a
noble family he was still the youngest son and landless. The prizes he had won on the tourney circuit
would count for nothing with her father and he would
consider him to be a poor bargain in the marriage market. Remy St Leger was the one thing a father took
pains to avoid—a landless, penniless knight. And if
that wasn't enough she would do well to remember
that he was five years younger, and so very handsome.

It was true that he had taken a fancy to her, but
what chance did she have of holding him? She had
little hope for a marriage based on lust, for as the years
passed his lust would wane, as her hair faded to grey
and her waist thickened from childbearing. For a moment she was delightfully enchanted by the tantalising
thought of bearing Remy's child. She had always
longed to hold her own babe in her arms, and she
could easily imagine that babe to have blond hair and
blue eyes. But then she returned to the tormenting
facts, that reminded her painfully why a marriage between her and Remy would be impossible.

Besides, she would not take the risk of having her
poorly mended heart broken again. And that fear was
the greatest deterrent of all. With a sigh Beatrice
turned over onto her side and sought solace from her
woes in sleep.

'Mother says you are to dress and come downstairs
for supper.'

Beatrice groaned and burrowed deeper into the
covers.

'Oh, do, please, dear Beatrice. I have missed your company this day and there are minstrels and acrobats come to the hall. We saw them at the fairing as we returned from our hunt and Mother invited them home to play for us. And Sir Richard bagged a fine stag, so all the men are in high spirits. There will be dancing.' Joanna added the last as a final lure, knowing well her cousin's love for dancing.

'Nay…' Beatrice shuddered '…I am too shamed.' For more reasons than she could truthfully admit.

Joanna clucked her tongue. 'Come now, no one thinks the worse of you because of Mother's outspokenness. Why, we have all borne the brunt of it at one time or another. Even Sir Kendall would likes strangle her after she learnt of his…' Joanna hesitated '…problem.'

Beatrice looked up with interest.

'Well, 'tis common knowledge that he has had little luck with the ladies lately.'

They laughed, but Beatrice wondered exactly what her young cousin was alluding to and whether it was proper that she should even know of such things. With a sigh Beatrice rose from her nest and allowed Joanna to help her dress, brush her hair and thread a pink ribbon through two thin braids on either side of her temples, the rest of her hair swirling about loose and lovely.

As they made ready the sound of music, laughter, and merry voices floated up the stairs. Joanna mentioned that a neighbour, Sir Vance, and his family had been invited to sup with them and it was quite a gathering, already well lubricated by drink, that sat down to eat. Beatrice was careful to avoid Remy's glance and seated herself at her usual place beside her father's chair, now occupied by Aunt Margaret. To her left was seated Sir Richard Blackthorn; Remy had been placed much further down the table, between the two daughters of Sir Vance, both plump, plain girls who almost swooned at the handsome young knight's unexpected company.

The minstrels played all through supper and Beatrice feigned a great interest in them, despite Sir Richard's deliberate attempts to divert her. He tried to engage her in conversation, but he was new to her aunt's household and she was a little wary of him. His lean face, dark brown hair and black eyes were not unhandsome to look upon, but there was something in his smouldering manner that unnerved her a little, as though he could see through her shift, or mayhap imagined her without it. Beatrice was not disappointed when her aunt claimed her attention and made enquiries about how they were managing since her mother's death.

After supper the trestle tables were broken down and put away against the far wall. Beatrice perched upon the settle beside the hearth, watching with a smile while Joanna and several other young girls urged the minstrels to play a tune they could dance to. They skipped into a carole, laughing and smiling, hands linked as they spun round in a circle.

It took some while for Beatrice to realise that Remy

was avoiding her as much as she avoided him. Though their glances collided several times, he did not once speak to her, and she did not encourage him with a smile. For once he was displaying some restraint and Beatrice thought it commendable, if highly unusual.

When the dancing began Remy sat himself down to watch Sir Kendall and Sir Richard arm-wrestle. He declined their challenge to contest them, pointing out his injured ribs. Sir Richard was insistent almost to the point of rudeness and Remy felt his temper flare.

Leaning against the warm wall beside the hearth, he watched while Sir Richard danced with Joanna, noting the man's keen interest. His hand was familiar on the girl's waist and Remy glanced to Lady Margaret, to see if she too noted this fondling. But Joanna's mother was too busy blushing and laughing at long-time-widower Sir Vance's attention. With her husband away to Wales Lady Margaret enjoyed a little male companionship and harmless flirting, revelling in the flattery that her own taciturn husband rarely bestowed upon her.

Remy drank deeply from the goblet of wine he held in one hand, and then he caught sight of Beatrice, sitting quietly on the settle. She was staring into the hearth flames, and he felt an ache in his chest as he gazed upon the features of her sweet face, her soft lips solemn. He thought he detected a bright shimmer of tears in her eyes, and wondered what sad thought it was she dwelled upon that caused her unhappiness. Despite his resolution to avoid her he shifted his frame from the wall and took a step in her direction, but he was waylaid and dragged off by the other men for a game of Hot Cockles.

It was a game he disliked, for it was often an opportunity for petty grievances to be vented. On this occasion it was to be a game only for the men. Sir Humphrey drew the short straw and was blindfolded. He knelt down and a circle formed about him. Then he had to guess who it was that struck him about the head. The blows started off with some restraint and there was much laughter as the men disguised their voices and became more enthusiastic about their task. Remy refused to participate and stood back, although when it came around for Sir Richard Blackthorn's turn he was greatly tempted to join in and administer a resounding clout.

It was a rough and tiring game and at its end the men gathered around a keg of ale to quench their thirst. The hour was growing late and jovial drunkenness was starting to turn ugly. Bess and another maid, Gillian, lingered as they served the knights with wine and seed cake. The maid caught Remy's eye and she gave him a smile, which he avoided, rasping a hand over the stubble on his chin as he pretended not to notice. The charms Bess offered, and he had on occasion enjoyed, now repulsed him. He pondered on this strange state of affairs, for he had a healthy appetite for bedsport that he had not failed to satisfy on a regular basis.

Overhearing a lewd conversation about several of the maids only served to remind him that most men were not averse to satisfying their lust with serving wenches. He tried his best to turn a deaf ear to it all, but when he heard mention of Beatrice's name his manner abruptly changed.

Sir Richard leaned against his shoulder, and enquired, his voice slurred and his eyes blood-shot, 'What know you of the Lady Beatrice? I have heard rumours that her brothers may have fallen in Wales. That makes her a wealthy heiress and I have the fancy to call myself Lord.'

Remy shouldered him away, his lip curling in distaste, 'Lady Beatrice is not a subject for conversation.'

'The thing is,' Sir Richard continued, ignoring the low growl of advice, 'she is no young maid, like Joanna—'

'Shut your mouth, Blackthorn,' snarled Remy, scowling into his mug of ale.

'Oh ho! What is this? Trespassing, am I?'

'Mayhap.' Remy shot him a hard glance.

'Oh, aye? I am wont to sample the goods before shackling myself for life. Have you? Is Lady Beatrice a good ride? Will she go on top?'

Remy shouted an oath, his temper finally goaded beyond endurance. He grabbed the front of Sir Richard's tunic in one fist, and snarled softly, 'Don't even *think* about her!'

'Or what?'

'Or I'll kill you!'

'Get your hands off me!' Sir Richard tossed his ale in Remy's face and in the next instant the two knights had toppled from their bench and were throwing punches at one another, Sir Richard's less than accurate, but Remy landing several with a satisfying thwack of his knuckles on soft flesh.

A shout went up, as several realised that a brawl was in progress. Sir Vance and his son jumped gleefully to their feet, being of the opinion that an evening's entertainment could never be better rounded off than with a good fight. Leaping into the fray, they joined in manfully as the hall erupted in a confusion of bellows, kicks, punches, eye-jabbing and stomping.

Lady Margaret sighed and beckoned for Elwyn to take Beatrice and Joanna away. Joanna protested loudly, but Beatrice was glad to escape the mêlée, horrified at the violence which men seemed to relish.

The next morning Remy received, in addition to his black eye, split lip and grazed knuckles, a severe tongue-lashing from Lady Margaret. He retreated to the bailey to exercise Walther, and refrained from pointing out to Lady Margaret that he had only been defending Beatrice's honour. It was on the tip of his tongue to say that he would not have Sir Richard Blackthorn anywhere near his daughter, but Lady Margaret was in such a fury over broken dishes and damaged furniture that a strategic withdrawal seemed wise. It rained and even Walther was little impressed with him.

From her window Beatrice watched as Remy put the big, black Hanoverian through his paces. She brushed her hair idly, leaning against the window embrasure and only half-listening to the chatter that ebbed and flowed from Joanna.

'I swear, coz, you have not heard a word!' Joanna complained and stomped across the room to snatch the hairbrush from Beatrice's hand and follow her dreamy gaze with an accusing glare. 'What on earth…? Ah, I see.'

Beatrice flushed, ''Tis not what you think.'

Joanna laughed, and put her arm around her cousin, giving her a gentle squeeze. 'Indeed? And why not? He's handsome, a fine knight, virile.'

'Young,' Beatrice sighed.

'What is a few years here or there? To my mind a younger man is far better than an old one, who will die and leave you a widow.'

'Young knights die too. In battle.'

Sensing at once the fears that plagued Beatrice her cousin murmured, 'Lightning never strikes twice. Does he know how you feel?'

'What?'

'Do you want me to murmur in his ear, or give him a token of your affection?'

'Nay!' Beatrice eyed her with some confusion. 'You—you do not mind?'

'Why on earth should I mind?'

'Well, I thought…you hinted that you had lost your heart.'

A peal of laughter burst from Joanna's shapely lips. 'Indeed I have, but not to that blond giant. 'Tis Sir Richard whom I love.'

# Chapter Five

A few days later the sky cleared and the sun came out. It was a lovely May day and Beatrice strolled in the pleasaunce, enjoying the warm sunshine upon her face and the soft scent of emerald grass and flowers growing in a colourful blaze of yellow and pink and purple. She stooped to examine the petals of marguerites and lupins, and inhale the sweet fragrance of cinnamon roses, glad for a moment of solitude to clear her confused thoughts.

A step sounded on the cobbled path behind her and a shadow cast itself over the flowers she was so intent upon. Beatrice straightened and turned about, her heart jolting as she came face to face with Remy. He too looked uncomfortable, and stared at his boots as he said gruffly, 'Your cousin Joanna said you wished to speak to me.'

'Oh, no, I did not, I—' Joanna! Beatrice cursed her silently. The scheming little madam had taken to heart her earlier, foolish words and sent Remy to her in the garden. When she had specifically stated that she wished to be alone! 'Well…' Beatrice hesitated, not wishing to offend him '…I think—' Indeed, she could not think at all, and struggled to find words, realising that if she was honest she was pleased to see him, to have the chance to clear up any misunderstanding between them. 'I thought that you and I—' She raised her eyes to his, silently pleading for his assistance.

He smiled slowly, softly. 'That we should take a stroll?'

'Aye.' Beatrice breathed a sigh of relief, and laid her hand on his arm as he held it out to her. They fell into step as they walked along the path, and Beatrice sought desperately for some civilised conversation; it seemed to her that all their previous encounters had been anything but civilised! 'It is a lovely day, do you not agree?'

'Indeed.'

'It has been a long winter.'

'Aye.'

'It is pleasant to walk in the garden and smell the flowers.'

Remy nodded and cleared his throat, a slight frown upon his brows. She was acutely aware of his tall presence, the warmth and scent of his male body, the corded muscles of his forearm beneath her fingertips.

'I hope you do not feel too unwell, Sir Remy, after your…' she hesitated '…disagreement with Sir Richard.' Her glance skimmed over his swollen purple eye and the cut upon his lower lip. She winced. 'You have not lost any teeth?'

He laughed. 'Nay, sweet Beatrice, I have not lost my teeth.'

His endearment affected her deeply and she stumbled on the uneven cobbles of the path. Remy quickly caught her about the waist. For a long moment they stood close together, staring at each other, he with a deep longing, she with confusion. Then Beatrice stepped back and they resumed their slow walk, all too aware of the windows of the castle that overlooked the pleasaunce; she had no doubt that several pairs of eyes watched them.

'Beatrice—'

'Remy—'

They both began at once, and laughed.

'You speak first,' he told her, and waited.

'Remy, I wanted to say…that is, what happened the other day, in my bedchamber, it will not, must not, ever happen again.' A blush stole over her cheeks and she glanced shyly up at him.

Her embarrassment enchanted him and he longed to pull her into his arms and kiss her lips that were now anxiously pursed, completely disregarding her words and wishes. He raised a brow, his smile rueful. 'Did my lady not enjoy being kissed? Not so long ago you begged me to do so, for you feared to become an old woman without ever knowing how it felt to be kissed by a man.'

Beatrice protested, her brows pulled together in a frown, 'That was different! My life was about to change drastically and I did not think that I would ever be part of this world, or ever see a man again after that night.'

'Indeed?' he said sardonically.

''Tis not chivalrous of you to bring it up! But—' now her temper was truly riled '—if past behaviour be the subject of our discussion then I have my own axe to grind!'

'Grind away, your ladyship.'

'Can you never be serious about anything?' she demanded, glaring up at him.

He shrugged, 'I am all yours, and all ears.'

Beatrice sighed in exasperation. 'It has come to my attention that you…' again she hesitated, she who was always so direct and easy in her speech '…it seems that you prevailed upon my father and took the liberty of asking him for my hand.'

'Aye. 'Tis true.' His tone implied that he was mightily proud of himself for this daring feat.

Beatrice was tempted to blacken his other eye. Drawing a deep, steadying breath, she asked between clenched teeth, 'Would it not have been good manners to have asked *me* first?'

'What?' He glanced down at her with genuine, wide-eyed surprise.

'Mayhap,' she said with a lofty tone, her nose tipped to the sky, 'I will not have you.'

'You will not,' he spluttered in confused outrage, 'have me?'

'Nay. If you went down on your knees today, Sir Remy, and begged me to be your wife, I would…' she held a hand to her heart and shook her head sorrowfully '…with the greatest and gravest of regrets, have to inform you that—oh!' Her sentence ended on a shriek, as Remy grabbed her hand and ran off with her down the path. 'Remy!'

Beatrice struggled to keep up with him as he dragged her along, ducked behind a high boundary of yew hedge and opened the gate that led out into the archery butts.

'Remy! What are you doing? Stop!'

He ran across a corner of the bailey and entered the cool shadows of the south tower, slammed the door shut and thrust Beatrice up against the wall. With his hands planted on either side of her head, the wall of the tower at her back and the even more formidable and solid wall of his chest before her eyes, there was no escape.

'What do you mean,' Remy panted, stooping to look down into her eyes, 'that you will not have me?'.

Beatrice swallowed nervously, her hands pressed to the hard warmth of his chest, stunned by his reaction. What had started off as a light-hearted exchange had now turned very serious indeed. 'Surely you must see,' she said softly, her eyes raised no higher than his tunic, 'that a marriage between us can never be.'

He uttered a curse then, demanding of her, 'And why not? I am a man, unwed, and you are a woman, also unwed. You cannot fault my lineage, for I am a knight of noble blood—my mother is a countess of Aquitaine. I see no great impediment to our joining.'

'Then you must be either blind or stupid! Besides the fact that my father would consider you to be unsuitable, being landless and penniless, I am not much better off. My dowry is gone and, as far as I know, the rumours that my brothers are dead are not yet true. I am unlikely to inherit any titles, and I have no manors and no gold, no silver, no jewels—'

'Stop it! Your dowry is safe. Your father tasked me

to retrieve it from the avaricious grasp of the Abbess, and it is now locked in your father's vault.'

Beatrice stared up at him, shocked. 'But—' She shook her head in confusion. 'Why did you not tell me this before?'

'Why do you think?' he counter-demanded, his glance fierce. Then he grasped her shoulders in both hands and shook her. 'It is not wealth I seek, damn it! 'Tis you alone! 'Tis you, Beatrice, that I want.'

She stared at him, full of doubt and mistrust, not only for his feelings but for her own too. She whispered, 'But why?'

For an answer he bent his head and kissed her. His lips were demanding, yet tender. He poured into her mouth all the passion that ignited him. Beatrice staggered, and he cradled her head with his large hand as the pressure of his kiss bore down on her slender neck. His other hand slid between her shoulder blades, pressing her into his body. She could feel the hard strength of his muscular torso against her soft female self, and her legs almost buckled with the startling joy of it.

At last he lifted his head and told her in a husky voice, 'That is why.' Then he went down on one knee and reached for her hand, gently holding her delicate white fingers between his palms. 'Lady Beatrice, would you do me the honour of being my wife?'

'Oh, Remy.' Tears sparked in her eyes, and then a sob burst from her throat. 'Please, get up.'

'Not until I have your answer.'

Swallowing hard, she dashed at her wet cheeks with her fingertips. 'Then my answer must be no.'

'But why?' He rose then, his fingers digging into

her waist as he clasped her to him, his eyes searching her face, 'Am I not handsome enough for you? I am young too, but no callow youth, and though I may not yet have my own lands I have been knighted, my reputation for valour upon the battlefield—'

She laid a finger on his lips, silencing him. ''Tis not you, Remy. It is I. Do you not understand that I am five years your senior? I do not care to lie awake at night while I wonder where, and with whom, my handsome young husband is spending his time.'

'Never!' he vowed. 'Once we are married I would be faithful to you unto death.'

'Indeed?' She smiled, with regret and sadness, shaking her head, her fingers closing over his wrists and urging him to release her. 'Let me go, Remy. 'Tis a fairytale you create, nothing more.'

'Nay, Beatrice!' He held her chin and kissed her again, pressing her against the wall, endeavouring to convey to her the depth of his emotion. Boldly his hand covered her breast and he pushed his knee between her legs. His other hand slid to her buttocks and lifted her against him, while his lips broke from her mouth and pressed hot, moist kisses down the side of her neck, 'Tell me you do not want me, Beatrice, as much as I want you!'

She arched her head back, shivering with pleasure at his touch, her skin on fire. 'Aye—' her voice was husky '—I want you, Remy. But lust is a poor basis for marriage and I will not shame my family by giving myself to you without the benefit of wedding vows. Nor will I condemn myself to a lifetime of misery and pain within them. For if I loved you as I once loved before, and I lost you too, the pain would kill me. I could not bear another such wound, for it goes too deep. I am too badly scarred to ever love again. Now,' she spoke more firmly and grasped his hands, lifting them away from her body, 'you must let me go. If my lady aunt were to find us so—'

'Then well and good,' he said roughly, anger at her refusal making him harsh. 'I have only to lift your skirts…' his fingers plucked at the fabric of her kirtle, baring her ankles, his voice hoarse and urgent '…and take you!'

'You would not dare.' Beatrice stared up at him with a gasp, suddenly reminded of his powerful male strength. 'And if you did dare, Remy, do you think I will thank you for such a brutal bedding, here upon the stairs of the south tower? It would be wrong and you well know it!'

'Aye, but you would have no choice but to make good the wrong by marrying me.'

'And two wrongs would make a right?'

He had the grace to hang his head in shame, his passion subsiding at her rebuke, and her resistance. Gently she stroked his cheek with her palm, and whispered, 'You will find someone else.'

'Nay!' He turned his head and pressed a kiss to the soft skin on the inside of her wrist. 'Mayhap my wooing has been too rough, too sudden, and for that I beg your pardon. I admit that I am no courtier, prancing about in pointed shoes and coloured hose. I cannot spout pretty poems, nor shower you with gifts and garlands of flowers, but…' here he drew a deep breath, and her heart ached at the catch in his voice '…know

that my feelings for you are true, Beatrice. I would
cut out my own heart before ever I would hurt or betray you.'

'Oh, Remy.' She longed to throw her arms around
him and surrender to his will, but she felt certain that
it would only lead to disaster for them both. She
brushed aside a lock of hair from his forehead. 'You
are too stubborn for your own good.'

Then she tore away from his arms and ran out of
the tower, tears blinding her path as she found her way
across the bailey to the keep, seeking refuge in her
chamber. Upon her bed she wept.

Despite the combined cajoling of both Joanna and
her aunt, Beatrice refused to attend the hall for supper.
Elwyn brought her a tray, but she ate little and sat in
a silent state of melancholy, staring into the fire flames
while Elwyn brushed out her hair. Her tears had long
since ceased, and now only a dull emptiness left her
still and silent.

'Tell me,' said Elwyn softly, 'why my little bird is
so quiet this eve?'

''Tis naught.' Beatrice smiled weakly. 'My usual
weariness at this time of the month.'

Elwyn shook her head, stroking the brush in long,
slow sweeps down the length of Beatrice's gleaming
hair. 'Nay, you can fool everyone, even yourself, but
there is nothing usual about my lady tonight.'

At that tears began to slide silently down Beatrice's
cheeks. She sniffed and wiped them furiously away.
'Do not give me sympathy, Elwyn, for I must be
strong and accept my lot in life.'

'Oh, aye?'

'Indeed. Decisions, once made, must not be broken.'

'How noble, my lady.'

Beatrice swallowed. She did not want to think about Remy. She must not doubt for a moment that she had made the right decision.

''Tis cold comfort,' murmured Elwyn.

Beatrice glanced up with a question in her eyes.

'Being noble will not warm your bed on a winter's night. 'Tis your birthing day next Lammas, is it not, my lady?'

'Aye.'

'And how old will you be?'

Beatrice sighed. 'You know well enough that I shall be thirty years old.'

'Aye. Thirty years old, Lady Beatrice,' Elwyn stated firmly, 'and if I were you I would grab hold of that handsome young Aquitaine that wants you so much, with both hands, before it's too late.'

'Hush,' Beatrice admonished her. 'What kind of a fool do you think I am? Aye, he wants me now, and, aye, maybe it will last for a year or two. But what then? He will cast me aside in favour of a pretty young thing, her face unmarred by crow's-feet about the eyes and her breasts firm and plump.'

'And are you God, to see the future so clearly? And even if it was so, and I greatly doubt that he would be so fickle, for even a doorpost can see how he cares for ye, then take the year or two and make the most of it! 'Tis better than nothing, better than the cold comfort of your noble and empty bed.'

With a sigh Beatrice snatched her head away. 'If I

was not so fond of you, Elwyn, I would punish you for your wayward tongue! Besides, Joanna will be up anon and share the bed with me.'

''Tis only truth I speak. Lies are easy to swallow, but 'tis the truth which oft times sticks in the gullet.' Elwyn helped her mistress to disrobe and climb up into the four-poster bed that awaited her, with warmed sheets turned down invitingly upon its vast expanse. ''Tis a shame indeed to waste all that space upon your cousin.'

'Be gone!'

Elwyn clucked and fussed, tidied the room and then retired to sleep upon her pallet. Beatrice listened to her gentle snores and lay awake for many hours, her thoughts in riot. When Joanna came to bed she was full of giggles and whispers upon the merits of Sir Richard, dwelling on the significance of his every glance and word. Beatrice sighed with relief when at last Joanna fell into a peaceful slumber.

That night her dreams were filled with anguish and longing.

She woke in the morning feeling unrefreshed. She dressed carefully in a gown of soft watchet trimmed with gold embroidery, her hair fastened in a matching net of fine gold mesh.

Slowly she descended the stairs to the great hall, and glanced about cautiously. She looked for Remy. She needed to see him, to speak with him, to gauge whether the feelings of her heart were truer than the reasoning of her mind. He stood with his back to her, and her heart did a little somersault at the sight of his tall frame, his blond hair slightly ruffled from the night's sleep and his voice husky as he spoke. He was occupied with his squire, as bedrolls were put away and instructions given for the day, but as he turned to wash his hands in a bowl of hot water offered to him by a serving maid, their eyes met. Again her heart did peculiar things, a pitter-patter that she was unfamiliar with, and she felt the warmth of a blush heat her face and spread throughout her limbs. How could one glance have such a strange effect? she thought, bewildered by emotions that were both unfamiliar and exciting all at once. She had to speak with him, but to summon him to her side would cause unwelcome comment, and, judging from the grim set of his face, she was not at all sure he would respond favourably.

Sitting down with Aunt Margaret and Joanna to break her fast, Beatrice idly crumbled a piece of bread, and wondered how she could achieve a secret meeting with Remy. Joanna would see it as a tryst, and be all too eager to conspire in the venture, yet she was reluctant to confide in her cousin, fearing that her tongue would wag. Listening to the conversation at table, she realised that plans were afoot to go hunting before noon, if it did not rain. She was not overly fond of hunting, but she thought an opportunity might be found to speak privately with Remy, whilst they were out in the forest. But then, she mused, if they were using hawks, as seemed likely when the discussion turned to the merits of goshawks and peregrines, no doubt they would keep to the open fields, which would afford little shelter from observation. She pondered on her dilemma and then noticed that Remy was staring at her across the width of the table. She was about to smile when he looked away, his expression stern, no doubt keenly aware of his rejection. Now she fretted anxiously, eager to make it known to him that all hope was not lost.

But then she faltered, afraid to commit herself, afraid to hurt him needlessly if she found that a great mistake had been made. Mayhap what she felt for him was little more than what he felt for her, and could be easily extinguished by a satisfying night or two in his arms. Her cheeks flared with bright colour at such a thought, but in all honesty she could not see herself creeping about in her nightshift, nor would she lower her high ideals and reduce them to mere carnal desire. What she wanted was love, true love, and Remy had made no mention of such, despite the overwhelming expertise of his kisses that left her in no doubt as to his passion. And yet to love again filled her with terror. She could hardly dare to believe that it could be true either. Did this man love her? What was there about her to love? She had loved William so deeply, with such a fierce ardour, and when he was taken from her the pain of that loss had made her ache with despair. She thought that she was one of those people who could love only once, who chose a mate for a lifetime, like a swan, and even if that mate no longer lived she was still bound to him by her heartstrings. William and his love had filled her life with such brightness that his sudden death had plunged her into a world of deep and endless darkness. Now, many years later, she lived in a world that was neither dark nor bright, but a dull safe warmth that sustained her need for survival. Dare she make any attempt to reach out for the brightness again?

It was imperative that she speak with him, in private, but it became very clear indeed that Remy was taking great pains to avoid her. By mid-morning she was seething with frustration, and just when she resolved to go to the armoury and confront him, heedless of the breach of etiquette she would be committing in so doing, another matter arose that took precedence.

Elwyn came to her chamber, where Beatrice sat with her tapestry frame and her restless thoughts, and announced that a messenger had arrived from Wales. Beatrice set aside her sewing and flew down the stairs. She came at a run across the hall, skirts and braids all flying askew in her haste. But she was halted in mid-stride, when her aunt held out a hand and said, ''Tis for Sir Remy.'

Beatrice gasped, and then watched while a servant was sent to the armoury to fetch him. She asked the messenger, 'Do you come from Wales?'

'Aye.' He shifted uneasily.

'Did Lord Thurstan send you?'

The messenger gulped and nodded, eyeing her nervously, but his torment was not prolonged as Remy came striding into the hall, tracking mud from his boots and his eyes narrowed in suspicion. At once the messenger turned to him and held out the parchment, relieved to have done his duty.

Remy studied Lord Thurstan's seal and then said tersely, 'Go you to the kitchen and have your fill of ale, and a meal.'

The messenger bowed and grinned his thanks, while Beatrice contained her annoyance, her lips thinned to a tight line as she wondered at how Remy dared to give orders in *her* hall.

Remy broke the red wax seal and then realised, with a flush of stinging embarrassment, that he could make little sense of the formal Latin script. He cast around and, seeing his dilemma, Lady Margaret carefully edged in by his elbow. She read the letter quickly, gasped several times, and looked with horror from Remy to Beatrice and back again.

'What is it?' demanded Beatrice, losing all patience and snatching the message from Remy's hand. She took it to the fire and by its light cast her eyes over her father's neat writing, chagrined that the one for whom the message was intended was still ignorant as to its contents. Quickly, however, all amusement was wiped from her face and she too gasped with astonishment.

'Well?' demanded Remy.

'My father has summoned you back to Wales,' said Beatrice slowly, 'and you are to take me with you.'

Remy stared at her in disbelief and then searched about the hall, until he found the chaplain. In two strides he was at Beatrice's side, and plucked from her fingers his letter. He thrust it at Father Thomas and commanded, 'Read this to me.'

With shaking hands the priest held the creased parchment, cleared his throat, squinted at the thick black letters and read out loud, 'Greetings to Sir Remy St Leger, from your liege, Lord Thurstan. I ask that you bring at once my only daughter. Bring too the medicine chest containing poppy juice. We wait for you at Carmarthen and wish you God speed.'

'Nay!' exclaimed Remy. 'I will not take a woman to Wales.'

'My father commands you.'

''Tis safe enough,' murmured Sir Kendall, 'by Carmarthen and the Marcher lands.'

'Aye,' agreed Sir Humphrey, 'and we will ride with you, as we are due to rejoin with Lord Robert now that we have safely delivered Lady Margaret to Ashton.'

Remy frowned, his mouth a hard line. He liked it not, and he cast a glare upon Beatrice that made her knees shake. 'Then pack and be ready, my lady. 'Tis not yet noon and we can make some distance before nightfall.'

Beatrice and Elwyn flew about the bedchamber in their haste to pack and be ready. Beatrice changed her kirtle in favour of leather breeches and a riding gown that was split both front and back. She sent a message to the stables for Bos to be saddled, brushing aside Elwyn's fears that she was not a rider skilled enough to handle the young stallion.

'He is swift and strong,' retorted Beatrice, 'and such a horse will I need if we are to keep pace with Walther.'

An hour later they assembled in the hall with five panniers and four saddlebags, and two baskets of food packed by Lady Margaret. Beatrice was making her farewells when Remy came striding into the hall to chivvy her along. He stopped and stared at her baggage, stifling the oath that sprang to his lips.

'What is all this?' he asked with feigned patience, waving one hand at the small mountain of luggage.

Beatrice frowned at him, wondering if he had left his senses in the bailey. 'Why, 'tis mine and Elwyn's belongings.'

'Elwyn? She will not be going. One woman is bad enough, but two, never!'

'But I must have my maid! Who else will attend me?'

'You will manage on your own.' He knelt on one knee and began ripping open the panniers, pulling out gowns and shifts and girdles, hairbrush, Bible, shoes, blankets, shawls, and piling them up on the floor. Then he tipped out the saddlebags and curtly ordered Beatrice to repack. 'Two saddlebags, my lady, 'tis all you can take. And make haste, we leave anon.'

Beatrice watched with her mouth gaping open. Her temper rose in a flash and she turned to berate him, but already he was striding out the door, shouting orders as he chased the ten men-at-arms who would accompany them.

Aunt Margaret clucked her tongue. 'These young men nowadays, so full of themselves.'

Elwyn bent to retrieve their scattered belongings and sort through the essential items that Beatrice would need: two clean gowns, two shifts, her monthly linens, hose, slippers, brush and Bible.

Fastening on her cloak, Beatrice turned to embrace her aunt. 'When I return Father will be with us, I am sure.' Then she turned to Elwyn and bade her farewell.

'Aye, mistress. Take you good care of yourself now.'

They kissed, then Beatrice hurried outside as Remy's squire hovered anxiously. A sharp breeze lifted tendrils of hair at her temples and the hem of her dark blue cloak. Beatrice ran lightly down the steps into the bailey and looked up at Bos, the fine bay stallion her brother Osmond was training to be a warhorse. He snorted at the touch of her fingers on his pink nose, pawed the ground and swished his tail. Beatrice swallowed nervously and looked around for assistance—Bos was so much taller than Willow and she was unable to mount on her own.

A shadow fell over her and Beatrice turned to face Remy as he came to stand at her shoulder, eyeing Bos grimly, hands on his lean hips in a belligerent fashion, 'Tell me that you do not intend to ride this creature.'

Beatrice took a deep breath, and drew herself proudly upright, glancing up at him with a spark of challenge in her eyes. 'Aye, I do intend to ride him. He is one of the best horses we have.'

'He is too strong for a woman. Take Willow.'

'She is old and slow. Bos will keep better pace with Walther.'

'Not if I have to stop all the time and pick you up from the roadside.'

'Nonsense! Bos is well mannered.'

'He will toss you,' warned Remy gravely, and then, with a sigh, seeing the stubborn set of her mouth, and not wishing to engage in a full-blown public argument, he put his hands to her hips and lightly lifted Beatrice up into the saddle.

Beatrice, caught offguard, gasped and quickly threw her leg over the saddle and settled her feet in both stirrups. Remy thrust her thigh up with his forearm as he ducked beneath the saddle flap to check and tighten the girth. In protest, Bos kicked with one back leg and Beatrice had to grab quickly at the reins, almost unseated before the journey had begun.

Casting her a sceptical glance with raised brows, Remy strode away and vaulted on to Walther. With a shout he wheeled the destrier and led the small party out of the gate, across the wide green meadow of the outer bailey and clattered across the drawbridge.

# Chapter Six

It became at once apparent that Remy would be their leader, despite the fact that the three knights belonging to Birchlea had the advantage in age, Sir Humphrey Stanhope being the eldest at twenty-eight. Remy set a fast pace, cantering swiftly over hill and dale towards Bristol and leading them through all the short cuts he had learned of on his previous journeys.

They had not gone far when Bos took exception to Sir Richard's horse riding close alongside him. He lashed out with his back leg and with his teeth took a chunk out of the unfortunate creature's neck. Sir Richard's horse screamed and during the ensuing fracas Beatrice lost her seat.

With a cry she hit the ground with a hard thump, banging her hip and elbow and flying hooves narrowly missed crushing her head. Remy swore and called the party to a halt, trotting Walther back and swinging down. He knelt in the road at Beatrice's side; with his hands running over her limbs he quickly ascertained that she was not seriously injured. Then he lifted her up by the elbow and said, stooping to peer into her face, ''Tis not too late to turn back. No doubt Willow will be pleased to see you.'

Beatrice jerked her arm free, and replied sharply, 'We go on.'

He shrugged, seized her so roughly that she gasped aloud, and lifted her into the saddle. Catching his eye and the slight smile on his mouth, as his hand lingered on her rump, she rather suspected he enjoyed picking her up. Beatrice snatched up the reins and took control of Bos, who jibed a little but respected her firm hand. Putting his head down, he flowed into a beautiful, smooth canter that scarce bounced Beatrice from the saddle. The other horses kept well out of his way.

By the time dusk fell they had travelled a good twenty miles, and Beatrice ached in places she never knew could ache. She longed to lie down and rest her weary body, and as they rode through wooded countryside she wondered where they would spend the night. But Remy had no intention of stopping just because the sun had set. Beatrice felt her anger rise again. She wanted to shout at him, hammer him with her fists, swear at him, but he rode ahead and she was helpless to do anything other than keep Bos under control and cantering onwards.

A cloudless night sky lit their way by star and moonlight and the spring evening was only mildly cool. Beatrice marvelled at the rare privilege she had been granted in sharing this experience, this company of men, when women were oft left behind, cosseted and sheltered within the dull safety of stone walls.

At last Remy called a halt, but only because the

horses were tired and needed to be cooled, watered and fed. They walked for some distance, and then turned off the main track and made camp in a sheltered dell amongst the massive trunks of an oak wood. Squires took care of the horses, while the knights quickly set about erecting canvas tents and making a fire.

They sat on fallen logs and ate a dry supper of cold meat, bread and cheese, washed down by wine or water carried in skins. Beatrice sat exhausted and silent, slightly apart from the men as they busied themselves with horses, tack, armour, their conversation incomprehensible as they muttered and grumbled and discussed the path ahead and the war in Wales. All she wanted was to sleep and she stood up, planning to find a tent and a sheepskin that would accommodate her.

The talk abruptly stopped, and the men looked at her. The light of the dancing flames fell upon her pale cheeks and the glow of her braided honey hair. Beatrice was acutely aware that she was the only woman amongst eighteen men, although the ten men-at-arms camped apart from them, in a protective ring about the inner core of the four knights, their four squires and, at their heart, Lady Beatrice of Ashton.

Remy rose to his feet, still chewing on a hunk of bread, as did Sir Richard Blackthorn, and Beatrice was trapped between the pair of them.

'I wish to sleep,' she whispered, glancing shyly up at Remy.

'Come, my lady,' said Sir Richard, taking her gently by the wrist, 'my tent is available to you.'

Roughly Remy seized her other wrist and for a moment Beatrice felt like a bone caught between two dogs, before Remy pulled her away and thrust her behind him. He held her with his left hand, while his right hand clasped the hilt of his sword and he announced in an implacable voice, ''Tis I Lord Thurstan entrusted with the safety of his daughter. Not you, Blackthorn. She will sleep in my tent.'

For a moment Sir Richard glared at the younger man, then he grinned, and swept an ornate bow as he backed away, 'As you wish.'

A tug on her wrist and Beatrice had to follow Remy, tripping in his wake over the rough ground. His squire ran ahead and flung aside the tent flap, fussed around arranging furs and sheepskins, showed Beatrice where he had put her saddlebags and begged to know if she required anything else.

'Your manners are better than your knight's.' She smiled at the boy, ignoring Remy's scowl at this insult. 'What is your name?'

'Nogood.'

'What?'

'His name is Nogood,' barked Remy and, with his hand in the small of her back all but shoved Beatrice inside the tent. 'Lie you down and go to sleep. We rise at dawn.'

Beatrice had thought she would lie awake all night, so strange was her bedchamber, with the wind banging on canvas, the rustle and snap of the woods all about, the smell of grass and the snort and stamp of horses close by. But she fell asleep almost instantly and only woke up once when the weight and heat of a large male body settled not two feet away from her. In one corner Nogood lay, judging by his snores, and Beatrice did not stir until he gently wakened her at first light. She suspected that her easy slumber had much to do with the fact that Remy St Leger slept beside her, and with his broad back for her door and his long legs for her walls she had felt safe as a babe within its cradle.

Remy watched her in the morning, with an inscrutable face, as they prepared to ride on. She stood in front of Bos, stroking his nose and talking softly to him. The stallion's ears were pricked as he listened, and he mumbled at her hair with his thick, velvety lips. Laughing, Beatrice fed him a crust of bread and Bos snorted, butting her gently in the stomach for more. Her lack of fear impressed Remy, for there were few women, especially one as small as Beatrice, who would not be frightened of the hot-tempered and powerful destrier.

Even though he knew her body must be screaming with aching protest at the unfamiliar exercise, he admired the way she made no complaint. Her walk was slightly hobbled as she moved to check girth and stirrup leathers and Remy was quick to be the one to assist her to mount, even though Sir Richard had attempted to reach her first.

Beatrice smiled her thanks to Remy and gathered the reins in one hand, turning Bos to join with the others. The day was much the same as the one before, although longer and more exhausting. Sometimes the men sang; often there was a joke and much laughter. She liked listening to them, even though their conver-

sation was sometimes not suitable for the hearing of
a lady.

Remy looked back often, not only to check on his
men and their progress, but to check that Bos behaved
and gave Beatrice no trouble. Or was that just an excuse to look at her lovely face? Her smile was so soft
and sweet, he thought, although always slightly
guarded. He wondered if she ever allowed herself to
let go of this elderly and formal constraint that she
wore like the mantle of an old woman. What would it
take to make her laugh so hard and so loud that tears
ran down her cheeks?

That night it was he who tossed and turned, while
she slept soundly in a nest of furs, a slender shape
beneath her covers, but the curve of one hip, as she
lay on her side, distinctly female.

On the third day they left England behind and entered Wales. Beatrice noticed a change in the men.
They became quieter, wary and vigilant. The countryside was now wild and treeless, rising to high mountain crags and swept by a noisy wind.

Sir Kendall rode alongside Beatrice and she asked
him, 'Tell me about the Welsh. Are they as fiercesome
as everyone says?'

'Indeed.' Sir Kendall nodded sagely, glad for the
opportunity to impress her with his knowledge, scant
as it was. 'They are not overly tall, but they are ex-
ceptionally sturdy and live outdoors in all weathers.
They throw javelins and spears and it is thanks to them
that we have adopted the longbow, which can fire an

arrow over a greater distance than our crossbows, and
with more accuracy.'

'Indeed.' Beatrice considered this information and
looked fearfully up at the barren hills circling them,
expecting at any moment to see hordes of angry
Welshmen aiming their arrows at her.

Remy, overhearing this conversation, twisted in the
saddle, with a frown for Sir Kendall. 'Have no fear,
my lady, for we ride through Marcher lands still. There
are no Welsh here who will attack us.'

Beatrice relaxed a little at this information, but,
judging from the continued wariness and quiet of the
men, as they rode in close formation about her and
looked constantly to left and right, she wondered how
truthful his assurance was.

That night they camped against the walls of a Cis-
tercian monastery, and had their first hot meal in three
days, seated at the refectory table of the monks' guest-
house. Remy made enquiries about a room for Beatrice, but it turned out there were none available, full
as they were with a large party of pilgrims on their
way to St David's. After the meal, she returned with
the men to their camp and settled herself for the night
in Remy's tent, while he sat around the campfire and
warmed himself with aquavit, hoping that it would
dull his senses. He must spend another night sleeping
alongside Beatrice and he was not certain that he could
endure the torment, or the temptation.

In the tent's dark privacy Beatrice sank down with
a sigh upon the nest of furs that Nogood had made
ready for her. After three days of hard riding her gown

and breeches stank of dirt and horseflesh. Glancing over her shoulder, making sure the tent flap was down, she pulled off her boots, her hose, her breeches and her gown. Clad only in her muslin shift, she climbed beneath the covers and settled her aching body with a sigh, wriggling her bare toes with delight into the spongy softness of a sheepskin.

Shadows from the men seated around the fire leapt gigantically against the cream canvas of the tent, and Beatrice watched these idly as her thoughts roamed. She heard Sir Kendall tell a joke about a maid and a monk that made her ears blush, although she didn't quite understand its meaning and was intrigued when Sir Humphrey admonished his fellow knight for its coarseness. Remy, however, laughed heartily and then the men were silent for a moment, conspicuously aware of the lady that lay not far from them.

Smiling to herself, her cheek pillowed on one hand, Beatrice fell asleep, her last thought being that the Welsh would not attack them here on the sacred ground of a monastery. When the others came to sleep she did not know, but when she woke again it was very dark and quiet, except for the distant howl of a wolf that had disturbed her from her sleep. She woke with a start, heart thumping, and reached out with one hand, hearing no snores and fearful of being alone.

She encountered the warm bulk of Remy's back. Reassured that she was not alone she turned over, facing towards him. She remembered her conversation with Sir Kendall and suddenly, in the black emptiness of a dark, wild night, she felt a return of her fears. What, indeed, was there to stop the Welsh from attacking them? Mayhap they were heathens and had no respect for the sanctity of holy ground, and there was neither moat nor battlements to protect them from whatever the hills harboured.

Stifling a small moan of terror she shifted closer to Remy, and he, his instincts honed with a soldier's alertness, woke instantly. He turned to her, his voice rough with sleep and rasped, 'What is it?'

His hand reached at once for his sword, but her cool fingers on his wrist stayed him. ''Tis naught,' she whispered, 'I was just a little…afraid.'

He lay back down, aware of her small hand and her bare arm as it slid past his when she tucked it back under the covers. 'Have no fear,' he answered softly, 'I will protect you with my life from all harm.'

In the dark Beatrice smiled. She could not help but voice her fears, 'But you are only one man, Sir Remy.'

With a chuckle, he lifted her hand and placed it upon the massive bulge of his bicep and whispered back, 'Aye, but what a man!'

Beatrice clucked her tongue at his boasting, but joined him in a soft chuckle, realising that he humoured her out of her fear. It seemed only natural when he reached out and dragged her pallet of furs closer, and she made no objection when their two separate sleeping spaces became one. For a while they were both silent and she wondered, judging from his deep, even breathing, if he was asleep. 'Remy?'

He grunted, and stirred. 'What?'

'Do the Welsh kill women, in battle?'

His eyes opened at that, although he could see nothing in the pitch dark. He did not want to frighten her more and tell her the truth: that the Welsh would not kill her, but rape her and take her captive. 'Nay, my lady, they do not kill women.'

She sighed thankfully, slightly mollified. 'How far do we still have to go?'

'We should reach Carmarthen by midday tomorrow.'

'I shall be very glad to see my father.'

'Aye. And he will be glad to see you.'

She smiled. 'Remy?'

He curbed his impatience, holding sleep at bay as he answered her yet again, 'What?'

'Where is Nogood?'

'On guard duty.'

'Would it...be very improper...if I asked you...to hold me?'

He smiled, 'Aye, my lady, very improper indeed.' But without further ado he reached out, opened both their covers, and pulled her slender body into the warmth of his.

Beatrice gasped as she met the furnace-like heat that his body generated, and realised, with a further gasp, that he slept naked. He, too, became aware that she wore only her shift and the feel of her silky limbs against him stirred his blood. But neither of them made any comment, and Beatrice settled herself with two inches of space between their bodies, her head pillowed against his proud bicep. She resisted the urge to rub her cheek against him and snuggle even closer to his heavy male body that towered reassuringly over her. A languid warmth flooded through her limbs and she relaxed trustingly beside him, eager once again for sleep.

'Beatrice?' whispered Remy, after some long while, probing to see if she was still awake.

'Mmm?' she murmured drowsily.

His reply was to press his lips to her temple, his fingers sliding up her arm to reach her chin, tipping her face up to his and finding her mouth unerringly in the dark, tilted to the perfect angle to meet his kiss. Beatrice sighed weakly, soft and pliant, unresisting. Whenever Remy kissed her she knew only pleasure, and so she lay quietly and let him. His ardour quickened and his mouth opened hers, his tongue sliding possessively in and joining with her tongue in a kiss of such deep intimacy that she quivered. She moaned and her arms slid around his neck, encouraging him to continue.

Whether it was the aquavit or the knowledge that tomorrow he must surrender Beatrice to her father, he did not know, but he only knew that he wanted more, much more. His fingers found the strap of her shift and slid it down from her shoulder, tugging at the fragile linen until her breast was bared to him and his hand settled upon the soft, high mound. His thumb brushed the velvet circle of her nipple and instantly it tightened into a bud.

Beatrice gave a gasp, startled at the touch of his fingers on her breast. He leaned over her, tucking her hips against his, the heavy bulk of his thigh sliding over her legs. His hand explored down the length of her body and cupped the round flesh of her buttocks, pressing her even closer to him. Beatrice lowered her hands to his chest, her heart drumming very hard. He kissed her again, long and deep, and then his mouth moved to her nipple and Beatrice exclaimed softly. She melted as he sucked and licked, shudders of pleasure vibrating deep within her. Her hands now clutched at his shoulders, holding on to him for guidance and support as he swept her along on a wave of excitement.

'Beatrice,' he whispered hoarsely against her cheek, 'I want you.' His hips pushed closer, the solid ridge of his arousal leaving her in no way uncertain of his need.

They both lay still, unmoving, struggling for breath, knowing that in the next moment all would be changed between them, and staring at one another in the dark as Remy waited for her consent and Beatrice hesitated to give it.

Suddenly the tent flap was thrust up. They both froze. Nogood came in and flung himself down upon his pallet, carefully putting aside his sword and boots. For a long time Remy and Beatrice lay entwined, until at last they heard Nogood's snores and carefully Remy drew himself away, and moved with great stealth to lie apart from her. He buried his long sigh of regret in the furs he lay upon and succumbed to the depths of sleep that reached out to claim him, before starting awake as a violent thought attacked him: God Almighty, he had almost deflowered Lord Thurstan's daughter!

Beatrice lay awake for a long time, hardly able to contain the thoughts that racked her for hours. How close they had come to breaking the bonds of honour that bound them so closely! If she had given herself to him, in that moment of heat and lust that robbed the mind of all reason, his conscience would no doubt have forced him into offering for her hand and she would have soon found herself wed to the handsome knight. And all she had sought to avoid would have been achieved, the price being a few moments of ecstasy. Thank goodness for Nogood and his unexpected arrival! For she still could not decide whether it was folly to refuse Remy, or folly to love him. Exhausted from the day's journey and wrestling with her thoughts she too, at last, fell sleep.

In the morning Beatrice found it difficult to wake. When she rose reluctantly from her bed she gazed upon Remy's empty pallet and was uncertain whether she felt disappointment or relief that they had been interrupted the night before. This morn she may well have risen a woman in the truest sense, but to surrender her virginity in such a manner seemed cheap indeed. She dressed with shaky hands and wondered how she would face Remy in the broad light of day, after such intimacy as they had shared last night.

The tent flap cracked open and Beatrice started, looking fearfully over her shoulder as she laced up her kirtle. She met Remy's glance, her brown eyes wide and accusing. He came in and knelt at her side, drawing her into his embrace, but she remained stiff as wood.

'I will ask your father again for permission to wed you,' he said softly, glancing down at her, wishing that she would look at him, yet when she did he flinched. They were aware of the men outside, their conversation conducted in hoarse whispers.

'Let us not argue that point again.' With both hands she tried to push him away, but he remained unmoving, and she glared at him, her lips still tender from all his kissing, her chin scraped pink from the rasp of his stubble. 'What makes you think I am more willing now to marry you?'

'Well…' he shrugged '…after last night—'

'It was a mistake, that's all.'

He captured her by both wrists and bent his head to look her in the eye, as he whispered fiercely, 'I will have you for my wife, Beatrice! Aye, last night was a mistake, for I wish to worship you with my body within the bonds of matrimony, but that does not mean the wanting has lessened.' He gave a low laugh, 'Indeed, my taste of honey has left me aching for more, but when I take you, when we finally join together, it will be as husband and wife.'

She turned her head away from him, flushing with embarrassment. 'Have you forgotten that in ten years' time I will be an old woman and you will be yet in your prime?'

'By the blood of Christ, what foolishness you speak!' He tilted her chin up to him, his blue eyes blazing. 'You are not the sort of woman to age, and I care nothing for a few years' difference. Why, to look at you one would think that you are no more than sixteen, and by this fuss you make I would say less, for you speak not with any wisdom.'

She was gratified, but not sufficiently enough to dissolve her doubts about accepting him, and rebuked him sharply, 'Nay, Remy, it cannot be.'

'Why?'

Her long hair shivered in a wave as she glared up at him. 'I have stated my reasons why. Do not press me further.'

'Is it...' it was his turn to blush as he hesitated to ask '...is it because of my strength? You fear intimacy with me because I might hurt you?'

'Aye, Sir Remy—' she seized upon the excuse '—I tremble at the thought of being bedded by you. I would be wiser to seek a wizened old man, one who is eager to do my bidding, as you are not.'

He bent to nuzzle her neck, whispering close to her ear, 'Aye, but he will not satisfy you as I would.'

She turned her head away from his kiss and pushed him back. Seeing that she would not easily grant him her favour, Remy released her. 'We are ready to ride, my lady, and the sooner we reach Carmarthen and your father, the sooner we can make all right.'

She was so self-conscious about the events that had occurred during the night that the mere thought of emerging in broad daylight caused a fierce blush to sweep up her neck. 'I do not think I can face anyone!'

'No one will know,' he assured her, but then he frowned with doubt as he eyed her swollen lips and rosy cheeks. 'Pull up your hood. I will make it known that you are belaboured by a cold.'

Beatrice waited until the very last moment before emerging from the tent, and strode quickly to Bos, looking neither to left nor right. Remy tossed her up into the saddle, but she did no more than glance at

him. Quickly the remains of the camp were broken
down, packed away and they set off.

Along the way Remy rehearsed mentally what he
would say to Lord Thurstan. He meant to impress
upon her father how deeply he felt for Beatrice, and
would make no mention of their premature intimacy—
that is, unless he had to.

Beatrice, too, considered what she would say to her
father when she at last saw him. But somehow she
could not focus her thoughts and was faced with a
bewildering array of mismatched, feeble sentences that
neither excused nor condoned Remy St Leger. Her
gaze strayed to his broad back and the column of his
tanned neck again and again. It was madness to consider a wedding. Sheer madness!

Shortly before midday they clattered into the small
town of Carmarthen and rode directly to the castle. A
sentry let them pass quickly enough as soon as he had
established their identity, and many turned aside from
their tasks to watch as their party swept to a halt in
the courtyard. Here they were greeted by Sir Giles
Radley and Beatrice embraced him tightly as soon as
she had dismounted. Her first question was for her
father, but to her dismay, over her head, Sir Giles
turned his gaze to Sir Remy and quite ignored her.

'Come this way,' said Sir Giles, leading them up
the steps and into the hall. 'Sir Remy, a word. My
lady, sit you down by the fire. I will order refreshments for you.'

Reluctantly, Beatrice sat on the edge of a broad,
polished oak settle placed at right angles to the hearth.

Her eyes were wide and wary as she watched Remy and Sir Giles stride away. They climbed a spiral staircase and were gone from her view. The hall was busy, and a maid approached her with a tray of wine and honey cakes. Beatrice accepted both gratefully and then sat up as a soft voice claimed her attention.

'Welcome, my dear, to Carmarthen. I am Lady Alys, wife to my Lord Haworth. I am chatelaine here—'

'My lady—' Beatrice rose quickly to her feet, dipping a curtsy as she set aside her goblet and half-eaten honey cake '—I beg you to take me at once to my father, Lord Thurstan.'

A shadow passed over Lady Alys's face and she laid a restraining hand on Beatrice's arm. 'In a moment, my dear—'

Alarm speared Beatrice. 'Nay! Now, at once. I will not be put off.' She ran across the hall and up the spiral stairs before Lady Alys could stop her.

Ascending quickly, tripping over the hem of her gown in her haste, Beatrice emerged into a narrow corridor brightened by the light spilling from an open door at the far end. She could hear muted conversation, and recognised the deep, beloved timbre of her father's voice. Calling his name, she burst into a room filled with people. Remy knelt on the floor beside a low cot, and it was he who turned with a shout and clenched fist, pointing with outstretched finger to the doorway.

'Get her out of here!' he roared, and at once Woodford and Fitzpons seized Beatrice about the waist and dragged her from the room.

She did not go quietly, kicking furiously, and shouting her anger. 'Damn you, Remy St Leger! How dare you do this to me? Father, it is I! Beatrice!'

In the corridor Lady Alys and two of her waiting women met them. They soothed, cajoled and manhandled Beatrice away and into Lady Alys's own chamber. Beatrice vented her rage, her voice nigh on a scream. It was not until Lady Alys administered a sharp slap that Beatrice subsided.

'Listen to me, girl,' said Lady Alys sternly, 'your father is gravely ill. In a battle with the Welsh he received severe wounds and we doubt that he will recover.'

Beatrice stared. Then she began to shake her head in denial of this tragic news, and to weep.

Remy's distress at the sight of Lord Thurstan was just as great, if not more than Beatrice's, as the full horror of his lord's fate became apparent. He lay behind a screen, shielded from the prying stares of servants, and bade near to him only those he most trusted. Remy was so privileged, and the young knight knelt on one knee beside the bed, his head bowed, and his heart heavy with the great weight of his sorrow.

Lord Thurstan's voice came in a croaky whisper. 'Beatrice must never see me like this. I will have your promise.'

'Aye, my lord. It is done.'

'And I would have you wed her. Quickly, for she will have need of a strong man to protect and defend her. With no word of her brothers, I must presume them dead and Beatrice will be forced by the king to take a husband of his choosing. The vultures will descend after my death and it is Ashton's bones they will pick over.'

Remy sighed. His speech, so carefully prepared, was cast aside; what he would not have given to have Lord Thurstan rise from the bed and knock him senseless at his audacity to dare ask for his daughter's hand! Remy cleared his throat and murmured, 'I thank you, my lord, for this gift, but—'

'Spit it out, boy. I am not long for this world.'

'Beatrice has not, will not—' Remy grimaced and shrugged his shoulders in Gallic fashion. 'In a nutshell, my lord, she has refused me.'

A snort came from the bandaged form of Lord Thurstan. 'Did you not tell me once that you are man enough to take my daughter?'

'Aye,' said Remy, doubtfully.

'Then take her! Her mother was just the same, and 'twas only maidenly foolishness. We raise girls to be pure and chaste and then instantly expect them to be whores upon their wedding night.'

'My lord,' protested Remy, 'I would never treat Beatrice so!'

'I know, I know.' Lord Thurstan sounded very weary indeed, and after a moment of silence broken only by his laboured breathing, he asked, 'Did you bring the poppy juice?'

'Aye.'

'Then ease me from this world into the next.'

Remy shook his head. 'Nay, my lord, do not ask of me that.'

'I have endured agony these weeks past, just so that

I might know Beatrice is safely wed. Call the priest
and make her your bride before the dawn, and I will
pass with no regret to heaven—or hell—as God sees
fit.'

'What you are asking, 'tis murder.'

'Look at me, Sir Remy! Take a long, good look.
They have butchered me beyond human endurance.
All I ask now is for mercy.'

Remy could not bear to look, his gaze glancing
away from the mutilated hands and feet. He could not
deny the truth of Lord Thurstan's words. He might
linger yet for weeks to come, suffering great agonies
of the body and mind.

'Come now, Sir Remy. I give you my daughter.
What greater price can I pay?'

'My lord, I would hasten to do your bidding and to
marry your daughter without hesitation and for nought.
But this thing, I cannot do.'

Lord Thurstan sighed. After a moment of careful
thought, he whispered, 'Very well. Then do me but
one favour. Bring the poppy juice and leave it here
beside my bed. I will sip it to ease my pain, and if I
sip too much, well, so be it.'

At last, an answer was wrung from Remy's husky
throat. 'Aye.'

'Go now and find Beatrice. The priest awaits. The
banns have not been read but we have special permission from the Bishop. Make this broken old man
happy and safeguard my daughter.'

'My lord,' Remy said, with tears in his voice, 'my
life is hers now and for always.'

# Chapter Seven

Beatrice lay upon Lady Alys's bed, spent and exhausted, her cheeks flushed and her hair dishevelled. Dusk had fallen. Her hostess had departed for supper in the great hall and Beatrice was left alone with her anger.

She heard the door creak open, and shrank into the pillows behind the drawn bedcurtains, unwilling to face Lady Alys, or anyone. She tensed at the sound of footsteps, and smothered her breath in the tasselled cushion she clutched to her chest as a comforter. The curtain parted and candlelight spilled in at the same moment as Remy's shadow fell across her crumpled form.

'You!' At once she sat up, then got to her knees. She hurled the cushion at his head and then, with a shout of rage, she pummelled the rock-hard expanse of his chest with both clenched fists.

Remy waited while she vented her fury, until at last she collapsed sobbing and he held her against his heart, stroking back her tangled hair as she sniffed and gulped.

'I want to see my father.' Beatrice whispered, with a mutinous pout.

'Nay.'

Her head jerked up and she glared defiantly. 'You cannot do this! I *will* see him.'

He gripped her arms and said bluntly, 'Your father is dying. It is best that you respect his wishes and do not attempt to see him.'

Tears streaked anew from her swollen eyes. 'I cannot believe that my father loves me so little that he does not care to see me!'

'Foolish wench!' Remy shook her, none too gently. 'He loves you so greatly that he desires only to spare you the pain of seeing him so grievously injured.'

'Oh, Remy! Tell me, are his wounds very bad?'

'Aye.' He looked away from her searching gaze, and then sought to impart his lord's commands without further ado. 'Your father has granted me permission to marry you.'

'What!'

'Aye. Make yourself ready, for we have special dispensation from the Bishop, and Lord Haworth and Lady Alys are ready to stand as witnesses.'

She stared at him with a look of horror and disbelief. 'Such haste. I would rather wait, my father…he may well recover.'

His blue stare was very hard upon her. 'Your father will not recover, and after last night, I did not think either of us would prefer a long betrothal.'

Beatrice flushed, and then suspicion dawned in her eyes as she stared up at him. 'All is clear to me now.' She spoke slowly, her voice husky from weeping.

'With my father dead and my brothers lost and pre-
sumed dead, I stand as heiress to Ashton, and you
stand to gain much as my husband.'

His fist flexed and he almost struck her upon the
face, such was his fury at her accusation. 'Is that how
you see me, Beatrice? A feckless youth prepared to
wed an older woman for the riches he might gain?'
With a frustrated sigh he thrust her away from him
and she fell back on the pillows. 'I will tell Lady Alys
that there will be no wedding.' He turned away, and
then glanced back, his face impassive as stone as he
told her, 'I have stripped myself bare of all pride for
you, Beatrice. I have fought other knights to defend
your honour, humbled myself before your father for
you, shown my passion for you, but you have made it
clear that you will not have me. So be it. I will not
ask again.'

He let the bedcurtain fall and she was left alone in
the dark. She heard his booted feet thump across the
wooden floor and the creak of the door as it closed
behind him. With a small cry Beatrice sat up and made
to run after him, regretting her harsh words, and then
she remembered that her father lay dying and it was
Remy who prevented her from seeing him one last
time. Her jaw set and she clenched her teeth. She
would wait, and then later, when the household was
asleep, she would find her father and hear from his
own mouth what his wishes were.

For now, she must bolster herself, and her rumbling
stomach and the weakness she felt from hunger reminded her that it was the hour for supper. Beatrice
crossed the room and tipped water from a copper jug

into a shallow bowl, set upon a carved oak coffer ready for Lady Alys when she should retire. She bathed her face, red and sore from crying, then tidied her hair with a comb, and went downstairs.

A minstrels' gallery, screened with an intricate lattice-work of cherry wood, bridged the passage between the private chambers and the stairs leading down to the great hall. Here Beatrice paused and gazed through a trellised pattern of unicorns and elves upon the scene below. She felt as though she moved in a dream, an agonising nightmare, and at any moment she would waken and find herself safe in her chamber at Ashton, with her mother sewing in the solar and her father roaring impatiently at his knights.

The hall was brightly lit with candles and the glow of a dancing fire in the massive hearth spread a cosy warmth. It was noisy too, with a cheerful hubbub of voices and laughter, a lute-player strumming a pleasant tune in one corner, and several wolfhounds tail-wagging as they sat to one side and resisted the urge to chase after scraps, for which they would be severely punished. She saw Sir Giles and Sir Baldslow eating with careful concentration, ignoring the antics of other diners; nearly all the knights from Ashton appeared solemn and sober. Beatrice longed to run away and hide in a dark corner, but she knew this she must not do. Her father would wish her to carry on as befitting the daughter of a Lord.

Remy was the first to notice her as Beatrice came down the stairs and he rose from his seat. Sir Giles looked up, then over his shoulder in the direction of Sir Remy's bright gaze, and he too rose.

'My lady.' Sir Giles gestured to a place beside him, and Beatrice sat down at the table, her eyes lowered and ignoring Remy, until he too was forced to regain his place.

Sir Giles piled her trencher with roasted fowl, ham-and-leek pie, crumbly Welsh cheese, and filled his goblet with sweet Spanish wine to share with her. Beatrice murmured her thanks, and forced herself to eat, knowing that she would need her strength for the coming night. She kept her eyes upon her food, thus maintaining a barrier to conversation, until Lord Haworth, having eaten his fill and succumbing to the nagging whispers of his wife, came to Beatrice and stood at her shoulder. He leaned forwards, and asked softly, 'Might I have a word, Lady Beatrice? Finish your meal and then I would be pleased if you would meet with me in the solar.'

Beatrice nodded, but her lips were pursed and she did not encourage Lord Haworth to make small talk.

He withdrew, eyeing his wife with a sour glance as they climbed the stairs. 'It be none of our business,' he hissed in her ear.

'Pish!' Lady Alys gathered her skirts in one hand. 'With her mother dead and her father soon to be, who else is there to advise the girl?'

'You can advise all you like, dear wife, but she will not listen. My understanding is that Beatrice of Ashton has never been biddable.'

Beatrice ate slowly and lingered over her meal, her thoughts thawing as the delicious food warmed her, and lifted her gaze to look around at the crowded trestle tables. She glanced across and further down the expanse, seeking a handsome face and a direct gaze of sky blue, but was a little piqued to find that Remy had gone. Suddenly there was no reason to linger and she wiped her fingers and mouth upon a linen napkin.

'Goodnight, Sir Giles.'

'Goodnight, my lady.' Sir Giles rose to his feet and made a bow to Beatrice, 'And do not distress yourself overly, for we stand ready to serve you as we did your father.'

Beatrice laid her hand upon his arm, and smiled. 'I thank you for your loyal service, Sir Giles, and I only hope that I prove to be as worthy a master.'

'Mistress,' corrected Sir Giles.

With a sigh, and a slight nod of her head, Beatrice left him and climbed the stairs to the upper floor. Further along the passage she came to the open door of the solar and knocked.

'Come in, my dear,' called Lady Alys from her seat before the fire, gesturing with one hand for Beatrice to sit in the other chair placed opposite.

Lord Haworth laid aside the letter he was perusing, cleared his throat and paced for a moment with his hands folded behind his back, before approaching Beatrice, stroking his dark beard pensively.

'I...we—that is, Lady Alys and I, felt that we should help you with your situation. Being young and—'

'I am twenty-nine, my lord,' said Beatrice quietly, gazing calmly at Lord Haworth.

'Quite. Indeed. But, nevertheless, you are without advisers who are mature and wise in the ways of the world. We know that your father was keen for you to wed this evening, but you have refused. The Bishop is ready and waiting, and my wife and I are more than happy to stand as witnesses. It would be in your best interest.'

Beatrice rose to her feet, a flush of anger staining her cheeks and firing her eyes with a bright gleam. 'My father has always left the decision to wed entirely up to me. He has never forced me, and I do not believe that he would force me now!'

'Most girls of your age and rank have been wed a long while and produced several children,' commented Lady Alys, her glance upon her sewing.

'That may be so, but I have been fortunate in that my parents had a care for my feelings in the matter!'

Lady Alys set her sewing down in her lap and stared at Beatrice. 'You have not the luxury of feelings! You will need a husband, however repugnant that might be to you, for 'tis a man your knights will need to lead them into battle, not your tender feelings!'

Beatrice gasped at her plain speaking, her conscience yet twinged by the truth of Lady Alys's words. 'I could lead them myself, as my father did!'

'Women do not ride into battle!' snorted Lord Haworth.

'Boadicea did.'

'And look what happened to her!' Lady Alys rose to her feet, her sewing finally set aside. 'Come, child, we are not your enemies.' She put her arm about Beatrice's shoulders and led her to the door, 'It has been a long journey for you and at the end a great shock to find your father such as he is. Rest now. Tomorrow we will consider the matter again, after you have had a good night's sleep.' She clapped her hands and a maid came stumbling along the passage. 'Show Lady Beatrice to the Blue Chamber and assist her this evening.'

Beatrice had no intention of meekly laying down her head and going to sleep. Not when she had such violent thoughts to wrestle with. But she gave the impression to the eager little maid that she was retiring for the night and allowed her to unlace her kirtle, put her into her nightshift and brush out her hair. Then she was left alone in the big canopied bed and Beatrice stared at the glowing fire until it was reduced to ruby embers and a hush descended over the castle. Doors ceased to bang, voices fell silent, and only the howl of the wind and distant wolves could be heard.

She rose from the warm bed and, shivering, slipped on her cloak and her leather shoes. Without even a candle to guide her, for she did not want to give herself away, she crept along the passage and up the spiral of stairs to her father's chamber.

After supper Remy took himself off to the stables to check on Walther. He prized his horse so greatly that he would not leave his care to the rough mercies of a stableboy. He made sure that Walther was warm and well fed, settled him for the night with a fond pat to the arch of his powerful neck and then crossed the bailey to regain the warmth of the keep. He shrugged off his cloak and threw down his bedroll in a vacant spot near the hearth, but hesitated before allowing himself to end his duties for the day and seek his rest.

Filling a goblet with wine, Remy sat on a bench and contemplated the fire flames, much as Beatrice did on the floor above him. He had long since left the vial of poppy juice close at hand for Lord Thurstan and he was troubled as to whether his lord still lived or not. He could not bear to think of him dying alone in a dark corner, and yet he did not want to intrude on his lord's privacy. Drinking deeply, Remy pondered, and then rose to his feet and loped with a silent tread upstairs, passing the upper floor that led to Lord Haworth's rooms, and continuing until he reached the passage leading to Lord Thurstan's chamber.

A candle flickered in the gloom. He waited for his eyes to accustom themselves to the dark, and then he walked slowly forwards, behind the screen. Lord Thurstan's shape seemed strange, until he realised that a female form lay slumped across him. The female, he realised after a few moments more, was Beatrice.

Remy dropped to one knee and seized Beatrice about the waist and jerked her away. 'What are you doing here?' he hissed.

Beatrice wiped her face as tears poured in a silent stream down her cheeks. 'He is…my father… he's…gone.'

Setting her abruptly aside Remy leaned forwards and felt for a pulse at Lord Thurstan's neck. There was none. With a sigh, and a prayer, he closed the unseeing eyes. 'He is at peace, God rest his soul.'

'And this?' Beatrice snatched up the empty vial of poppy juice and thrust it in Remy's face. 'This is your doing, is it not? Were you so eager to take me as wife that you would commit murder?'

At that his discipline broke and Remy slapped her face, with an oath that was not softly spoken and smothered her cry of shock and pain. 'At your father's deathbed you are yet still the shrew! What man in his right mind would seek to wed with you?'

Beatrice sucked in her breath, and scrambled to her knees, backing away a step as Remy too rose and stood towering over her. Then he grabbed her arm and forcefully ejected her from the chamber, dragging her along the passage and down the stairs, along yet more passages until he reached her chamber, where earlier he had placed her belongings. The door banged shut behind him and they stood facing each other like two snarling combatants upon the tourney field.

'Do you deny that you gave my father the poppy juice?'

'I do not deny it.'

'Then you have killed him!'

Remy was silent, hands on hips as he glared at her with narrowed eyes. 'You do not know how it was.'

'Nay, Sir Remy, I do not.' She tossed back strands of hair from her eyes and tilted her chin up to meet his gaze. 'And whose fault is that?' Her finger stabbed him in the chest. '*You* would not let me see him, *you* denied me the chance to hear from his own lips his final wishes, and now, because of *you*, he is gone and I will never be able to speak to him again!' Her voice broke; turning away swiftly, she covered her face with both hands and wept.

'Beatrice…' he took a step towards her, his voice

gentle '…I am sorry. But I did as I was commanded—indeed, as your father begged. His injuries were so grievous—'

Beatrice whirled about to face him. 'I did not see, he was already gone when I reached the chamber. Tell me, what were his wounds?'

'It is best that you do not know.'

With a low shriek of rage, Beatrice demanded, through gritted teeth, 'I wish everyone would stop deciding what is *best* for me! Tell me, or I will go up, pull back the covers and look for myself.' She made to rush past him, but his large hand moved quickly and fastened around her upper arm, halting her in mid-stride, jerking her backwards.

He stooped, their noses almost touching, blue eyes glaring into brown, and then he told her, softly and without emotion, 'The Welsh had hacked off his right hand and both of his feet.'

'Oh, God!'

'How he has survived so long I do not know. The loss of blood, the infection—'

She held her hands to her ears. 'Enough.'

'Aye. 'Tis not pretty, but you wished to know and now I have told you. On his deathbed your father begged me to take you for my wife, but until *you* beg me—' this time it was his turn to stab his forefinger into her chest '—I will not do so. Goodnight, Beatrice. Go to bed and let there be no more disturbance this night, for we all need our rest. In the morning we must prepare for a funeral, and then we depart to fight the Welsh who did this atrocity.'

'I will ride with you.'

'Nay. You will stay here, where it is safe and there are walls and women to care for you.'

'But I would see the men who murdered my father punished!'

Remy smiled grimly, a dangerous light in his eyes. 'Have no doubt—we will track them down and slaughter them like the vermin they are.' At the door he swept her a bow. 'Goodnight, my lady.'

Remy hurried away to inform the priest of Lord Thurstan's death and that he should make preparations for a funeral on the morrow. Then, at last, he rolled himself in his blankets before the fire hearth and sought oblivion in sleep.

When he had gone Beatrice clutched at the bedpost for long moments, her heart hammering very fast. So much had happened in so short a space of time! What was she to do? And what path did she follow on the morrow? Marry Sir Remy? How greatly she was tempted, but he had spoken of pride, of honour and passion, and had made no mention of love. Over his head hung the suspicious cloud of her father's death. How could she trust a man who might have had a hand in hastening her father to his grave? And what were his reasons for doing so? She could not bear to think that there was anything other than honourable intentions, but of this she could not be sure. And with neither trust nor love, there was no hope of happiness in the lifelong union of marriage.

Wearily she tossed aside her cloak and shoes. She climbed up into the bed and lay beneath the covers, clutching her rosary and praying for the departed soul of her father, too exhausted to weep, until she fell asleep in the middle of her third Hail Mary and knew no more.

The morning dawned bright and clear, a fine day with a hint of summer. Birds sang loudly and, hearing them, Beatrice found it hard to believe that her own world had changed so completely, and yet that of others remained the same. Birds still sang, the sun still rose, maids laughed, and knights swaggered with their swords slung about their hips.

Her movements felt slow and heavy as she washed and dressed and braided her hair. Lady Alys came and after a brief embrace spoke of the funeral, set for midmorning.

'I would prefer to take my father back to Ashton.'

Lady Alys grimaced. 'It would not be wise.'

They both recoiled from dwelling on the nasty image of a corpse rotting in canvas as it was transported on a long slow journey south, and with a small nod of her head Beatrice agreed to a funeral to be held at Carmarthen and without delay.

'Come, my dear.' Lady Alys took her by the arm, and led her downstairs. 'Let us break our fast and do honour to your father's memory. He was a great man and much loved.'

Condolences came in a steady stream, from Lord Haworth, the resident knights and their ladies, from the priest and Bishop, from her own men—Sir Giles Radley, Sir Hugh Montgomery, Grenville, Woodford and Fitzpons, and, of course, Sir Cedric Baldslow. She hid her shudder of revulsion as he bent to kiss her hand and murmur his regrets. He looked her deeply in the eye for a long moment as they both realised that she stood—until her brothers were proved to be alive—both heiress and unwed, a ripe fruit for a hand daring enough to make the plucking.

Sir Richard Blackthorn came and tendered his sympathy and she smiled as he gallantly offered his services should she need assistance. Beatrice thanked him and did not notice the scowl that marred Remy's handsome features as she favoured Sir Richard with her smile.

If that was the way of it, thought Remy, God help Ashton! But he controlled the slow burn of anger within his chest and stooped to publicly make his condolences to Beatrice.

She blushed as he kissed her hand and held it for several moments, whispering for her ears only, 'The Bishop stands yet ready for a wedding.'

'Would we wish to celebrate our marriage, in years to come, on the day that we mourn my father's death?'

He smiled wryly, outwitted. 'Then, my lady, we might set a date for the future?'

'I thought you said that you would not ask me again and, besides, what man in his right mind would want to marry a shrew such as I?'

Remy almost laughed, but saw that she was most earnest and would not appreciate his humour. He bowed deeply. 'True, my lady. But I am willing to shoulder the burden, as your father wished.'

'Sir Remy,' whispered Beatrice through clenched teeth, 'I would rather marry a…a…' He eyed her with brows raised and head tilted to one side as she struggled to find words vile enough. With a frustrated moan, she jerked her hand from his clasp. 'I have matters to attend. Go from my sight.'

'Your wish is my command.' He smiled grimly as he backed away.

Beatrice went to don her cloak and collect her rosary and bible, before joining Lady Alys and walking with her to the chapel across the bailey. The funeral mass was well attended, yet overly long and tedious. Clouds of incense billowed out and a plaintive chant sung by several young pageboys tore at Beatrice's heart. At its end her father was carried to his final resting place on the sacred hill beyond the castle walls, and many of the townspeople stopped to stare and cross themselves as the funeral party went by.

After the burial there was to be no respite for Beatrice. She longed for the solace of her chamber, to be alone and sit with her mind vacant of all thought, but it was not to be. There was the mid-day meal to get through and then a great commotion as many of the knights, under the leadership of Sir Giles Radley, donned their armour and prepared to ride out to track down the Welsh.

From the steps of the great hall Beatrice watched as her father's men mounted their horses. She waved her scarf in goodbye, and for a long poignant moment her gaze held with Remy St Leger's as his horse pranced to the gate. Then he saluted her with one hand, swung about and was gone from her sight. She felt utterly alone.

At last, she retired to her chamber and sat in a chair by the window, watching thin clouds scud across the sky as the sun journeyed along its afternoon path. Her mind was like a pool hidden deep in a dark forest—it seemed that there was nothing there and all was quiet and still, but beneath the surface all manner of life existed.

By evening Beatrice had made her decision. She would go home to Ashton, and for this purpose she would enlist the aid of Sir Richard Blackthorn to escort her, as her own knights were gone in pursuit of the Welsh. She resolved to speak with him at the evening meal, and all being well she would be home before the week was out.

Supper was a subdued occasion, out of respect for her loss, and in the hushed atmosphere there was little opportunity for Beatrice to talk privately with Sir Richard. In the end, she was forced to invite him to accompany her for a stroll around the pleasaunce, an engagement she would much rather have avoided as gossip-mongers put their heads together and watched as they left the hall.

The evening was warm and the buds of flowers were just unfurling in the pleasant garden as Beatrice strolled slowly beside Sir Richard. Carefully, she sought to broach the subject uppermost in her mind. In the end, she decided there was no need to prevaricate and spoke directly.

'Sir Richard, I am anxious to return home and you have kindly offered me your assistance should I have a need. I ask you then, kind sir, if you would escort me to Ashton.'

Sir Richard stopped and stared at her for a long moment. Then he bowed and reached for her hand, pressing a kiss upon it as he said gravely, 'My lady, I would be delighted to escort you, but I am not free to do so. We ride at first light to join with my Lord Robert.'

'But—'

'It is by direct order of the King.'

Beatrice searched his face with her eyes, trying to decide if he spoke truthfully or whether he was just playing a dangerous game with his own safety in mind. There was no clue from his bland expression and she turned away with a heavy sigh, freeing her hand from his clasp. 'I see.'

'My apologies, Lady Beatrice. But there is naught I can do. King Edward is in need of reinforcements against the Welsh and his campaign takes prior claim over…' He hesitated to be blunt.

'Over the petty affairs of women?' Beatrice finished for him, an acid tone to her voice. 'Very well. You have no need to grovel, Sir Richard.'

He flushed. 'If I could, I would, be assured of that. May I suggest that you apply to Lord Haworth?'

She inclined her head with what little dignity she could muster. 'I shall do so.'

Her instincts were that such a request would not meet with any favour, and she was right. Lord Haworth was polite but firm in his refusal, stating that he could not spare the men to escort her homewards.

For several days Beatrice seethed in frustration; there was something distinctly odd about the blank

wall of refusal that she came up against time and time
again from all quarters. She was convinced that a con-
spiracy was afoot to prevent her from leaving Wales,
but exactly why she was uncertain.

Four days after the funeral Beatrice emerged from
Mass to find a party of monks dismounting from their
mules in the bailey, with heartfelt murmurs and groans
of relief.

'Good day, Father,' Beatrice greeted one of the
monks, noting from his plain garb of brown wool that
they were Benedictines. 'Have you journeyed far this
day?'

'Good day, my child,' exclaimed the monk loudly,
as he rubbed his aching backside, with great relief to
have his feet upon *terra firma*. 'We have come from
St David's, where we have made our pilgrimage. Are
you the chatelaine of this keep?'

'Nay, indeed. It is Lady Alys you should apply to,
although I am sure you are most welcome. Come, I
will show you to her.'　　'Thank you, sweet girl, you
are most kind. Father Dennis, bring the others, this
young lady will show us the way.'

'Very good, Father Clement.'

Beatrice escorted them all the way across the bailey
and up the rise of stone steps that led into the great
hall, surrounded by five Benedictine monks, all ton-
sured, some overweight and overtired, others gaunt
with earnest piety. She asked carefully, 'It is a great
undertaking to make a pilgrimage to St David's. I hear
that the journey is so perilous across the wild land of
Wales that it would be easier to make one to Rome.'

'Indeed, child.' Father Clement sighed heartily. 'Yea, though I shall walk through the shadows of the valley of death, I shall not fear. Thy rod and thy staff shall comfort me.'

'Psalm 23?'

He smiled and patted her hand, nodding in agreement.

Beatrice asked her next question carefully, 'And where is your home, Father? Have you very far to go?'

'Our monastery is near Bath. A week's ride from here. Not too far, yet far enough.'

As they entered the hall and stood before the warming flames of the hearth, Beatrice was already concocting a plan, but she bided her time as Lady Alys approached and introductions were made. Bath was only twenty miles from Ashton; could she manage to persuade the monks to take her with them, and could she manage to travel the remaining miles alone? She had no desire to repeat the dreadful occurrence of her last solitary journey. This time there might be no Remy St Leger to rescue her.

She pondered on these thoughts during supper and did not rush to make any request of the Benedictines. Indeed, she even resolved to sleep on the vexing matter, and, as she lay awake hugging her pillow, she wondered whether it was wisdom or cowardice that prevented her from making a decision. It might be many weeks before another suitable escort, or any escort for that matter, might happen along. She had better grab the chance while it was still within her grasp.

* * *

With that thought in mind, upon rising in the morning and joining with the monks in the chapel for early prayers, she touched Father Clement upon his sleeve and asked, in a taut whisper, if she might have a private word with him. He showed no surprise or reluctance at her request and, in the shadows of the cloistered gardens, she quickly told him of her predicament and her desperate need to return home.

Father Clement nodded his head slowly, mouth pursed, florid jowls vibrating. 'Certainly you are most welcome, although we can offer you poor protection, for we are not knights, but I am certain the banner of God shall guard you as it has us.'

'Oh, thank you, Father, I am most grateful!'

'Providing,' he said sternly, arresting her joyful reaction, 'providing that Lord Haworth and Lady Alys give their consent, for I would not want my order to be accused of abducting rich young females.'

'Certainly.' Beatrice uttered the word glibly, without a trace of the deceit she knew she would have to practise in order to leave Carmarthen. She promised that she would tell the Haworths of her departure, but in fact she had no intention of doing so. She hoped, somehow, to slip out of the gates unnoticed.

'We shall leave shortly after we have broken our fast.'

'I shall be ready, Father.' Beatrice hurried away, calling over one shoulder as she skipped across the bailey, 'Thank you, Father.'

She ran up the steps and then forced herself to walk modestly and quietly across the great hall, afraid to attract any undue attention and most anxious to avoid

Lady Alys. Any questions from that shrewd woman and she would crumble like a Christmas pudding!

Arriving in her chamber somewhat breathless, Beatrice ran about gathering up her possessions, stuffing them into her saddlebags and now grateful that Remy had been so severe about her baggage. She had no need to call a waiting woman to assist her; throwing on her cloak, she endeavoured to hide the bags beneath its concealing folds. Then she crept down the stairs and observed the hall before attempting to sneak across it. As she had hoped, the maids were busy setting up the trestle tables and tending to the dogs, and Lady Alys could be heard scolding some unfortunate fellow in the kitchen as she chivvied preparations for the first meal of the day. Most of the men were about their business in the armoury, bailey and stables, and those two that remained dozed before the fire with eyes closed, besotted from too much drink enjoyed on the previous eve.

Her footsteps were swift and silent as she crossed the hall. Then she was out the door and across the bailey, hurrying in the direction of the stables. Here she ordered a stableboy to saddle Bos and bring him out to her, and she was a little daunted as he emerged from his stable dancing from foot to foot, snorting and chafing at the little exercise he had been given these five days past. Walther came to the door of his stall and poked his head out to see what all the commotion was about and, seeing Beatrice, he snickered. He had been left behind, together with all the other destriers of the English knights, who were relying upon sturdy Welsh ponies; far too many of their own warhorses,

imported at great expense from France, had been lost
to the Welsh. Beatrice ignored him, swallowed nervously and was just about to throw up her saddlebags
upon Bos when the stentorian boom of the sentry
guard echoed across the yard. She gave a guilty start,
thinking that her subterfuge had been detected, but it
soon became apparent that she was not the subject of
interest.

The main gates, always kept securely shut and
barred, creaked open and a small party stumbled in on
foot. Beatrice watched, her eyes narrowed as she
looked the distance. Then, as recognition dawned, she
dropped the saddlebags and ran.

'Sir Giles!' she called, picking up her skirts in both
hands and forcing her legs to run faster.

The knights, leaning with weary exhaustion upon
their knees or each other, looked up as she ran towards
them. There was Woodford and Montgomery too, and
the other two knights belonged to the Haworth household, she knew not their names, but all of them were
filthy with mud and blood, haggard with exhaustion,
and horribly bereft of their weapons and horses. But,
as she stood staring at them, there was only one question that desperately needed an answer. 'Where is Sir
Remy?'

Sir Giles looked up at her with a grave expression,
'He is taken, my lady. The Welsh have captured him.
Along with Baldslow, Nogood and three of the
Haworth knights.'

'And the others? Grenville? Fitzpons?'

'Dead. They are all dead. They only let us go to
bear a message of ransom.'

Beatrice pressed a hand to her mouth, stifling her gasp of horror. From the corner of her eye she saw the Benedictine monks emerge from the hall and move towards their mules, ready to embark on their journey south and homewards. Beatrice groaned. It was one thing to leave, knowing that Remy was alive and well and off doing what men loved to do best—fight—but quite another to leave knowing he faced a fate of almost certain death. Damn you, Remy St Leger!

With clenched fists Beatrice watched as the gates were opened for the monks to depart. Father Clement approached leading his mule by the reins. She murmured her excuses, and then waved them goodbye.

# Chapter Eight

'Nay!' thundered Lord Haworth. 'I forbid it! We will not pay ransom to those thieving heathens! And you will not ride out to meet them. The King has ordered the Welsh prince, Llewelyn ap Gruffydd, to pay homage to him, and he has failed to do so. Now Edward has amassed the largest army since King William came from Normandy and will take Wales by force. It will mean forfeiture of my demesne if the King finds out that we have paid ransom monies to the Welsh.'

'Do not say nay to me, my lord!' shouted Beatrice in return, spinning so fast upon her heel that her skirts flew about in a swirl. 'Are these not my very own knights? If I wish to pay ransom, then I will do so. If I wish to ride out and meet the Welshman and pay him his thirty pieces of silver into his dirty little hand, then I will do so. By God, I will do so!'

She ran to the solar door and wrenched it open, but was halted by the roar that exploded from Lord Haworth.

*'Young woman!'*

Beatrice paused, and turned to glance over her

shoulder. Lady Alys came up to her and placed her arm around Beatrice's shoulders, gently guiding her back into the room.

Lord Haworth sighed heavily. 'Lady Beatrice, you try my patience!' He held up his hands to hush her protests. 'Listen to me for a moment. A knight knows well enough the price he may be called upon to pay in service to his king. He is not afraid to die.'

'I will not let Remy die!' cried Beatrice, her control breaking and the words bursting out upon a sob. 'I beg you, my lord, please. Please help me. I will do anything. Anything at all. I have the money to pay the ransom, and I will even pay ransom for your knights as well. Then the King cannot judge you.'

Lord Haworth again sighed deeply, torn between his duty and his conscience. He would gladly see returned safely home his three knights, but the price was too high. 'I cannot spare any men to ride out and pay the ransom, and risk their capture too.'

'I will go myself.'

'Nay! Impossible.'

'Why?' pleaded Beatrice, pressing her advantage. 'With or without your permission, Lord Haworth, I leave before midday to secure the release of my knights.'

Beatrice turned then and marched resolutely from the solar, despite the pleas and cajoling of Lady Alys and Lord Haworth.

Sir Giles Radley sat sprawled in a chair before the fire hearth in the great hall, clutching a goblet of hot spiced wine. He sat up as Beatrice approached.

'How much?' she demanded, breathless, pushing back the strands of hair that she had disturbed in her heated and agitated argument with Lord Haworth. 'How much do they want?'

'A hundred pounds.'

'Well...' Beatrice sighed with relief '...that is not beyond my means.' Her father had left a coffer of gold coins, to pay his men and purchase their food and lodgings, as well as armour, weapons and horses.

'Each.'

'What?'

'A hundred pounds for each man.'

Beatrice calculated that even three hundred pounds was well within her means, but then she remembered her rash offer to free the Haworth men as well—the ransom monies would be six hundred pounds. That was a fortune indeed. And she did not have it readily to hand. She raised her eyes to the ceiling, as though she could see through it to the solar above and the furious Lord Haworth, bitterly regretting her argument with him. Now she would need to humble herself and beg him to reconsider and provide the money to free his own knights. It occurred to her that this task was best suited to someone Lord Haworth was more agreeable to listening to—in short, a man. She turned to Sir Giles, and after some persuasion on her part, some sighing and eye-rolling on his part, he reluctantly rose to his aching feet and went off to engage Lord Haworth in a serious discussion.

Satisfied that Sir Giles would not fail her in his task, Beatrice went off to make preparations for her journey. She hurried to her father's chamber. In the doorway

face and neck in a hot embarrassing tide. Lady Alys started to fan herself and complained that she felt faint, stumbling to seat herself upon the settle by the fire, while Lord Haworth stood with arms akimbo and a mighty frown upon his face. But he remained silent. Then Sir Giles came forwards and made his bow to Beatrice.

'My lady, we are ready to depart.'

Remy woke with a start. He had been dreaming, a bright, vivid dream of a silver lake glinting with sunshine, a blue sky, a shaded oak tree, beneath which he lay upon a velvet cloak with Beatrice. Her hair had been unbound, flowing like a golden river of dark honey over her bare shoulders. Her body had been pale, and soft, and inviting. Love had been shining in her eyes as he had leaned over her...and that was when he had awoken, his mind unable to accept so untrue a fact. Love did not shine from her eyes, and no doubt he would never lie naked with Beatrice of Ashton!

He did not want to open his eyes and remind himself of where he was. But his other senses did that for him. His big body ached, cold and cramped as he lay upon the dirt floor of a hut, the soft snoring and disgruntled sounds of his companions as they too shifted uneasily in their sleep making him all too aware that he was held captive by a Welsh chieftain. He cursed himself for a fool over and over again. He had thought himself invincible, having survived many battles and never been captured before. True, it had taken five of these heathens to bring him down from his horse, and two he had quickly despatched to their maker before Sir Giles had called for them to put up their arms, seeking to save lives with surrender.

They had been vastly outnumbered and taken by surprise. One moment the craggy hillside had been deserted, the next swarming with hundreds of bare-chested, dark men in kilts and armed with bows and spears. Their bows were formidable, long as a man, and the Welsh had nocked up fresh arrows with light-ning speed. Their faces had been painted and their wild war cries were savage incantations that chilled the blood of the stoutest men. He glanced at Sir Cedric Baldslow, asleep sitting up with his back against the wall, his head nodding on his chest. Even Sir Cedric had blanched as the tide of Welsh warriors had washed over them.

Dawn came creeping slowly, lifting the swirling mist that he spied between cracks of the poorly plas-tered walls. Indeed it would take little effort for him to smash his way out of this dark, stinking prison, but beyond there were dozens of Welshmen on guard. Be-sides, they had been led here bound and blindfolded and he knew not his way out of this mountain lair.

He wondered if it was too late to pray. He began a plea and then his mind wandered, again to Beatrice. How he regretted their bitter words and how he longed to take them back! He should have dragged her to the altar, kicking and screaming if needs be, and married her, and made her his wife in both body and name. Warmth seeped through him at the thought of bedding Beatrice and he stifled a groan.

* * *

Mid-morning they were brought a scant meal of coarse brown bread and whey. The men chewed, some muttering, complaining that it was fare fit to break good teeth. The day had brightened, and as their guards passed through the open door, Remy could see a cloudless blue sky. Then a shout echoed around the hilltop cluster of huts and the Welshmen gathered about one of their clan who came running into their midst, panting and pointing back down the valley.

The Englishmen craned their necks to take notice, but the door was swiftly kicked shut and barred. Sitting up, Remy nudged Sir Cedric in the ribs and nodded to the doorway. The men stilled their grumbles and looked up eagerly, hope stirring.

'Do you think 'twas a messenger?' asked Remy.

'Mayhap,' grunted Sir Cedric.

'I am certain Lord Haworth will do all he can to rescue us,' chirped Nogood, his expression woeful as he looked to Remy.

'Aye.' Remy tried to give the boy some comfort. 'It will not be long now.'

His personal feeling was that they would not live to see the sunset, and he sat back in stoic silence, his mind working constantly on the possibilities of escape. So far, none had presented itself. He sighed, and closed his eyes, his thoughts again wandering to Beatrice. Would she shed a tear when news of his death reached her? Mayhap she had been right to refuse his suit. Had she not already suffered too deeply over the death of a betrothed? He vowed then that, if ever their freedom was won, he would not plague her with his ardour, no matter the cost to his own yearning heart.

* * *

It was not long before the Welshmen came and dragged them from the hut. Their hands were tightly bound behind their backs, four of the swarthy, stocky Welsh attaching themselves to Remy as he towered over them all. Again they were blindfolded and led down the narrow mountain track across the spine of high hills.

Remy wondered at their haste, as they were urged none too gently to hurry. The Welsh chieftain, Gwyn ap Iestan, told them that a party of knights had been scouted approaching, and hinted that their ransom was to be paid. In the valley below they were led to a grove of birch trees and hidden between the thick undergrowth of bushes lining the banks of a small tumbling stream, spanned by a wooden bridge.

It was dim and cool in the shadows, here at the bottom of the valley, affording the Welsh concealment. The captive English knights chafed at the waiting, impatient now to snatch at the freedom that was only a breath away. Surely their release had been secured?

Remy did not readily believe that honour was yet to be upheld by the Welsh in their dealings with an ancient foe. Their blindfolds were removed and he lifted his head from the cloying dirt and watched as Gwyn ap Iestan deployed his men. Although he could not understand the Welsh language, he was familiar with their hand signals, the same he would himself use to give orders when an ambush was being planned and all noise had to be suppressed. His foreboding only grew as he recognised the flanking movement the Welsh used to send men off to the rear of the approaching cavalcade. They intended to encircle the English from behind, cutting off their retreat and no doubt slaughtering everyone, taking the ransom monies and leaving no trace of their foul deeds.

Over the sounds of swirling water and wood pigeons cooing, Remy and the other knights detected the faint yet familiar sounds of harness chinking, and horses blowing as they climbed the path leading through the forest. As they craned their necks, their faces came alight as the flag of St George appeared above the crest of the hill below them, and then the bearer and his horse, followed by two knights and four men-at-arms.

'God bless ye, Lord Haworth,' muttered one of the Carmarthen knights.

'Nay,' said Remy, squinting at the pennon that followed and held aloft by a small young knight, 'those are the colours of Ashton.'

A spear jabbed him in the back and he rose to his feet, as he and the other knights were led out of the bushes and on to the river bank. On one side of the bridge sat the Welshman Gwyn ap Iestan upon his sturdy mountain pony, and on the other side the party of knights clattered to a halt and sat rigid upon their horses, banners held proud and tight in wary gauntlets.

They were a paltry few, thought Remy, but he had no doubt that Lord Haworth could not spare even this handful of men to rescue them. One, Remy cast an upwards sidelong glance at, who looked little more than a pageboy. Then he looked again and his head jerked up as, in an instant, he recognised the soft brown eyes of Beatrice.

His mouth opened in slack horror. He almost called out, then quickly realised the folly of so doing. Silently he ran through his repertoire of curses, heaping all manner of vile names upon the slender young knight who was in fact a woman. God have mercy! If the Welsh made this discovery… His face paled visibly and quickly he turned away, pretending to stumble, hanging his head down low to hide the emotions that seized him.

Now that the prisoners had been brought forth the negotiations began. The young knight leading the English signalled with one gauntlet and an older knight—in fact, Sir Giles Radley—nudged his horse forwards and began to speak. The Welsh sneered at this high-handed tactic and made several rude remarks about the noble lord who deigned not to speak aloud. But Remy knew that it was not arrogance that prevented Beatrice from speaking. The moment the little lordling spoke, the Welsh would know they had in their midst an English lady. Sweat trickled from beneath his arms and his heart beat very fast. He bargained with God, making all manner of rash and foolish promises, if only the Almighty would see this matter through quickly and allow Beatrice to depart safe and sound.

At last the small leather chest containing six hundred pounds was exchanged and the English knights had their bonds cut. They were shoved forwards and none tarried upon that wooden bridge.

Reaching Beatrice, Remy flashed her an angry glare. She smiled, greatly pleased with herself, and this only enraged him further. Spare horses had been brought along and Remy vaulted up into the saddle, turning to Sir Giles Radley to hiss a dire warning, ''Tis a trap! Look to the trees.'

'Fear not,' Sir Giles whispered in return, wheeling his horse about as the party moved off at a smart trot.

'They mean to ambush us in the woods!' said Remy, urgently trying to impress upon Sir Giles the situation, but again he was met with calm reassurance. Had they all gone mad? thought Remy, wishing he had a sword latched about his waist and feeling as powerless as a babe. How would he defend Beatrice from the Welsh when he had no weapon?

Dappled sunlight streamed through the canopy of lime-green leaves overhead as they moved off, harnesses creaking and ringing, the clop of hooves muffled by the soft mossy earth of the track. Remy looked to left and right, and then, suddenly, the Welsh were upon them, loosing a volley of arrows. He gave a shout of warning, but already Beatrice had spurred her horse forwards and was galloping past him, whilst the other knights reined in.

'We must flee!' shouted Remy, his glance following after Beatrice and yet knowing full well it was his duty to remain with the other knights and fight, as Sir Giles drew his sword. 'Nogood, follow my lady and stay with her!'

Nogood spurred his horse and set off in pursuit of Beatrice. Then, as the Welsh charged at them from the bushes on either side of the track, the silhouettes of mounted English knights darkened the hilly rise edging the woods. A ringing hiss of steel silenced the birdsong and startled the Welsh, as many swords were drawn from their scabbards, followed by the hoarse bellow of an English war cry.

The ground trembled and the woods echoed with a sound like thunder as the knights galloped towards them, expertly threading their way through the trees with all the skill of battle-seasoned cavalry.

'What the devil...!' exclaimed Sir Cedric.

Sir Giles grinned. ''Tis Lord Henry, the new Lord of Ashton, come to our aid.'

But this was not the moment for explanations and Sir Giles quickly broke open the leather pack hidden beneath his saddle flaps and tossed out swords as the Welsh came at them with their spears and javelins, their longbows letting fly arrows at the rate of a dozen a minute. With a jubilant shout Remy raised his sword and threw himself into the fray of battle.

From her safe distance Beatrice let the reins drop upon Bos' withers and he bent his neck to crop at the emerald grass tufting upon the hillside beyond the woods. She could hear the ferocious ring of steel, the shouts of men and the shrieks of horses. With a gasp of stifled pain she leaned forwards, in a vain attempt to escape the burning agony that seared her body. The first arrow had struck her left shoulder, the blow softened by the chainmail of her bishop's mantle; the second had found her right hip and was deeply embedded.

'My lady!' Nogood exclaimed in horror as he pulled his horse up alongside her, and he eyed the arrow shafts protruding from her body.

With a soft cry she turned to him. 'Nogood, help me.'

Quickly he dismounted and hurried to reach up and support her before she fell and caused more damage. 'Hold on, my lady,' he begged softly, looking over one shoulder in the direction of the woods. 'Sir Remy will be here in a moment, and then we can lift you down.'

She nodded, her brow beaded with sweat. Gradually, as Nogood's arms ached and her grip on consciousness weakened, she hung doubled over Bos' shoulder, her forehead resting on one knee. Darkness reached out to claim her, but she fought to resist it, knowing that if she fell from Bos now the arrows would drive deeper into her body and she would not live; and she wanted to live, she wanted to see Remy, to speak with him. She must hear from his own lips his denial that he had ought to do with her father's death. She tried to keep her thoughts busy, reciting psalms and prayers, and then her mind wandered and she remembered this morning, which seemed so very long ago now.

They had not been far from Carmarthen when they had met with her brother Hal upon the road. He had with him twenty mounted knights, all of them crack campaigners who had been with King Edward on Crusade to the Holy Land. They were the finest cavalry fighters that England could muster and had at their command fifty men-at-arms. When Beatrice had explained that several Ashton knights had been taken captive by the Welsh tribe who had butchered their father, Hal had been only too eager to avenge his death.

They had ridden off together, formulating a plan

along the way in which Beatrice would meet with the Welsh, hand over the ransom monies and secure the release of their knights, whilst Hal encircled the woods with his men and attacked from the east and western flank. Her brother had impressed upon her the importance of getting out of the way when the fighting began, and had been half-inclined to leave her behind. But Beatrice had insisted that she ride along, without revealing that there was one knight in particular that she had to see, safe and sound, and free. Now, she could only wait, and pray that all was going to plan. Pray that her brother reached her before it was too late.

'Nogood?' Beatrice whispered.

'Aye, my lady?'

'If...' She hesitated, and then forced herself to go on. 'If I should die—'

'Nay, my lady!' exclaimed Nogood. 'You will not die. You must not! Why, Sir Remy will thrash me if you do.'

Beatrice tried to laugh, and managed only a weak smile. 'He would not do such a thing. Methinks he is a master much loved.'

'Aye, indeed. But you are his lady love, the other half of his heart. If you were to die, then his life would not be worth living, and neither would mine.'

At that Beatrice started to cry, silent tears running down her cheeks and dripping on to her hand, there to run in salty rivulets upon the blood that had seeped from her shoulder and down her arm.

'Hold on, my lady,' implored Nogood. 'Listen—' he cocked his ear, glancing back '—all is quiet. The fighting is over. They will be here anon.'

It was some long moments more before Sir Giles and Lord Henry emerged from the trees, followed by the other knights. They were grim, panting with the exertions of the fight, wiping bloodstained swords and sheathing them. Sir Giles looked about to take an accounting, noting with satisfaction that there were many cuts and bruises, but their armour had stood them in good stead. A shout then distracted him and he spurred his horse towards Nogood.

Remy wiped his face with a battle-blackened hand and sheathed his sword. He too looked up at Nogood's desperate shout. As he saw Beatrice slumped over her horse with two arrow shafts jutting from her body, he let loose a profanity and urged his horse into a gallop. He overtook Sir Giles and was the first to arrive, pulling up with a suddenness that caused his horse to snort.

'God Almighty! Beatrice!'

'Careful!' Sir Giles dismounted too and reached to the other side of Beatrice, together with Lord Henry. 'Gently now.'

Remy, being the tallest, reached up and carefully lifted Beatrice down from Bos. With a professional eye he examined the arrows and where they had implanted. 'We must get them out.' He raised his eyes to Sir Giles, and to another knight whom he did not know and looked at him with a question in his eyes.

'This is Lord Henry,' said Sir Giles, 'my lady's brother.'

A muscle tightened in Remy's jaw. He felt his anger rise like a red-hot flame, ready to burst out and sear this careless brother to ash. Now was not the time to question why he had brought his own sister into such a dangerous situation. Turning to Nogood, Remy gave his orders. 'Build a fire and boil water. Find out if anyone has any aquavit, and bring it to me.'

He exchanged a long look with his squire. Having attended Remy on many campaigns, and attended to his wounds, he knew well enough what each item would be needed for. Nogood rushed to do his bidding, while Remy gently lifted Beatrice and carried her to a makeshift bed beside the track, which had been thrown together by a combination of several cloaks.

'Beatrice?' Remy whispered, laying her down upon her front.

'Mmm?' Her lashes fluttered, but she was barely conscious.

'I must remove the arrows. It is your only hope.'

She nodded, and gasped with renewed pain as she was jolted into awareness by the sound of Remy's dagger ripping away her cloak and tunic. Cold air struck her flesh and she moaned.

'We should take her to Carmarthen,' murmured Sir Giles.

'She will not make it,' replied Remy brusquely. 'We must do this now.'

Lord Henry, known as Hal, cleared his throat. 'Do you know what you are doing?'

'Nogood, where's the aquavit?' demanded Remy, ignoring the question.

His squire came running, having secured a small flask of the strong alcohol from one of Lord Henry's knights. Remy splashed a drop liberally over the two wounds and then said, 'Tell me when the dagger is red-hot.'

'What are you going to do?' demanded Hal.

'After the arrows have been removed, I must seal the wounds.'

'By God!' exclaimed Hal. 'You cannot mean to take a red-hot blade to her flesh? You will kill her!'

'If I do not, then the wound will bleed and rot. She will die of the fever.'

'You will scar her for life!'

'Aye, but at least she will have a life!' Remy glanced down at Beatrice, her face turned to one side. Her chainmail coif and linen lambrequin had been removed and he leaned over and stroked her cheek, brushing back tendrils of hair. He wondered whether to give her aquavit to dull the pain, or knock her out with a blow to the head. Either choice had little merit, for the strong spirit was not usually imbibed by ladies and might well make her retch, and he feared a blow from his fist might cause her further injury. He hoped that once he began extracting the first arrow, the pain would be so excruciating she would faint anyway.

Beatrice felt his breath upon her cheek as he whispered, 'This will hurt, sweeting, but it must be done.'

She tried to smile, but was too weak. And then pain such as she had never known in her life pierced her senses and she screamed, eyes snapping open, her hand lashing out and four nails digging deep into the nearest arm, which happened to be Nogood's. Remy drew the first arrow from her shoulder, and Beatrice, to all their relief, collapsed into unconsciousness.

* * *

When they reached Carmarthen dusk was falling.
Beatrice was taken at once into the care of Lady Alys
and a local wise woman, who with her skill had managed to keep alive Lord Thurstan beyond expectation.
Now it was his daughter who received such tender
care.

For several days Beatrice tossed and turned in the
grip of delirious fever. Her wounds had been cleanly
dealt with, and now her body fought to overcome the
shock and pain. She was hardly aware of anything, yet
sometimes through the hot mists she heard voices, the
chanting of prayers, and felt upon her brow the touch
of cool lips. Her hand reached out blindly, and found
a strong clasp, drawing from it the strength and comfort that she needed.

Remy stayed with her, despite the clucking disapproval of the women, who tried to chase him away
while they undressed and bathed Beatrice, but he
would not go. He feared that if he left her side for a
moment, he would never see her again. Lady Alys,
taking pity upon the knight and having knowledge of
a matter that involved him deeply, allowed him to
stay. She ordered a servant to attend to Sir Remy,
bring him hot water to wash with, food and wine to
sustain him, and all his needs were met within the
same chamber where Beatrice lay in a great four-
poster bed. She looked so small and fragile within its
vast expanse that he, knighted for his valour, trembled
with fear.

By the morning of the third day it became clear that
Beatrice would survive. The dangerous heat left her

body and she fell into a deep, quiet slumber. At last, exhausted, Remy left her and went downstairs to the great hall. He sat in a chair beside the fire and fell asleep.

When he awoke he opened his eyes to find Lord Henry standing with arms akimbo and surveying him with a narrowed gaze. Remy sat up and rubbed the sleep from his eyes, his first reaction being, 'Beatrice? She is well?'

'Aye—' Hal nodded '—she sleeps peacefully. We have not yet been introduced, but I know who you are. Remy St Leger, the Aquitaine.'

Remy rose to his feet and made his bow. After all, besides being Beatrice's brother this man was his new liege lord. 'At your service,' he murmured, noting that, whilst there were few men who equalled his height Lord Henry was one of them.

Hal smiled, if somewhat grimly. 'I have heard much about you, not least of which your reputation upon the battlefield. I hear that you won your spurs at the age of sixteen and my father—' Here he stopped and his frown deepened. 'When my sister is fully recovered I would speak with you both.'

'My lord?' questioned Remy.

'For the moment it must wait.'

Hal turned on his heel and strode away, leaving Remy to gaze after him with a perplexed expression. A servant touched his elbow then, and he turned to answer him.

'My Lady Beatrice is awake and asking for you.'

'Thanks be to God,' Remy murmured and took a

step towards the spiral stairs that would lead him to her chamber, and then stopped.

God had been good indeed, and he must not forget the promises he had made to the Almighty, nor the vow sworn on a Welsh mountainside to spare Beatrice further anguish. With a regretful sigh, he said to the servant, 'Tell my lady that I am glad she is well, but I have other duties to attend to.'

The servant bowed and went away to do his bidding. Remy stood uncertainly for a moment, a new experience for one always so sure in his deeds. Then he went out to the stables and spent some time with Walther, who snickered a welcome at the sight of his long-lost master.

Beatrice opened her eyes slowly. Her head ached and her eyes were slow to focus as she looked about the chamber. Carefully she stirred, and moaned as pain flooded every part of her. A soft step sounded upon the floorboards and Lady Alys came to her bedside, and leaned down to stroke her forehead with cool, soothing fingers. 'Welcome back to the world, Beatrice. You had us all worried.'

'How long—?' Her voice cracked and Lady Alys brought her a cup of water, which she sipped and then tried to speak again. 'How long have I been ill?'

'Three days. Sir Remy did well to remove the arrows as swiftly and cleanly as he did, or I fear you would not have survived. You will have scars, of course, but they will cause you no great inconvenience.' She smiled then. 'Boadicea would be proud of you.'

Beatrice smiled weakly in response. 'I would like to see Sir Remy, and thank him for saving my life.'

Lady Alys signalled to a servant and sent him with a message to summon Sir Remy, but when the maid returned to say that Sir Remy had conveyed he would be unable to attend her, Beatrice felt a keen disappointment.

All that day she drifted in and out of sleep, forcing herself to swallow the nourishing broth that Lady Alys insisted would help rebuild her strength. Her eyes closed wearily and she slept away most of the day. That evening she asked again for Sir Remy, but he sent apologies for his absence and she felt the first stirrings of bewilderment. It was her brother who came to her bedside, pulling up a stool as he sat down and clasped her slender hand between both of his.

'How glad I am to see you, Hal,' she whispered, still very weak and tired. 'We have missed you these many months. How is Osmond? Is he well?'

'Aye—' Hal nodded '—he is in Chester with the King. I have been given special leave by his Majesty to go home, and see to Ashton now that Father...' he hesitated, a shadow passing over his brown eyes '...has passed on. I am sorry, little sister, that I was not here to help you shoulder the burden of his loss.'

Her fingers tightened in his clasp. 'You had little choice in the matter, Hal. Your duty was with the King.'

'Aye.' Then Hal shifted uncomfortably on his seat, and looked at Beatrice carefully, gauging if she was ready to hear the news that he must impart. 'Beatrice…' He hesitated, wondering if he should wait awhile, but eager to have the matter resolved.

'What is it, Hal?' Beatrice questioned, with a little frown. 'Do not fear to speak. My body is greatly weakened, but my mind is as strong as ever.'

He smiled at that, remembering the wilful little girl who would always seek to play with her older brothers. 'There is a matter, of a delicate nature.'

'I am listening.'

'Well, it seems that our father made a new Will before he died. Lord Haworth sent it to me while I was marching with the King, seeking my response. I advised him to keep you here at Carmarthen, and made arrangements for a leave of absence as soon as may be.'

'Ah,' said Beatrice, realising now that she had not imagined the efforts to detain her at Carmarthen. 'And what does this new Will contain that troubles you so deeply?'

Hal took a calming breath, barely able to control the anger he felt about the contents of his father's Will. 'I am sure Father meant well, but he was obviously not in his right mind, towards the end.'

'Tell me!'

'It seems…' he hesitated, and then went on in a rush '…it seems that Father has left you his estate at Hepple Hill in Wessex, on condition that you marry Remy St Leger within thirty days of his death.'

# Chapter Nine

The following morning Lord Henry called a meeting, which he was willing to hold in Beatrice's bedchamber, but she insisted upon rising from her sickbed. She dressed in a kirtle of maroon, the deep colour accentuating her pale features. Bryony braided her hair and assisted Beatrice with an arm about her waist to make the short journey from her chamber to Lord Haworth's solar. Here her brother greeted her and together they stood by the window, whispering.

'We need not tell him,' said Hal urgently, observing his sister's profile as she gazed out of the window and down upon the colourful flowerbeds of the pleasaunce.

Beatrice cast him an exasperated glance. 'What purpose would that serve? He will find out eventually, with Father's Will registered by the court clerks, and then we would have the King's sheriff riding upon us with a writ. Nay...' she laid a hand upon her brother's arm '...I would urge you, Hal, not to be devious.'

The door opened and Lord Haworth and Lady Alys joined them. Beatrice moved to seat herself in a chair before the fire hearth, feeling tired already. She leaned her head against the high, carved back of the chair, flexing her shoulder as it throbbed with pain. They waited for the last guest to attend their meeting, and Beatrice hoped that he would not be so foolish as to refuse her brother's summons, as he had refused her own.

When Remy arrived in the solar, he opened the door cautiously and peered in. He had the distinct feeling he was in for a reprimand, but he could not recall any misdemeanour of late that warranted such. Seeing those already gathered in the solar, and their sombre faces, only increased his wariness and he was ready to be on his guard.

'Come in,' called Hal, 'and close the door.'

Remy did as he was bade and came to stand in the middle of the solar. He glanced at Beatrice, noting how pale and drawn she appeared. She should be resting in bed, and he opened his mouth to suggest as much when Lord Henry turned to him suddenly and said, 'Sir Remy, do you know of Hepple Hill, my father's estate in Wessex?'

Surprised at this odd question, Remy nodded slowly. 'Aye. Lord Thurstan sent me there to assist in the training of a unit of men-at-arms that we brought with us to Wales.'

'And would you say it is a fine estate?'

'Aye.' Remy frowned, puzzled. 'It has a well-fortified keep with four towers, a moat, and a wide meadow that afforded twenty men to practise their archery, swordsmanship and—' He stopped suddenly, 'Why do you ask? Are they under siege?'

'Nay.' Lord Henry strode to stand beside his sister and laid his hand upon her shoulder. 'We are gathered here to inform you of the terms of my father's Will.'

'Indeed.' Remy stood with hands on hips, wondering if Lord Thurstan had been kind enough to bestow upon him a token; he hoped that it was his sword, for it was a fine weapon that he had oft admired.

'It seems that my father has gifted Hepple Hill to Beatrice, on condition that she marries you within thirty days of his death.'

Remy digested this news slowly, uncertain whether he had heard right, and a little confused as to what reaction was expected of him, or, indeed, what he himself felt. Then Beatrice spoke for the first time, her voice very soft.

'Tell him all, Hal, for it would be unfair to let him have only half of the whole truth.'

Hal cleared his throat, clearly annoyed. 'If either of you refuses to consent to the match, then Hepple Hill is yours, for all time, and for all your successors by your lawful wife other than Beatrice. Do you understand what this means?'

Beatrice held her breath tensely while she waited, wondering nervously whether Remy had fully comprehended all the implications.

'Let me see,' said Remy, pacing the floorboards, 'if I have this right. If Beatrice and I marry, she will inherit Hepple Hill?'

'Aye. And with it goes the title Lord Pensax.'

Remy slanted him a narrowed gaze, wondering if he was funning, but he decided there were more im-

portant issues than an oddly named lordship. 'And
what of children born of this marriage?'

'They will be her successors in title.'

'And I will own nothing?'

'As her husband you will own whatever Beatrice
holds for her lifetime.'

'And if I do not choose to marry her?'

'Well—' here they came to the crux of the matter
'—it seems that my father held you in such great es-
teem that he has gifted you Hepple Hill outright in its
entirety, with no entailments. It is yours to pass on to
your successors, but only if born of a marriage to another woman.'

Remy stared at Lord Henry, wondering what on
earth Lord Thurstan had been thinking of. If he married Beatrice, he would own nothing for his lifetime
except what she owned, but if he did not marry her
he would be a very rich man indeed! He glanced at
the tense faces ringed about the room, at Beatrice with
eyes downcast. After some long moments of silence,
enlightenment came. If he truly loved Beatrice he
would be willing to forfeit all riches, and that was
what Lord Thurstan wanted to secure for his daughter.
A love match. But after careful musing, he realised
that there was a loophole, one that Lord Thurstan had
not, apparently, covered. He became aware then that
Lord Henry was talking to him.

'Naturally, I need not point out to you that I do not
desire a rich estate like Hepple Hill to be lost forever
to Ashton. It has been part of this family since the
time of King William. If you are unwilling to wed with

Beatrice, then I can offer you compensation, in exchange for the title to Hepple—'

'I am not unwilling,' said Remy quietly, his gaze reaching to Beatrice across the width of the room. 'But what say you, my lady?'

She looked up then, a slight gasp escaping from between her lips. She stared at him in confusion. Perversely, all night she had tossed and turned and wept, certain that Remy would not refuse this chance to gain for himself his own lands. She opened her mouth to speak, and became aware of the pressure of Hal's fingers squeezing the bones of her shoulder. If she refused to marry Remy, he would be furious, and she did not dare think what her life would be like after that, living under his roof, at the mercy of his dictates, which might well include marriage to a man he chose for reasons other than her happiness.

Remy approached brother and sister with a menacing scowl, noting the hand that clutched at Beatrice's shoulder and her slight wince as Hal's lean fingers tightened imperceptibly.

'Step away from her,' said Remy curtly. He was not wearing his sword, but his fists clenched.

Hal looked up, neither faint of heart nor intimidated by Remy; indeed, he was the taller of the two. He took a step towards Remy, 'You dare to speak to me so? I, your liege lord?'

'I seek no quarrel, but I would have Beatrice free to answer without duress.'

'She is free, damn you!'

'Then step away from her.'

The two men glared at one another, and Beatrice

feared that they would come to blows. She held up her hand, signalling to them both that she was ready to speak.

'Hal, I would ask that you allow Sir Remy and I a moment alone, to discuss the matter.'

'What is there to discuss?' protested Hal, turning to look at her. 'You told me last night that you were not averse to the marriage.'

Beatrice blushed, avoiding Remy's eye. 'Please, Hal. Just a few moments, 'tis all I ask.'

'Come, Lord Henry,' cajoled Lady Alys, taking him by the arm and leading him to the door, 'let us arrange some refreshments.' She beckoned to her husband and the trio left the room.

The silence that followed in their wake was deafening. The only sounds were those of the fire flames crackling in the hearth and Remy's footfalls echoing across the floorboards as he approached her. She looked up shyly. His eyes searched her face. She had suffered so much pain, he could not bear to be the cause of anymore.

'What will you have me do?' he asked her quietly.

'I cannot say. You must make your own choice.' She glanced down at her fingers entwined in her lap.

'I know well enough that you will not have me as your husband. Is that not so?'

'It is not that I do not want you, but I fear that I would make for you a poor wife. I fear to love again, Remy, you know that well. I am older than you, and I have scars that mark me as unlovely. How could I ask any man to take me as his wife? Now the conditions of my father's Will only makes it more difficult.

And there is too the manner of his death, that greatly concerns me, and your part in it.' Here she looked up at him, hardening her gaze and waiting for his answer. She prompted him then. 'Tell me that there was nothing underhand, or malicious, in your dealings with my father, Remy, and I will let the matter rest.'

'Will you, Beatrice? Is this not another feeble excuse to avoid facing up to your own feelings?' She flinched at his words, looking away from his steely gaze, but he pressed onwards. 'I tell you with hand on my heart that I did no more than your father asked of me. He begged me to pour the poppy juice between his lips, but I could not do so. Then he asked that I leave the vial close at hand, so that he might ease himself from the hell of this world to the peace of heaven. How could I refuse the dying request of a man I honoured?'

Beatrice cast her gaze to her lap, nodding slowly, believing him at last. 'Nay, I see now that you could not have done otherwise.' She was silent for a long moment, digesting this information, releasing the doubts from their harbour in her mind. 'But...' here she looked up at him again, before saying carefully '...you must refuse to marry me, Remy, and then you will secure for yourself a grand estate.'

'And your brother will kill me at the first chance he has!'

Beatrice gasped. 'Nay! I will make Hal promise never to cause you harm.'

'And what of my family? My children?' He dropped to one knee and unclasped her fingers, taking one small hand into his large palm, momentarily distracted

and enchanted by her delicate white fingers, his thumb
tracing the outline of pale blue veins. Then he forced
himself to concentrate, and returned to the matter at
hand. 'What of my wife? For I assure you, Beatrice,
I will not live celibate until I die. I will take a woman
to wife; if you refuse me, then I must choose another.
Is that what you want? Do you wish to see me wedded
to another woman? Joanna, mayhap?'

At that tears stung her eyes and she shook her head.
'Please, Remy, do not torture me so. I offer you freedom and riches, yet you are too stubborn to take
them!'

She began to cry in earnest then, for she could not
bear to think of him with another woman. With a muttered oath Remy put his arms around her waist and
drew her into his embrace. She sobbed against his
neck, and he stroked her hair, whispering endearments,
pleading with her to stop.

'Shh, sweetheart.' He held her away from him and
wiped her face with his thumb, 'There is another option, one that your father obviously did not consider.'

Beatrice sniffed and looked up at him, her lashes
spiky with tears. 'What do you mean?'

'The Will states that we must marry within thirty
days from the date of your father's death. Then you
will inherit Hepple Hill.'

'Aye. That is so.'

'But it says nothing about an annulment. We could
marry, but if we do not...' he hesitated, seeking a
polite description for the act that he envisaged with
such passion '...if we do not consummate the mar-

riage, then we can have it annulled after the thirty days has passed. If that is your wish.'

She stared at him wide-eyed, puzzled. 'But why? Why would you do that? You stand to gain nothing.'

'I would gain the knowledge that you are safe. You need not live at Ashton under your brother's roof and at his mercy. No doubt he too will take a wife, and what would become of you then?'

Beatrice shook her head doubtfully, chewing her lower lip as she pondered his suggestion.

'What say you, my lady?' He chucked her under the chin, hoping to draw from her an answering smile. 'Shall we call your father's bluff?'

She smiled weakly. 'He will not be pleased.'

'He had no right to play God with our lives, no matter how good his intentions.'

'Aye.' She nodded in agreement. 'Then let it be so.'

Remy rose to his feet, taking a deep breath and suppressing the exclamation of triumph that threatened to erupt from him. By hook or by crook, Beatrice had agreed to be his wife!

The door opened then and Lord Haworth came into the room, followed closely by Lady Alys and Hal. Beatrice rose to her feet, and together she and Remy turned to face them.

'Well,' demanded Lady Alys, 'is it good news?'

Hal snorted. 'That depends on what you mean by good news.'

Remy took Beatrice by the hand and drew her close to his side, announcing, 'We are to be married.'

'Oh, wonderful!' exclaimed Lady Alys.

'Excellent,' agreed Lord Haworth.

Hal nodded, giving Beatrice a look that congratulated her in more ways than one.

'Well, then,' said Lord Haworth, 'shall I call the Bishop?'

'What?' exclaimed Beatrice, alarmed.

'He has been waiting ten days now to perform this wedding,' Lord Haworth muttered grimly.

'Oh.' Beatrice tilted back her head and looked up at Remy. It was too sudden. She was not ready. 'I— I—' she stammered and then seized upon an excuse. 'I want to be married from my own home, at Ashton.'

'Nay, Beatrice,' said Hal, anxious that no delays jeopardise Hepple Hill, 'what difference does it make where the ceremony is performed?'

Beatrice swayed then, suddenly feeling exhausted and unable to cope with further argument, and she pressed a hand to her brow. Quickly Remy supported her with an arm about her waist.

'Can you not see she is in no fit state for a wedding? We will wait until we reach Ashton. No doubt,' he said brusquely, turning to Hal, 'you had planned to depart for home soon anyway.'

There was some discussion upon the merits of waiting or rushing through with the marriage ceremony, but at last Remy won out.

'At least,' said Hal impatiently to his sister, 'I trust you have no objections to a public announcement of the betrothal?'

'Nay,' Beatrice whispered. The room tipped and swayed and she feared that she might faint. And then she felt strong arms slide beneath her knees and around her back, her feet leaving the ground as Remy lifted her up into his arms. She linked her hands behind the strong column of his neck as he secured her against his chest, and she was greatly tempted to lay her head down upon his shoulder.

'Come,' clucked Lady Alys, 'to bed with you, young lady.' And, with a reproving frown for Lord Henry, 'This matter is dealt with, my lord. A betrothal is as binding as a marriage. Let your poor sister rest now.'

'Aye,' agreed Lord Haworth, 'I will call the clerks and have the marriage contracts drawn up. There can be no doubt then that either party shall renege upon their agreement, to which we stand as witnesses.'

'Indeed.' Hal bowed to Remy, who stood at the door with Beatrice in his arms. 'By your leave.'

Remy nodded his head in acknowledgement and, striding from the solar, carried Beatrice to her bedchamber. As they traversed the passage they had a moment alone and she glanced up at his face, noting his clenched jaw and the muscle that ticked in his cheek.

'You are displeased?' she murmured.

He kicked open her chamber door, and set her down upon the edge of the great four-poster bed. 'Not with you,' he answered curtly, sitting down beside her and cupping her face in his palm, a smile unclouding his eyes. 'I believe it is tradition to seal a betrothal with a ring, and a kiss. I have no ring to give you, but I have a kiss.'

He leaned down, but she stayed him with one hand upon his chest. 'I fear you have made a poor bargain. What if...' She hesitated, then pressed on, 'What if we are unable to obtain an annulment, for whatever reason?'

'We will cross that bridge when, and if, we come to it.' He spanned her waist with his hands, urging her closer, and angled his head to kiss her.

Beatrice allowed herself a moment of surrender. The feel of his lips moving upon hers made her heart beat faster, and she sighed and relaxed against him. His ardour quickened and he made to open her mouth wider, but a discreet cough at the door forced him to withdraw and release her.

Lady Alys came into the room with a quick step, hiding her smile. 'Now, Sir Remy, enough of that. My husband bids that you join him in the hall to celebrate this joyous occasion.'

Remy rose, with a grin and a bow for Lady Alys. 'Take good care of her, my lady, for I would hope that a speedy recovery shall lead to a speedy wedding.'

'Aye,' agreed Lady Alys with a teasing glint in her eyes, 'and speed is of the essence.'

Remy laughed, bowed to the two ladies and withdrew. Lady Alys watched his impressive male form as he walked to the door, and then turned to Beatrice and sighed. 'You are a lucky girl indeed.'

Beatrice felt a fierce heat creep up her neck and cheeks, embarrassed that Lady Alys should be so indiscreet as to allude to the obvious male charisma that Remy exuded. This was but one of her many fears—the attraction Remy held for women, all women it seemed, no matter their age. With a sigh she allowed Bryony to undress her and in her nightshift she slid between the covers of the bed and lay back against a pile of soft pillows. Her glance strayed to the scar behind her shoulder, the skin pink and puckered. She knew that the one upon her hip was bigger and just as ugly. Thank goodness Remy had agreed that their marriage was not to be consummated, for she could not bear to have his fingers touch her body and know that such scars would almost certainly repulse him.

Downstairs in the great hall the household was gathered for the noon meal. At its end Lord Haworth hammered the hilt of his dagger upon the table boards and called for quiet. He turned to Lord Henry and invited him to speak. Hal rose from his place.

'On this day,' he announced, in a deep clear voice that echoed around the crowded hall, 'Sir Remy St Leger has made his pledge to my sister, the Lady Beatrice, and they shall be married.'

A cheer went up, the loudest echoing from all the Ashton knights, who drummed their knuckles upon the table to show their approval. Sir Giles exclaimed loudly, ''Tis high time we had a bit of good news.'

Remy accepted the many congratulations that came his way, some of the knights pounding him hard upon the back. As the commotion subsided he took a deep draught of the fine wine that Lord Haworth had ordered brought up from the cellar, and across the table met the brooding gaze of Lord Henry. Slowly, Remy set his goblet down, and rose from the table. Deliberately he strolled to an alcove beside the fire hearth and turned to look directly at Lord Henry. His silent challenge was taken up, and Lord Henry joined him.

'My lord,' said Remy, with mock servility, 'spit out what chokes your gullet.'

Lord Henry eyed him impassively, respecting the fact that it was not often he came eye to eye with another man and mindful of Remy's reputation. He had entertained the idea, as he journeyed from Chester with his father's outrageous Will burning a hole in his pocket, that he would challenge St Leger and settle the matter of Hepple Hill in the age-old tradition of hand-to-hand mortal combat. But now, having met Remy, having seen him perform in battle against the Welsh, he had spurned the idea as foolhardy. Hal considered himself to be a good knight, and a good swordsman, but he was no match for the likes of St Leger, who was not merely good but superior.

'Come now, my lord,' prompted Remy with impatient sarcasm, 'let us have it out, for we are to be brothers, and I for one have no quarrel with you.'

Lord Henry muttered under his breath, 'I'll wager you don't.' But then he said in a louder tone, 'All is very rosy for you, St Leger, in your garden. Hepple Hill is a fine estate.'

''Tis not mine. It belongs to Beatrice.'

'Indeed. And that puzzles me. Don't mistake me, I love my sister, but I cannot for the life of me see why you have agreed to marry her. If I may speak bluntly, why would a man such as yourself choose to hide behind a woman's skirts?'

Remy narrowed his eyes, but controlled the spark of anger that leapt too quickly in his breast. Then he smiled, slowly. 'If we are being blunt, then I will tell you. Sometimes, the only way to lift a woman's skirts is to stand behind them.'

Lord Henry stared at him for a moment, aware that to speak so of a lady was a grave insult. He considered striking St Leger, but then, instead, he began to laugh. He laughed so loud and so hard that others standing nearby turned to stare at them. Remy stood with hands on hips, eyebrows lifted and a wry grimace upon his lips. He did not think his comment was all that amusing—indeed, he had expected a blow and would have welcomed a fight to break the tension between them.

At last Lord Henry wiped the tears from his eyes and controlled his guffaws of mirth. He patted Remy consolingly on the shoulder. 'Here I was thinking that you had some grand political scheme, and all it really is…' he laughed again '…is lust.'

Remy scowled. The joke had worn thin long ago. He thought Lord Henry should be defending his sister's honour, instead of laughing about it. He shrugged off the hand on his shoulder, his stance turning belligerent, and muttered, ''Tis not mere lust I feel for Beatrice.'

'Indeed?' Lord Henry sobered then. 'You are aware, I trust, that she is a good few years older than you?'

'Aye.'

'And that she still feels a deep devotion to William de Warenne, her betrothed killed in battle years ago?'

'Aye. But I think 'tis a great exaggeration to say that she still has feelings for him. 'Tis mere loneliness that has caused her to be loyal to his memory, and loyalty is a quality I greatly value.'

'Indeed?' Lord Henry gave him a look that was almost one of pity. 'Then I wish you good luck, Sir Remy, for it will take a bold man to overcome the disadvantages that you face. I trust,' he said with a note of warning, 'that you plan no harm towards my sister? For Hepple Hill shall return to Ashton upon her demise, should she be childless at such time, and you will stand to gain nothing if that is the route you plan to follow.'

Through clenched teeth, his blood hot with anger at this insult, Remy replied, 'Have no fear. If harm should come to Beatrice, it shall not be by my hand. I intend to give her only happiness and joy in our marriage.'

Lord Henry looked the knight up and down, noting the handsome face, the muscular, broad-shouldered body, and the sensual curve of his mouth. 'No doubt upon her wedding night Beatrice will swoon from all this joy and happiness.'

For the first time Remy smiled, and he said softly, with great amusement and a sweeping bow, 'My lord, I shall do my best!'

Holding out his hand, Lord Henry invited, 'Come, let us put aside our unfortunate beginning. We are men of the same mettle and I think we could well be friends.'

Remy nodded his agreement and shook hands with Lord Henry, for never was he one to hold a grudge and he could find no other fault with his brother-to-be except a ruthless dedication to his family's welfare, that in truth was to be commended.

Five days later they left Carmarthen and embarked upon their journey southwards, and home. There had been some delay to their departure as Lord Henry had insisted that he would not leave his father buried in Wales. Members of the clergy had muttered with misgivings, but the greasing of holy palms with a generous donation had ensured their blessing and Lord Thurstan was removed from his grave. A coffin of gleaming oak bound with brass received his remains, and this was placed upon a covered cart.

Thus encumbered, and as Beatrice tired easily, the journey was slow. She rode upon a gentle palfrey while Nogood had the unenviable task of riding Bos, whose temper had little improved during his idle days in Wales.

So large a party could not be easily accommodated at inns along the way, and most nights they camped under canvas, secure in the knowledge that only a fool would dare attack when the odds were vastly against them. With the country awash with lawless bands and mercenaries intent on winning their fortunes with King Edward in Wales, too little care could not be taken and the English knights, together with their men-at-arms, were confident yet vigilant.

Many times Beatrice felt Remy's gaze upon her, as they rode along, as they watered the horses at a tumbling silver stream, as he lifted her up into the saddle or helped her dismount. Sometimes, when they were seated about the campfire eating a cold supper of bread and cheese, his stare seemed speculative, and she wondered what were his thoughts. At other times, she could not mistake the warm glow of desire that softened his hard male features and relaxed his mouth. It was then that a tingle crept up her spine and flushed across her skin, but she could not decide whether it was fear for the future and her irrevocable commitment to be his wife, or excitement at the prospect of Remy St Leger being her husband.

By this time it was mid-June, and surprisingly hot. Lord Henry fussed and fumed at their slow progress, anxious to reach Ashton and have his sister safely wedded before the thirty-day deadline elapsed. Already nineteen days had passed since Lord Thurstan had passed away.

On the fifth day they paused to water the horses beside a river and Beatrice lifted the heavy weight of her braided hair away from her neck, damp tendrils clinging to her overheated skin. She felt great pity for the men, roasting in their leather tunics and mail armour. The heat at midday was intense and on the horizon a great bank of dark clouds loomed. A stiff breeze whipped up and rustled the leaves of the willow and elder trees lining the river bank. A storm was promised before the day was out.

'We can cross here,' said Lord Henry, eyeing the dark green waters of the river blocking their path, 'it will save us some time.'

Sir Giles urged his horse forwards and advised, ''Tis safer if we travel up to the causeway, my lord. These rivers may look benign, but beneath the surface there can be strong and dangerous currents.'

'Nonsense,' replied Lord Henry, 'get the wheels off the cart, and float it across. The horses can swim well enough and it will save us a great deal of time. Before nightfall we might reach Ashton.'

'What of your sister?' said Remy quietly. 'Would you put her in danger?'

Lord Henry turned to Beatrice with a casual smile. 'She is an excellent horsewoman and I have no doubt she will fare better than most.'

'My lord—' Sir Giles tried again to make his protest, but to no avail.

Lord Henry urged his horse down the bank, his spurs forcing the wary animal onwards as he lowered his head to the swirling waters, snorting and blowing and stepping gingerly as firm earth gave way to sliding mud. With much shouting and hard riding Lord Henry urged his destrier on and rose dripping and triumphant upon the far side. He waved his arm and urged the rest of his party to follow.

Whilst the knights assisted most of the men-at-arms to cross, Sir Giles and Remy stayed to see the wheels removed from the cart bearing Lord Thurstan's coffin, and set half-a-dozen men to guide it as they floated it across the river.

'Beatrice,' said Remy, wheeling Walther about, 'you are to go last and I think 'twould be better if you rode pillion with me.'

'Nay.' Beatrice smiled, taking up her reins. 'I would not wish to burden either you or poor Walther.'

''Tis no burden,' he replied impatiently, his frown lowering over eyes that warned her against entering into a quarrel.

Beatrice held fast and turned Bos—she had taken pity on Nogood and let him ride the palfrey that day—

towards the riverbank. She did not relish the prospect of riding him through the swirling waters, which were not overly deep and reached to shoulder-height on most of the horses, but she did not want Remy to think her a simpering ninny. She must trust Bos to carry her safely, however grave her misgivings. When her turn came Remy tried again to persuade her to dismount and ride with him, but Beatrice gave a little laugh, that sounded nervous even to her own ears, and urged Bos forwards. He did not like the idea of getting wet, and made much protest, snorting, throwing his head up and down and causing Beatrice to feel unsure of her seat. Perhaps it was her mistrust that communicated itself to the stallion, for suddenly he reared, with a melodramatic shriek and wildly rolling eyes, and with a startled cry Beatrice fell.

She hit the riverbank head first and was momentarily stunned before she rolled and fell into the water with a splash. The spot was a little off the chosen crossing path and deeper than expected. A swirling current snatched at her with hungry fingers, dragging her down into the river's dark depths.

Beatrice fought desperately, opening her eyes beneath the water and peering up at the faint green glint of sunlight above her head. She kicked hard with her legs and flailed with her arms, suddenly emerging out of the watery grave that threatened to claim her. She screamed, and waved her arms, frantically calling for help.

Remy had plunged Walther into the river the moment Beatrice had hit the water. Now he desperately urged the powerful destrier onwards and followed the swift flow downstream, shouting to Beatrice. He wondered whether to throw himself into the river and swim after her, but he resisted the temptation and relied upon the greater strength of his horse to carry him ever closer.

'Beatrice!' shouted Remy, trying to catch her attention before she ducked beneath the water again. 'Look ahead! There's a fallen tree, grab it! Beatrice, grab the tree!'

He could not be sure that she had heard him. She screamed again, choked on a mouthful of water and disappeared.

Remy cursed. For this he would kill Lord Henry!

Frantically he searched the smooth glide of water as it flowed along, and then at last he saw her head pop up. She grabbed hold of a branch protruding from the fallen tree trunk that had crashed down during some long-ago storm and wedged between an outcrop of boulders. She clung to it with both arms and looked back over her shoulder, gasping and panting.

'Remy!'

'Hold tight! I'm coming. Don't let go.'

With urgent words of encouragement Remy guided Walther towards her and then, at last, he managed to grab hold of Beatrice by her kirtle and dragged her across his saddle bow.

Beatrice coughed and spluttered, retching as she hung upside down. Her legs trailed in the water and she clung to Remy's knee with both hands, terrified of falling back into the river.

'Hold on,' Remy urged, 'we'll be out of this in a moment.' He turned Walther towards the far bank, searching for a safe place to climb out of the treacherous torrent, the brave horse holding his head up high and swimming with the current as it flowed along. At last Remy chose a suitable spot and Walther found his feet, rising up out of the river with a snort as he clopped up the steep slope, halting beneath a great oak tree to shake himself off and turn his head enquiringly towards his master. Remy praised him and patted his neck and then he lowered Beatrice to the ground and dismounted himself. He grasped her by both arms and demanded, 'Are you all right?'

Beatrice nodded weakly, still gasping for breath, and then she turned, fell to her knees and quietly ejected the contents of her stomach.

'Damn him!' exclaimed Remy, slamming his fist into his palm. 'Damn the son of a bitch!'

'Remy!' Beatrice remonstrated with him, as she rose weakly, her hair clinging wetly to her head and her lips a bright crimson against the wet pallor of her face.

'When I get hold of him I am going to thrash him in the manner he deserves!'

Again she exclaimed his name, and stared at him with horror. 'Hal is your liege lord. You dare not lift a finger to him.'

'And why not?' he demanded of her, stooping to glare into her eyes. 'Manners and good sense are obviously two lessons he has never been taught.'

'Nay!' Beatrice took a step towards him and laid a hand on his arm. 'That is not so. It has been a difficult time for Hal, away from home these many months, and now our father's death, and he is saddled with the burdens of an estate he had not so soon expected. This—' she waved her hand at the river, at her sodden clothing, at poor dripping Walther '—this was merely his eagerness to reach a home much missed. Please, Remy, I beg you to seek only peace with my brother.'

'Indeed?' he muttered beneath his breath, glancing down at her for a long moment, her soft-spoken words of reason cooling the molten lava of his rage. His mood calmed, and with a sigh, taking her arm in one hand and Walther's reins in the other, he began to walk off upstream, towards the rest of their party, some distance away, muttering darkly, 'Your precious brother still has much to learn.'

# Chapter Ten

Beatrice spent an uncomfortable afternoon in her sodden kirtle, the wet fabric chafing against her tender skin and her hair dripping continuously as a shower broke upon them and Hal insisted they push on.

'Hot food and warm beds await us at Ashton!' he goaded the men, urging them forwards.

She watched with disquiet as Remy rode close by her with a scowl upon his face, his glance for her brother as sharp as the edge of his sword. She wondered how to convince Remy that his anger should be extinguished, before it led him astray.

The storm passed over and the afternoon brightened as golden sunshine beamed out from behind the clouds. They were very close to home now, and Lord Henry sent a messenger on ahead to give warning of their arrival. A relieved cheer went up when, at last, the towers and walls of Castle Ashton came into view.

Hearing the jingle of harness and the beat of many horses trotting by, the local tenants came running from their cottages. They waved and called out a greeting to their new young lord, and then sobered as Lord

Thurstan's coffin trundled past, making the sign of the cross and muttering a prayer for his departed soul.

It was eventide when they plodded across the drawbridge, wet and weary and cold. The cart bearing Lord Thurstan's coffin drew up before the doors of the chapel and their chaplain, Father Thomas, greeted them solemnly upon the steps.

Remy helped Beatrice to dismount and then he joined with Sir Giles, Sir Cedric and Lord Henry to bear the coffin upon their shoulders and carry it into the chapel, where it was laid to rest before the altar. The dim interior was glowing from the flickering light of a dozen candles, and Father Thomas swept away any demons with clouds of incense from a brass burner, swinging it to and fro upon a chain. He chanted prayers for the departed soul of his liege lord, and the chapel quickly filled with knights and servants eager to pay their respects.

Beatrice stood to the fore, beside her father's coffin, shivering in her wet dress and shoes, her hair a damp coil upon her shoulder. Remy eyed her with concern, noting her pale cheeks and her frame racked by shudders. He moved to stand behind her, his arms encircling her waist and drawing her back against her chest.

She looked up over her shoulder, and welcomed the warmth that emanated from his tall frame, seeping into her very bones until some of the deep chill melted away. But still she continued to tremble, bone weary and distressed as once again she was forced to live through her father's funeral rites.

Remy said, 'My lady, at this rate you will not be fit for a wedding in a month of Sundays. Go you to bed.'

Beatrice shook her head, 'My duty is here.'

'Your father would be the first to see you take better care.'

Lord Henry turned then and frowned, admonishing them for their whispers as the priest intoned his Latin liturgy.

Seeing this, Remy told him, 'She is exhausted, she should retire.'

Beatrice looked to her brother, and when he nodded it irked Remy that she obeyed her brother's authority and not his own. He watched with narrowed eyes as Beatrice disappeared into the dark shadows of the chapel, accompanied by Elwyn, who greeted her with an embrace and took her away to her chamber.

Elwyn fussed over her charge, caring for her as she always had since Beatrice was a young girl. She was of a mind to have her take a hot bath, but Beatrice refused.

'Let the knights have the water, Elwyn, for they have had a long five days, sweating in their armour. I will bathe on the morrow.'

In front of a roaring fire in her bedchamber a grumbling Elwyn helped her to strip off her wet garments and rubbed her down with towels soaked in hot water, fragrant with rose and lavender petals. Submitting to these brisk ministrations, Beatrice asked Elwyn how she had fared these weeks past.

'Oh I be all right, my lady,' muttered Elwyn, picking up discarded garments from the floor.

Beatrice looked at her sideways, noting her disgruntled expression. 'Come now, Elwyn,' she said with gentle encouragement, 'if all is not well I would hear why.'

But Elwyn would not be drawn and insisted on dressing Beatrice in her nightshift. Obediently Beatrice raised her arms, like a child, and Elwyn made to don the soft linen, but her hands were stayed and, with an exclamation of horror, she demanded to know, 'My lady, what has happened to you? What are these scars you bear?'

Beatrice felt an anguished heat colour her face and she told Elwyn of the attack in Wales. Then she asked, peering over her shoulder with a small frown and grimace, 'Is it very bad, Elwyn? Have you any creams to make their livid marks fade?'

Elwyn made a strangled noise in her throat, and folded Beatrice into the comfort of her embrace, rocking her slender frame. 'Oh, my little lamb, you might have died! I might never again have had you home to love and to hold.'

Beatrice was deeply touched by her maid's devotion, she who had been like a second mother to her all these years past, and she waited patiently, patting Elwyn's broad back with one palm and murmuring, 'Do not distress yourself, dear Elwyn. It is naught and here I stand before you, hale and hearty. But now I am scarred without as well as within. How it sorely grieves me to be so maimed.'

Taking hold of her self-control, Elwyn huffed a sigh and set Beatrice away. 'What nonsense! You were always the most beautiful lady at Ashton, and always will be.'

Beatrice laughed. 'Such blind loyalty! How lucky I am!'

Briskly Elwyn set about dressing her mistress in her nightshift, and a rose-brocade robe, then bringing a bowl of clean warm water for her to wash her face and hands with. She served Beatrice with a meal of hot broth, thick with chunks of chicken meat, carrots and swedes, accompanied by soft white bread.

Having eaten her fill, Beatrice sat back with a contented sigh, and then returned to the question of what vexed her faithful nurse. 'Dear Elwyn, tell me what it is that troubles you,' pleaded Beatrice.

'Well…' Elwyn folded her arms over her bosom, and gave Beatrice a direct look '…I hear my lady is to be married.'

Beatrice laughed then. 'Is that all that has your nose out of joint?'

'Well, I thought I would know of such a thing long before any pageboy!'

'Who told the pageboy?'

'The messenger Lord Henry sent on to say you were on your way and to make ready.'

'You can hardly blame me for that, Elwyn.' Beatrice rose from her chair, resisting the weary ache of protest from her tired body, and reached out her arms to give Elwyn a hug. 'I would have told you the moment I had the opportunity. Besides—' she tossed the mane of her still damp hair '—'tis only to Sir Remy.'

'Only!' exclaimed Elwyn, 'What a peculiar thing to say, my lady, and I would have been much surprised to hear that you were going to wed anyone else!'

Beatrice bit hard on both her lip and her words,

thinking that for the moment it would be prudent not to reveal the pact she had made with Remy St Leger. She was going to be married, but she would not be a true wife and that knowledge gave her little cheer.

'Now,' said Beatrice briskly, 'what else can you tell me? Has there been any difficulties or disputes whilst we were away?'

Elwyn had a mutinous pout to her mouth, sensing that Beatrice was being secretive and not liking this new experience. 'Well, Cook has been selling small packets of salt and flour behind your back.'

'Has he indeed!' exclaimed Beatrice, marching to the door. 'Let us put a stop to that at once and remind Cook of his duty.'

Downstairs in the great hall most of the knights had come in, having discarded their armour and weapons in the armoury, and were now sitting down at the trestle tables to enjoy the same chicken broth and white bread that Beatrice had. Lord Henry had ordered wine and ale to be served in celebration of their homecoming and, spying Beatrice as she came down the stairs, he raised his goblet to her.

'Your health, sister!' he exclaimed.

Beatrice wondered if he had already imbibed a little too generously. 'Hal, there is a matter I would discuss with you.'

'In a moment, little Bee.' Hal sat down and a large steaming bowl of broth was set before him, which he applied himself to with relish.

Not wishing to disturb her brother further, Beatrice asked, 'When you are done, please meet with me in the kitchens, for there is a serious matter to be attended to.'

'Very well.' Hal tore off a chunk of bread and dipped it into his bowl, sighing and closing his eyes with pleasure as he ate a decent hot meal for the first time in days.

Leaving him to enjoy his food, Beatrice went to the kitchens at the rear of the hall and as she entered she noted that the curtains were drawn on the bathing alcove. She could hear the splash of water and a giggling female voice.

'Oh my, Sir Remy, I 'ave missed ye sorely!'

Beatrice froze. That voice belonged to one of the serving maids, a young strumpet by the name of Bess. She moved quickly and quietly, and jerked open the curtains. Remy sat in the bathing tub, steam rising up all about him, and Bess leaned over him as she scrubbed his back. They both looked up, she fancied with a guilty start, and Beatrice felt her heart plummet. Not yet wed and already another of her fears making itself known—that Remy would find the attractions of other women too hard to resist.

In truth, Remy had been about to dismiss Bess. He had no desire for her and knew that he would never betray his betrothed in any way. But now he looked at Beatrice with cold challenge and raised eyebrows, daring her to make comment as Bess stood with her hands upon his naked shoulders. He leaned back, his powerful torso tapering down into the water and revealing just a glimpse of his hips. Would Beatrice be jealous? He very much hoped so!

'You may go,' said Beatrice in a cold voice, and

she waited until the maid had bobbed a curtsy and fled.
Then she closed the curtains and approached the bath-
ing tub with slow steps, trying to look only at his eyes.
'What was that all about?'

Remy shrugged, and reached for the bar of soap
abandoned by Bess. He lathered it up and soaped under his arms, and then his chest with a lazy circular
motion, his blue gaze all the while holding with Beatrice's wide brown eyes. 'She helped me to wash.
Nothing more.'

'It didn't sound that way.'

'Indeed? How did it sound then, my lady?' He
leaned his head to one side and waited for her answer.

'Well…' Beatrice blushed fiercely, and stammered,
'It—it sounded to me, well, like…'

'Like what?'

'Like you and she…'

'What?' he persisted, gliding the bar of soap over
one muscular thigh, his eyes watching hers and the
blush that burned her cheeks as she followed the
movement of his hands.

'As though you knew each other!' Beatrice exclaimed.

He laughed, setting aside the soap and rinsing his
chest. 'Of course I know her. She's Bess, one of the
serving wenches.'

'You know what I mean! You have…'

'Yes?'

'Lain with her!'

Remy shrugged again. 'What if I have?'

Beatrice exclaimed her anger and frustration. She
took a step towards him, intending to deal him a slap,

but he caught her wrists and pulled her closer still, and she had to brace her knees against the edge of the wooden tub, lest she fall in and join him in his bath water.

'I will not tolerate such vile behaviour, Sir Remy!'

Remy transferred his hold of her wrists into one hand, easily encircling their narrow width, and moved his free hand to grasp behind her thighs, forcing her to sink down upon her knees. He brought her face closer to his, their noses almost touching, their lips just a breath away.

'I admit,' he whispered, 'that to lie with a woman tonight would greatly please me, but I will not cause you any shame. I assure you that between now and the day of our annulment the only woman I will give my attentions to is you, sweet Beatrice.' He kissed her then, his lips moving slowly and thoroughly, before raising his head and asking, 'That is still what you want, is it not?'

She blinked and stared at him for a moment, her senses swimming on a dizzy tide. 'What is?'

'An annulment. You do not wish me to, er...' he hesitated delicately '...perform the rights of a husband on our wedding night.'

She tried to snatch away from him, confused, but he held her, his fingers gentle yet implacable. 'We had agreed that you would not. Do you go back on your word?'

'Nay, a knight does not break his promise, especially one given to a lady. But you have not answered my question, Beatrice. Is it what you want? To be a wife *and* a virgin?'

'You should not speak to me so!' protested Beatrice.

He smiled lazily, enjoying her blushes, heartened to see some emotion upon the usual pallor of her constrained countenance.

'Please let me go!'

His hold slackened, 'On one condition.'

She eyed him suspiciously, 'And what would that be?'

'Finish what Bess has begun.'

'You mean, scrub your back?'

He laughed, 'Aye.' Then he planted a quick kiss on each hot, rosy cheek, his eyes full of mischief. 'That is what I meant.'

Beatrice suspected that he was mocking her, but she rolled up her sleeves and did as he asked. Her fingers rinsed the soap from his broad back, gliding over the hard muscle compacted on either side of his spine, smoothing across his shoulder blades, and rubbing at a stubborn speck of mud at the base of his neck. Stooping over him, she noticed goosebumps flare across his golden skin.

'Has the water gone cold, Sir Remy?' she asked, 'Shall I call for hot?'

'Nay,' he replied, his voice somewhat strangled. 'Go now. I will finish by myself.' He hunched forwards as she stepped out from behind him, not wishing her to see how her soft touch, her nearness and her elusive scent of flowers and female had aroused him. With some chagrin he concluded that the unexpected sight of rampant male vigour might be a shock to an innocent maiden. He jerked his head at the curtain and said curtly, 'Go!'

Beatrice eyed him with a puzzled frown, and then left, pulling the curtains closed. There was an agonised groan from Remy and the sound of water splashing, but before she could call out if all was well her brother came into the kitchen, and she went with him to deal with their thieving cook.

When she returned, with the unpleasant knowledge that on Hal's orders the cook would receive no wages for a year and ten lashes on the morrow, there was no sign of Remy. She went into the great hall, but she did not see him there either and with a resigned sigh she turned for the stairs leading to her chamber.

'Wait,' said Hal, detaining her with a hand on her shoulder. 'I have spoken to Father Thomas. It is agreed that you will be married on Midsummer's Eve.'

Beatrice turned sharply to face him and exclaimed, 'But that is only five days away!'

Hal shrugged, biting on a plump pear that he had purloined in the kitchen, and wiping the juice from his chin with the back of his hand. ''Tis ample time to send out messengers to our guests. And it takes little time to don a gown and march to the chapel. What did you expect, Bee? There are only ten days left before the deadline expires and St Leger inherits Hepple Hill.'

'Oh, Hal!' exclaimed Beatrice crossly, her patience with men utterly worn. 'You and Hepple Hill! Why, 'tis enough to make me ill!'

She stomped off and retired to her chamber. As she prepared for bed she told Elwyn how fast approaching was her wedding. Climbing up into the familiar and much-missed comfort of her own bed, she snuggled down beneath the covers and sighed, asking the age-old question, 'What on earth shall I wear?'

After his encounter with Beatrice, Remy took himself off to the armoury, hoping to cool his blood as it sang through his veins with hot ardour. He found Nogood and set him to sanding down his sword, answering the boy's questions about war while he paced about restlessly, testing various weapons. He balanced a patula in one hand and a pavade in the other, trying to decide in a desultory fashion whether he preferred the short sword or the long dagger. He set them aside and tried to turn his mind away from the memory of two small female hands gliding over his back. It was a difficult task and Nogood did not receive the best of his attention.

Sir Giles came in then and looked askance at Remy. 'What do you here? Should you not be in the hall getting better acquainted with your brother-to-be?'

Remy grunted, and hefted down a poleaxe, taking undue interest in its curved blade. 'He and I do not seem to be well matched.'

'Too well matched, more like.' Said Sir Giles with frank candour, eyeing Remy carefully. 'And where is Lady Beatrice? Should you not at least be spending time with your betrothed?'

'She has retired.'

'Then do you the same. It has been a long day and most everyone is bedding down in the hall.'

Remy looked at him with a frown. 'You seem

overly concerned about my welfare, Sir Giles, and while I thank you for it—'

Sir Giles clapped him on the shoulder heartily, and grinned. 'I know well your problem, lad. I am not so old that I do not know how it is to lust after a woman. 'Tis not only bridegrooms that fret with impatience.'

Remy coloured beneath the hue of his tan. Sir Giles knew only the half of it!

'But you must contain yourself, Sir Remy, for I would not see my Lady Beatrice dishonoured because of your lack of restraint.'

At that implication his temper flared and Remy set aside the poleaxe with a crash. 'Do you think I am so pea-brained as to do such a thing?'

'I fear, my brave young knight,' said Sir Giles gravely, hiding his grin of amusement, 'that at the moment you are thinking with every part of your body *except* your brain.'

When Beatrice awoke in the morning she lay for a long time just listening to the sweet melody of birdsong and enjoying a beam of sunlight that slanted across her bed from the window, the shutters having been left open during the warm summer night. She sighed and smiled, aware of a pleasant, delicious thought that hovered at the back of her mind, yet not quite awake enough to appreciate what it was. And then she remembered.

She was getting married!

After all these years she was going to be married. And then another thought brought her awake as surely as if cold water had been thrown in her face. She sat bolt upright, staring wide-eyed about the room and yet seeing nothing at all.

Remy St Leger would be her husband!

She groaned. And held her head in both hands. Gnashed her teeth and groaned again. Then she paused and held her breath, her thoughts darting about. Was there a way out? Could she delay the wedding, feign an illness mayhap, even have it cancelled altogether? Nay, her brother would go mad and drag her to the altar in her nightshift, ill or not ill. Huffing a violent sigh, she flung herself back against the pillows. There was no way out, leastways none that she knew of.

The door creaked open and Elwyn came in. Beatrice greeted her good morn and then noticed the garment draped carefully across her outstretched arms. She recognised it at once. The pale golden hue of the pure silk had scarcely faded after all these years.

'My wedding gown,' whispered Beatrice, and then she looked up at Elwyn with an accusing glint in her eyes. 'I thought I had told you to dispose of it after...' she hesitated, for it had been many years since she had said his name '...after William died.'

'Well, I could not bear to and thought it best to wait a bit. I kept it hid, safe and sound, sure that one day you would wear it. Now, at long last, you will. Of course, I didn't expect the waiting to be so long,' Elwyn said with a smile, 'and you are not as plump as you were at sixteen.'

Beatrice gasped, affronted, 'Thank you, Elwyn.'

'Never mind, we have five days in which to fatten you up. A man likes to grab hold of a good handful, you know.'

Beatrice had been about to make a retort, when suddenly she sobered and the smile vanished from her face. She remembered the pact. Their marriage was to be annulled. As far as Remy was concerned he would not be grabbing a handful of anything!

'Come, my lady,' chivvied Elwyn, worried by the dismal look upon Beatrice's face, 'you know I only jest. You are quite lovely just as you are and I have no doubt this gown shall fit you perfectly. Shall you try it on?'

'Nay.' Beatrice sat up and pushed back the covers. 'Hal was most insistent that we not delay this morn, as he wishes to see our father laid to rest.' She padded across the floor and shrugged on her robe. 'Is my bath ready?'

'Aye, my lady.' Elwyn laid aside the wedding gown and picked up a hairbrush, attending to the snarls and tangles of Beatrice's long hair swirling about her hips. 'What will you wear today?'

'I think the dark blue kirtle.' She put on her slippers and then went downstairs to the bathing alcove.

It was sheer delight that engulfed her as Beatrice slid down into the hot water. She sighed, her skin rippling with pleasure. She noticed the goosebumps rising on her forearms and thighs and could not help but remember how the same had appeared on Remy last evening, when he too had bathed in this tub. Leaning her head back, she pondered on this: had he also felt pleasure? She cast her mind back and remembered that she had been washing his back, her fingertips moving over the broad expanse of his muscles. A sudden wondrous truth hit her—he had liked it! He had enjoyed her touching him.

Elwyn came in then and began to wash her hair. Beatrice closed her eyes, hiding her secret thoughts, mindful that her cheeks were flushed not only from the hot bath water. When Elwyn had finished rinsing her hair, and went off to see what Cook had to offer in the way of a meal for her mistress, Beatrice lay back to return to her thoughts, so very new and interesting in their content. Her gaze strayed to her own body, and she could not deny that it felt different since she had known Remy. Her breasts felt firmer and tingled with sensation, her face always seemed to be aglow with a blush when he was near, and even her heartbeat strayed from its normal steady pattern! How could this be? she wondered.

Just then the curtain slid open and Beatrice, expecting to see Elwyn, glanced up with little surprise. Then she jerked forwards with a startled exclamation, crossing her arms protectively across her bosom.

'Sir Remy! You should not be in here!'

He smiled slowly, his eyes roaming in a leisurely inspection of her naked limbs, her slender hands and long, water-sleek hair covering well her female attributes.

'Is aught amiss?' she asked, as he stood there, silent and staring, and with one hand quickly covered the scar upon her shoulder, satisfied that her long wet hair and the lapping water concealed the other behind her hip.

'Nay.' He cleared his throat and forced himself to

look away. 'Your brother is anxious that you meet him in the chapel. He sent me in search of you.'

'You could have sent Elwyn with a message.'

'Aye. I could have.'

'But you did not?'

He shook his head, glancing at his boots, at the far-off beams of the roof, and then back to Beatrice, hardly able to resist the urgings of his body and mind.

'Why?' she asked, relaxing a little now, enjoying the novelty of holding such power over a man and curious to learn how to wield it. Of course, she reminded herself quickly, she would not torment or bait him, and she would send him on his way any moment now. 'Sir Remy?'

'What?' He noticed that she sat back and that her arm had eased its clasp across her bosom. His head began to swim as he caught a glimpse of rosy nipples. Boldly he took a step towards her, and seeing the slight smile upon her lips, the amused gleam in her eyes, he took several more and was close enough to kneel down beside the bathing tub and take her face between his hands.

Beatrice looked at him, her breath quivering from between parted lips, and she murmured, 'You must go.'

'Aye. But I had to see you. There is never a moment to be alone with you.'

'Why would you want to be alone with me?' she asked, with too much bright innocence, her lashes fluttering.

He chuckled then, wise to her mood. 'You are teasing me, my lady.'

She shook her head, feeling the pressure of his large fingers on her cheekbones. 'I, an old maid, teasing a worldly knight such as yourself? Surely not!'

He laughed outright and so did she, and then she gasped as his lips captured her own. His mouth moved fiercely on hers, persuading hers to open, and Beatrice suddenly wondered if she had gone too far. She was naked, and knew that her strength was no match for his own, should he choose to take matters further. But even while this thought was running through her mind, she felt his tongue slip inside her mouth, and she gasped again. She opened her eyes, and found his blue gaze watching her, taking note of her reaction. His tongue moved, touching with hers, stroking the sensitive roof of her mouth. A groan of sheer pleasure escaped from her throat and she moved her hands to his neck, fondling the smooth skin with her fingertips...

A piercing scream suddenly rent the air. Elwyn entered the bathing chamber and they sprang guiltily apart. She began beating Remy about the head and shoulders with the linen towels she had brought for Beatrice.

'Be gone, you wretch! How dare you! Get away from my lady, she is not yours yet!' Elwyn spluttered with outrage.

Remy rose quickly to his feet, raising his palms in defence and throwing Beatrice a look that brimmed full with regret and farewell. Beatrice laughed and remonstrated with her maid.

'Elwyn, stop that at once! You will do damage to my betrothed.'

Elwyn snorted, 'Nothing could damage that great lummock!' She shooed Remy away and jerked the curtains closed, muttering beneath her breath, 'I turn my back for five minutes and the two of you…' And then she turned to her mistress with a broad grin. 'I take it, then, that you have changed your mind about him? Not too young and handsome now, is he?'

Beatrice deigned not to reply, and retreated behind a tranquil mask of silence. Quickly she climbed out of the water, dried herself and dressed, rubbing at her hair with a towel. 'Help me, Elwyn, for Hal is waiting in the chapel and you know how he froths at the mouth with impatience.'

'Aye. And where does he get that from, I wonder?'

Beatrice smiled, 'He is very much like Father, is he not?'

'The spitting image. Here now, my lady, let me braid your hair and tuck it up, so, for it will take an age to dry.'

There was no time to break her fast and Beatrice hurried across the bailey to the chapel. This was an event she was not looking forward to, and it somehow felt false to her, having buried her father and grieved for him once already. The chapel was crowded, thick with a haze of incense, and she had to shoulder her way through to the front. She murmured an apology to her brother and to Father Thomas for her tardiness.

At her side Remy leaned forwards and whispered, 'You smell nice. Have you been bathing, my lady?'

She dug her elbow into his ribs, admonishing him with a frown to be quiet. He feigned a wince, greatly amused and delighted with this playful side to Beatrice that he had always suspected lurked beneath the solemn surface. Just then a laugh escaped from Remy. For so long now the tension between them had been too intense, and release, however inappropriate and unwanted, could not be stemmed.

'For the love of God!' exclaimed Hal, turning to them both and holding up a hand to Father Thomas, asking him to pause. Then he pointed a finger at the chapel door. 'You two, begone!'

As they made a rapid move to escape, needing no second bidding, Hal said sharply, 'Sir Giles, see that Lady Beatrice goes to her chamber, and Sir Remy to the armoury, for I will not have disgrace and scandal fall upon this household!'

As the two guilty parties threaded their way through the crowd, Remy managed to find Beatrice's hand. Upon the steps, before Sir Giles reached them and whisked her away, he raised her hand to his lips and kissed her knuckles.

'Adieu, my lady.' His eyes were full of promise and Beatrice left him with several backward glances, wondering how five days could suddenly seem like an eternity.

Late that afternoon Beatrice went to the holy ground where her father had been laid to rest, in a grave beside that of her mother. She knelt down and placed a bunch of flowers upon the mound of freshly turned earth. She felt sad, yet peaceful, resting her one hand upon the damp earth as she spoke aloud.

'Forgive me, Father, I meant no disrespect this morning in the chapel. It didn't have as much meaning for me as it did for Hal. After all, we already gave you a splendid funeral in Wales. But I trust that you know my heart will ever be full of love for you, and the good father that you were. I am happy to know that you are with mother, and together you shall rest in eternal bliss. Father…' she hesitated, struggling with the words that burdened her heart and her soul '…I do not know why you have gone to such lengths to ensure that I take Remy St Leger as my husband, but I hope your reasons are sound. I cannot deny that I have feelings for him, but is it right? Is it good?' And here she sighed her final, most urgent question. 'Will it last?'

Only the wind whipping across the fields, and the creaking of the trees, and the trill of larks, answered her. Beatrice sat for a long while beside her father's grave, basking in the bright sunshine and the tranquillity of the graveyard. When at last she rose and strolled slowly back to the keep, she felt peace enter her soul, even though her questions remained unanswered.

# Chapter Eleven

Two days before Midsummer's Eve the wedding guests began to arrive. First of all came Aunt Margaret, accompanied by her husband Lord Robert and foster-daughter Joanna, as well as several household knights, Sir Richard Blackthorn amongst them. Other relatives from as far away as Yorkshire and Norfolk came too, as well as two representatives from the court of King Edward, whose permission for the marriage had been sought and obtained.

The pale golden limestone walls of Castle Ashton and the leaded rooftops of her towers gleamed in the bright summer sunshine. Heraldic banners and pennons were hoisted aloft from every bastion, and from the crenellations facing the drawbridge over the moat bright banners in the household colours of Ashton, crimson and green, were hung in great swags.

Inside the castle there was a bustle of activity. The steward engaged many serfs in decorating the keep and the chapel with garlands of fresh flowers and ribbons. The Cook, chastised and eager to make amends, sweated night and day in preparing whole carcasses of roasted beef, venison and boar. On the wedding menu would also be oysters, lampreys and jellied eels, savoury and sweet pies, fruit cakes, jellies and blancmanges, subtleties of marzipan and spun sugar, as well as huge platters of wafers, nuts and cheese. Down in the cellars the butler worried about bringing up enough barrels of wine and ale to see them through the feasting of Lady Beatrice's wedding.

There was a feverish air to this busy hive, and Beatrice was only too happy to seek the refuge of her bedchamber, yielding to Aunt Margaret's strictures that she should remain in seclusion as much as possible until her wedding day. It was here that a pageboy came to her with the message that Father Thomas wished to see her. She was not unduly surprised, for she had expected some sort of lecture from their priest upon her forthcoming nuptials. Beatrice set aside the occupation of her tapestry embroidery—intended to soothe her tortured thoughts but, indeed, was of little comfort—and hurried to meet with the good father in his own chambers, attached to the chapel.

Father Thomas followed the teachings of St Augustine. He was kindly and well loved, his sparse frame and greying hair a familiar sight about the countryside as he rode to give mass and alms and comfort where he could. But there was also healthy respect for his rigid views, which were believed to be divine and imparted direct from God. No one thought to argue with, or against, Father Thomas, and Beatrice prepared herself mentally for a diatribe upon the merits of being a good wife and what her duties to her God, her Church and her husband would be, in that order.

'Ah, my lady.' Father Thomas looked up as Beatrice entered his spartan quarters, and he laid aside his quill beside the holy transcript he was penning. He rose from his bench and went to greet Beatrice.

'Father,' Beatrice murmured, and kissed his hand.

'Come, let us sit.' He indicated two chairs placed beside the open shutters of the narrow windows, overlooking the small cloistered garden that banked on to the chapel. ''Tis a lovely day. Listen to that birdsong. Enchanting.' He turned to Beatrice then, giving her a moment to settle herself, and smiled gently, 'No doubt you are looking forward to Midsummer's Eve.'

'Indeed,' Beatrice murmured, her eyes straying to a bed of sweetpeas and lavender humming with one or two bees and butterflies that flitted about.

Father Thomas cleared his throat then, linking his hands in his lap. 'There are several matters I wished to discuss with you, my lady. It is my understanding that this marriage to Sir Remy St Leger has come about in rather an unorthodox manner. I wish to ask you a question and…' he paused and then spoke more firmly '…you must answer truthfully. Are you entering into this marriage of your own free will? You realise that a marriage cannot be valid if it is entered into without the full consent of either party.'

Beatrice stared at him for a moment. Then she nodded and said softly, 'I am willing, Father.'

'Good, good.' Father Thomas nodded, his glance straying to his abandoned penmanship and clearly anxious to hurry on with his agenda. 'Now, it is my duty to remind you that marriage is a holy sacrament. It is binding for both your lifetimes. The Church, and especially the teachings of St Augustine, believe that a marriage blessed before God is a spiritual union and should not be sullied by—' he coughed and avoided her wide eyes '—by carnal lust. I have written out for you the days when you should avoid relations with your husband.'

He handed to Beatrice a small piece of parchment and she read, with dismay and wonder, the rather long list. It included Sundays, feast days, the Lenten seasons of Easter, Pentecost and Christmas, before receiving communion, while doing penance, during the time when she had her monthly flow, when she was nursing a baby, and not during daylight. Most amazingly of all, Beatrice thought, she was not to have relations with her husband on her wedding night. Stunned by this list, she wondered when it was that married couples were allowed to be intimate and how on earth anyone managed to become with child! She folded the piece of paper and laid it upon her lap.

'I must also tell you that the holy union of marriage was encouraged by the church to prevent excessive lust. You must endeavour to be always faithful to each other and you should not indulge in relations for any reason other than procreation.'

Beatrice felt her cheeks burning with heat. This very explicit and detailed lecture was not what she had been expecting, and she glanced anxiously towards the door, hoping for an escape.

'And yet so saying,' continued Father Thomas, 'you are both under an obligation to also fulfil your marital debt.'

Beatrice stared at him in confusion.

'The bond of marriage,' explained Father Thomas, 'affords you rights over your husband, just as he has over his wife, as far as the marital bed is concerned. You are just as entitled to demand that your husband fulfil his duties in attending to your needs and desires, as you are obligated in attending to his. For though the Church does not encourage carnal lust, it is better for it to be fulfilled within the bonds of holy matrimony than, well, outside it. Do you understand?'

Beatrice nodded, gulped, and suppressed the riot of thoughts that had suddenly stampeded through her mind. Her needs and desires? She had never considered their existence before!

'Do you have any questions, my lady?'

Meekly Beatrice shook her head. She had many questions but none that she had the courage to voice out loud! And besides, what would be the point, for surely theirs would be a marriage in name only?

'Excellent!' Father Thomas was delighted that the matter had been dealt with so speedily, and he rose from his chair, ushering Beatrice to the door. 'Be so kind as to send Sir Remy to me, please, my lady. I will say to him exactly what I have said to you.'

'Indeed?' croaked Beatrice, clutching her piece of paper. 'Will he have a list like mine?'

'Oh, yes.' Father Thomas was very pleased with her demure and pious response to a lecture that quite often brought forth a torrent of angry questions.

'Reading is not his strongest skill, Father,' she warned.

'Have no fear, I shall read it out for him.' He patted her shoulder, 'I wish you every joy in your marriage,

Lady Beatrice, and look forward to seeing you on the steps of the chapel on Midsummer's Eve.'

Remy rose from his chair and paced the room for a moment. Then he turned to Father Thomas and exclaimed, 'This list is ridiculous!' He threw it down on the floor. 'When God created Adam and Eve he made them naked and in such a way that they could enjoy each other! As much as they liked, whenever they liked!'

Father Thomas sighed. This was not going as well as it had with Lady Beatrice, he feared. 'I cannot deny that. But we have advanced since the Garden of Eden, Sir Remy, and now we have certain rules by which we live, for our own good.'

Remy swore then, beneath his breath. He leaned towards Father Thomas and demanded in a tetchy tone, 'Then tell me exactly when I am allowed to have "relations" with my wife? By God's teeth, the whole thing is absurd!'

Father Thomas restrained his own reaction to the young man's temper and asked, with as much patience as he could muster, 'Sir Remy, have you never practised abstinence? It may do your soul some good.'

'There's nothing wrong with my soul!'

'Please, sit down. There's no point getting so upset. It is only a guideline, for your spiritual welfare. If you choose not to follow it, and no doubt that would not be unusual given the nature of man, then that is your own choice.'

Remy flung himself down in his chair. 'Have you any idea how hard it has been to find favour with

Beatrice? And now this—' he flung his hand at the offensive list discarded upon the stone floor '—this will no doubt ensure that I never lay a finger on her. For she is pious, you know, she wanted to be a nun.'

'I know.' Father Thomas smiled, for he had been chaplain at Castle Ashton since the birth of Lord Henry thirty-two summers ago.

'Just when I thought her heart had melted and that all would be well.' Remy fell into a brooding silence then. After a few moments, he suddenly sat up right and asked, 'Why must we wait three days after the wedding to have intercourse?'

'Because you have received the holy sacrament of communion. It is out of respect for God that you wait.'

Remy grunted, none too pleased or convinced. And then another thought occurred to him and he asked, 'On what grounds could a marriage be declared invalid and annulled?'

'Well, if either party were already married. Are you, Sir Remy?'

'Am I what?'

'Already married. Do you have a wife?'

'Nay! Of course not.' Remy scowled, his chin propped upon one hand.

'Well, then, if the marriage was entered into without willing consent from either party.'

Remy was silent then, uncertain whether Beatrice was truly willing or not.

Father Thomas was by now beginning to feel a little bewildered. 'Might I ask why you would want to annul a marriage that has not yet taken place? And to a woman you obviously love.'

'Love!' snorted Remy. 'That tiny word does not even begin to describe how I feel. What else?'

'Well, if the marriage was not consummated because you were impotent...' the priest looked the virile, muscular knight over with a doubtful glance '...or if your wife could not physically accommodate you to enable it to be consummated. Of course, on such grounds the guilty party would not be allowed to remarry, for fear of casting such a situation upon a second spouse.'

Another long silence ensued. Then Remy said slowly, 'Father, if I tell you something now it would be in confidence, would it not?'

'You wish to make a confession?'

'Aye. Of sorts.'

'Then I am bound by holy vows never to reveal to others what you tell me.'

'Then I confess to you that Beatrice does not want me for her husband, but her brother has forced her into the marriage so that the family will not lose Hepple Hill. We have agreed that the marriage will not be consummated and that an annulment will be applied for as soon as the thirty days of her inheritance have passed.'

Father Thomas frowned. 'Is that what she told you? She will not allow the marriage to be consummated?'

'Well...' Remy shrugged '...not in so many words.'

'Then mayhap it will not be so. Women are strange creatures, Sir Remy, and my advice would be to take every aye and every nay with a pinch of salt. Lady Beatrice does not strike me as an avaricious type, more interested in wealth than in love, and she is certainly no timid maid unable to speak her own mind. If she was so determined not to marry you, then she would not do so. It seems to me that her heart is very much yours.'

Remy sighed heavily. 'Her heart is a fortress, Father. One that I have laid siege to with every weapon in my possession. To no effect.'

With raised eyebrows Father Thomas enquired, 'With every weapon, Sir Remy?'

He coloured and cleared his throat. 'Well, not that. It is certainly easier to acquire a wife by rape, but distasteful.'

'For whom?'

'For us both!'

'I am glad that you are aware of that truth. I have known Lady Beatrice since she was a babe and I have a great fondness for her. She has suffered such great hurt over the years and borne it all with grace and dignity. It is time she knew some happiness, and I trust that you will be patient and diligent in giving it to her. It must be obvious to you, Sir Remy, that as a battle-hardened warrior your physical strength is far greater than hers. I beg that in the heat of your passion you will treat her with gentleness. Now…' Father Thomas rose from his chair and escorted Remy to the door, along the way retrieving the all-important list and pressing it into Remy's hand. His parting words were much the same as those he had given to Beatrice. 'I will see you on Midsummer's Eve upon the steps of the chapel. Fare thee well.'

On the evening before Beatrice's wedding day all the ladies met in the solar, while the men kept to the hall, each to celebrate the couple's last night of maidenhood and bachelorhood in their own way. Aunt Margaret had given orders to her husband to ensure that the bridegroom did not become overly drunk and unable to rise to his feet on the morrow. Nor to fall foul to any pranks that might jeopardise his attendance, which, in her experience, had happened to an unfortunate cousin in Norfolk some years ago—the bridegroom had drowned in the moat, having been dared to swim across it naked and was too drunk to remember that he could not swim.

Since her meeting with the chaplain, Beatrice had been pensive, and it had not gone unnoticed. Her aunt and her cousin, other ladies who were relatives, friends and neighbours, now tried to put her in good cheer for the great day fast approaching. The door was barred, food was spread out on a table, cushions on the floor and it was an occasion to indulge in gossip and sweetmeats, advice on how Beatrice should do her hair and what flowers to wear and what to say to her guests after the ceremony.

Gradually, as the evening wore on and the wine loosened tongues, the talk turned to more important matters, namely what Beatrice might expect on her wedding night. However, Beatrice rose then and flounced away, clearly annoyed and discomforted. She hastened to the door, saying that she had the headache and wished to retire, and whilst some whispered spiteful comments that she was too old to appreciate a man like Remy St Leger, others were more tender in their concern.

Aunt Margaret signalled for Joanna to remain with

the other women, when she would have followed, and
pursued Beatrice to her bedchamber. There she found
her niece sobbing into her pillow. Gently, Aunt Margaret put her arms around Beatrice and drew her into
a comforting embrace, stroking back tendrils of hair
from her brow and asking quietly, 'What is it you fear,
Beatrice?'

'Naught!'

'Come now, 'tis obvious that there is much troubling you.'

'Nay, Aunt, let me be. It is truly naught.'

Her aunt sighed, but persisted, knowing full well
the family trait of stubbornness. 'Is there some vice
about Sir Remy that disturbs you?'

'Nay, indeed! He is all that is good. Why, if anything, he is too good, too handsome!'

Aunt Margaret began to have an inkling then of the
problem, and probed carefully. 'Is it that you fear he
will hurt you? It is true he is tall and strong and heavy
with muscle, but he is a courteous knight, and I am
sure he has learned to have good manners in his relations with a lady, especially his very own wife.'
Then, in the absence of her departed mother, Aunt
Margaret decided to speak more frankly, for which she
was renowned. 'There may be some pain, for you are,
after all, a virgin. But the pain will not last longer than
a moment or two.'

Beatrice sniffed, and calmed her sobs, whispering,
'It is not that. I do not fear him as a man.'

'Then what is it?'

'Oh, Aunt, look at me! I am no young maid, firm
and plump! And I have scars from the Welsh arrows!

They are hideous. What will he think if he touches me?'

'If?'

Beatrice bit her lip. She must not reveal their secret pact. It seemed a moot point, however, as she doubted whether either one of them intended to keep it. Or was she mistaken? She cried out in anguish then, 'Half of me wishes to run far away from him and never let him near, and the other half wishes to have him take me, possess me, love me, just as much and as hard as he can! I know not which half is the more shameful, nor which half to give!'

'There is no shame in love,' said Aunt Margaret gently. Her eyes fell upon the folded parchment on a coffer, which she had noticed Beatrice reading and re-reading often in the past day. She asked shrewdly, 'What did Father Thomas say to you yesterday?'

'Oh, I expect it was his usual speech for brides and bridegrooms, but it was disheartening. I did not know that there were so many restrictions upon—' Beatrice blushed fiercely '—physical relations.'

'Only in the mind of a priest.' Aunt Margaret picked up the paper and read it, then she folded it up and placed it back on the coffer, 'If you want my advice, I would put this list away somewhere, and only refer to it when it suits your purpose.'

Beatrice looked at her aunt with some confusion. 'And when would that be?'

Her aunt smiled, and wiped her tears with her sleeve. 'That you will learn for yourself, my child. Now,' she spoke briskly, 'I want you to stop all this nonsense. Tomorrow is your wedding day and God knows we have waited long enough for it. You must sleep now, so that you will awaken in the morning fresh and glowing with the radiance of a beautiful bride. And,' she raised her voice and overruled Beatrice's protest '...I want you to ask yourself a serious question. Would a handsome young knight like Remy St Leger fall in love with you if you were not the beautiful and intelligent woman that you are?'

Down in the hall the antics of the men were far less restrained. Heavy drinking had been indulged in since supper time and the roar of noise as men laughed, sang, shouted at one another and danced with several exotic women brought in for the occasion—jingling with brass bangles and clad in scanty veils that revealed more brown flesh than they covered—was enough to keep Father Thomas locked in his own chamber and the pageboys packed off to the armoury.

Remy, however, sat at a table with his head propped in one hand and glumly staring into his goblet of wine. Several attempts to get him to dance with one of the mysterious Moorish girls failed and Sir Giles rallied the other knights to cheer him out of his misery.

'Why so glum?' demanded Sir Giles as he sat himself down beside Remy and waved his hand about the hall. 'All this is in your honour, and yet you do not appreciate it.'

Remy sighed. 'I have received bad news.'

'Indeed?' Sir Giles sobered, concerned now that the wedding day was about to be ruined. 'From home?'

'Nay. From Father Thomas.' Remy held up the crumpled sheet of parchment he had been given. 'I am about to be married to the most beautiful woman I have ever set eyes on, have desired her for so long that even my bones ache, but it seems that once we are married there are only two or three days in the year when I might actually bed her!'

For a moment Sir Giles stared at him, at the list, and then he began to laugh, quietly at first, and then so loud and so uproariously he almost fell off the bench. It was not long before others demanded to know the joke and when, through fits and gasps and splutters of mirth, Sir Giles acquainted them with Remy's troubles, the entire hall began to rock with laughter.

Then the parchment list was purloined and a great ceremony was made of its burning, which resulted in several scorched fingers. Lord Robert and Sir Giles both sat themselves down and convinced Remy that no one took much notice of the Augustine teachings.

'Indeed,' cried Lord Robert heartily above the drunken revelries, 'if men obeyed the teachings of the Church there would scarce be enough babes born to populate a tavern, let alone a country. Cheer up, old son, we—' he waved his arm magnanimously around the hall '—us, this grand company of lords and warriors, we hereby give you permission to take your wife as often as you like!'

There were hearty cheers to this, and Remy began to thaw. He allowed his goblet to be refilled, little knowing that it was spiked with aquavit. He went so far as to enjoy watching the acrobats and the jugglers and the dancing girls, but drew the line as a silky veil slid around his neck and a pair of voluptuous, dusky-skinned breasts jiggled before his eyes. He pushed the girl away and with a throaty laugh she leapt up on to the table, her long, shapely legs twisting and turning in a dance designed to lure and entice.

A dozen men hammered their fists on the table, encouraging the dancer, but to no avail. Remy was not tempted by her. In the end, as she finished her dance in a frenzy of whirling arms and legs and gossamer veils, it was Sir Cedric that yielded to temptation and carried the girl off over his shoulder to a dark corner in the bailey.

Meanwhile Sir Richard Blackthorn had gathered together a small group and they whispered out of earshot of the guest of honour, planning their next round of bedevilment certain to shake Remy out of his iron mask of self-control. But first they needed him drunk and to this end they plied him with more wine, liberally laced with more aquavit. It took a while, but eventually Remy began to join in with the antics and frolics.

It was usual at these events on the eve of a wedding to play a joke upon the bridegroom, or urge him into a dare to prove his manhood. It was decided by a few that to 'tar and feather' the hapless groom about various parts of his body would be a splendid jest. The tar was made up in the kitchen, a busy place as the Cook hurried to prepare all the food for the feasting tomorrow. Amidst much laughter a harmless mixture of raw egg whites, honey, flour and vinegar was whipped up in a large bowl, the feathers plucked from a goose hanging in the larder. Yet somehow, whether by accident or a-purpose, the whole jape went awry.

It was later alleged that someone—and there were only two suspects, one of whom claimed to have been busy with a dancing girl in the bailey—added real tar purloined from the armoury.

Remy was far too drunk to appreciate what was going on, but he did manage to prevent the rowdies from 'tarring' him about his private parts and they had to make do with his chest and his head. As far as Remy was concerned the joke was not particularly funny and he fought the howling jackanapes off with a few cuffs and elbow pokes, but when they seemed intent on ripping open his chausses, matters turned nasty. A brawl erupted. Remy knocked out two guests within quick succession but he was abruptly yanked out of the fray by his brother-to-be and Lord Robert, who feared his wife's wrath should the groom appear at the chapel door on the morrow with a black eye at best, a broken nose at worst.

They retreated to the bathing alcove in the kitchen, where hot water was poured and engaged in much jovial scrubbing while the mess of feathers and 'tar' were removed. Laughter quickly died when the concoction could not be shifted and Remy started to bellow his fury. Hands on hips, brows creased in puzzlement, the men stood about staring at Remy, a peculiar sight with his hair all clumped in black spikes and his chest no better off. Someone suggested goosegrease, another linseed oil and both were tried in a vain attempt to rid Remy of his unwanted adornments.

'Fetch Elwyn,' instructed Lord Robert of Nogood.

Reluctantly Nogood went upstairs and tapped upon the solar door, only to be told that she had retired to bed with her mistress some hours ago. Nogood retreated, fearing that the ladies would ask him why he sought her out. For some long, thoughtful moments he stood before Lady Beatrice's door. What to do? he wondered in an agony of indecision. At last, he dropped to his knees and gently, carefully, creaked open the chamber door. On hands and knees he crept across the floor, until he reached the pallet upon which Elwyn slept, at the foot of Lady Beatrice's bed. With great stealth, he gently shook the maid awake.

Elwyn nearly jumped out of her skin with fright when she saw Nogood hovering over her. Mindful of Beatrice asleep in the big bed—it had been no easy task getting her settled this night—she did not utter a sound, but with a great sigh left her warm pallet, struggled into her kirtle and went with Nogood down to the kitchen.

'Oh, my Lord!' Elwyn held both hands to her mouth when she surveyed Remy standing half-naked in the bathing tub, disconsolate and red-raw on his chest and shoulders from the furious scrubbings that had failed to remove the sticky stains of black tar. There was no amusement in Elwyn as she stood staring at him. And then she announced, 'The only way is to shave.'

'Not my head!' protested Remy, aghast.

'Everything!' Elwyn sent Nogood off to fetch a razor and she began rolling up her sleeves, shooing from the alcove all the worthless spectators. She lathered up soap into a thick foam and spread this on Remy's chest.

With plenty of soap, hot water and a sharp blade Elwyn managed to scrape from his skin every last speck of tar. Unfortunately most of his hair went with it. Feeling as naked as a newborn babe Remy rinsed and dressed. She thought he was about to weep as he complained, 'I look like a Hun mercenary. When Beatrice sees me tomorrow she will either laugh herself sick, or run from me screaming in terror.'

Elwyn refrained, when she woke in the morning, from telling her mistress what awaited her. Beatrice was jittery enough as it was and Elwyn feared that just about anything would cause her to dig her heels in and refuse to go through with the ceremony. She insisted that Beatrice have a bite to eat and a little warm milk infused with valerian to soothe her nerves. Then she set her mistress down in a chair beside the open shutters and had Beatrice read her Psalter out loud, in particular Psalm 101.

'I will sing of your love and justice; to you O Lord I will sing praise. I will be careful to lead a blameless life…'

Diligently Elwyn attended to her ablutions, making sure there was plenty of hot water, scenting it with her favourite lavender and rose petals, brushing out Beatrice's hair until it gleamed and, finally, dressing her in the beautiful golden silk kirtle. It fell in soft folds about her slim figure, the V-shaped neck banded with pale cream and honey-coloured ribbons and perfectly displaying her delicate collarbones and slim throat.

Elwyn had fashioned a circlet of flowers—pink roses for loveliness, daisies for innocence, forget-me-nots for fidelity—laced with matching ribbons. She placed it upon the bride's head and stood back to admire her mistress, quite speechless at the picture of loveliness that was Beatrice.

The morning had passed so quickly that Beatrice could scarce believe that it was time to go down to the chapel. She took several deep calming breaths, thanked Aunt Margaret and Joanna as they gathered about her and complimented her. With her rosary beads in one hand Beatrice descended to the hall.

The wedding guests formed two rows from the keep door to the chapel, between which Beatrice walked, accompanied by her brother, her aunt and uncle and cousin. The ground was strewn with petals and the knights raised their swords to form a protective arch over her head. Beatrice smiled to left and to right, surprised at how calm she felt. The great day had dawned. For so long she had awaited her wedding and she was determined now to enjoy it.

Upon the steps of the chapel several people were gathered. Sir Giles was standing as groomsman to Sir Remy, in the absence of his own relatives who were far away in Aquitaine; and, although notified, they would not know of the wedding for some many weeks to come as a messenger sped towards them.

Beatrice looked ahead eagerly. Her wedding gift to Remy had been a set of new clothes. A soft white shirt and an embroidered tunic in fine royal blue linen, with matching chausses and a belt of enameled pigskin. She faltered a little when she could not see him. She saw Father Thomas and Sir Giles, and a tall, broad-shouldered man who looked familiar, and who wore the clothes made for her groom, yet his hair was so

close shaven you could see his scalp. He turned then
to watch the advancing bridal party, and Beatrice felt
a gasp escape from between her lips. Her eyes wid-
ened. It was Remy! Why had he shaved his lovely
golden hair? He looked like a stranger. A cold, hard-
faced, dangerous stranger.

Beatrice stopped. Something was wrong. She did
not think that she could go on. Her eyes moved from
examining his naked head and went to his face. She
saw the anxiety mirrored there. She saw the colour
flood his face, and then ebb to pallor as he watched
her falter.

Hal gripped her elbow, and squeezed. He urged her
onwards, and whispered in her ear, 'There was a mis-
hap last night. Do not fret, his hair will grow back
again.'

Now they were by the first step, and Beatrice had
to lift her gown with both hands and mount them. She
lowered her eyes, careful that she should not stumble
and make of herself a fool, but as she reached the top
and came to stand beside Remy, she could not bear to
raise her eyes and look upon him. Then, sensing his
pain emanating from the warmth of his tall frame, she
could not further increase his torment by ignoring him.
She turned to him then and raised her eyes to his.
Seeing the fear in his bright blue eyes, she smiled.
Relief flooded his gaze and he reached out and took
her left hand in the palm of his left.

'You are so beautiful,' he whispered.

A blush warmed her cheeks and there were murmurs of approval from the guests as they gathered
nearer and watched the lovely bride and her hand-

some, if somewhat shorn, bridegroom. Some had feared this moment and there were many with sore heads and queasy stomachs this morn, but at last the marriage ceremony began and Lady Beatrice was joined in holy matrimony to Remy St Leger.

# *Chapter Twelve*

In the great hall of the keep the newly married couple sat themselves down in their places of honour upon the dais. Lord Henry called for a toast, and the company drank to the good health of Lady Beatrice and Sir Remy. Then the feasting began and servants brought in the first course, groaning beneath the weight of the trays piled high with oysters and mussels and crabs, jellied eels, lampreys, salmon and trout. One entire trestle table against the side of the hall was piled up with a veritable wall made from rounds of fresh manchet bread, sliced in half and to be used as trenchers, a fresh one per guest for each course. There would be six courses and the eighty guests leisurely enjoyed each one.

Beatrice picked at her food, aware of the nervousness that roiled in her stomach, her eyes often straying to the heavy gold band upon the fourth finger of her left hand, and to her new husband seated beside her. The first shock of Remy's appearance had not quite worn off and each time she looked at him she was startled anew. He looked older, very much the hardened warrior who had won his spurs at a young age, and Beatrice wondered if she had imagined the tenderness that Remy had displayed in days gone by. Tonight, what would happen?

Remy was not ignorant of the emotions that plagued Beatrice. They were written plainly upon her face, obvious in her silence and the wary look in her eyes when he spoke to her. He repressed a sigh of frustration. He had hoped to see just an inkling of joy upon her countenance. He could not disguise his own satisfaction and jubilation knowing that now she was his wife. She belonged to him. She was his to do with as he wished. Or was she?

With these doubts and questions subduing the bridal couple, they rose with some reluctance when called upon to initiate the first dance of the evening. A band of minstrels had been engaged by Lord Henry and they played a pretty tune upon their lutes, gittern, flute, drums and rebec.

As Remy took her hand and led her about in a pattern of intricate steps, she kept her eyes lowered. Yet still she was aware of him and he seemed so very tall and broad shouldered. Her hand disappeared in his large palm and she was acutely aware of the warmth and strength of his fingers as he twirled her about. He was a better dancer than she had been led to believe, and did not step on her toes or the hem of her trailing gown, a feat upon which Remy congratulated himself, his eyes watching her every move.

She looked so small, he thought, her head barely reaching to his collarbone. Her slender frame in the lovely golden gown seemed immensely fragile and he experienced a nervous twinge at the thought of doing with her what had been uppermost in his mind from the moment he had first kissed her, all those weeks ago at the Red Lion inn. He was now fearful that he might crush her dainty ribs, bruise her skin that appeared soft and pale and delicate like the dewy white petals of a magnolia. He forced away such heady thoughts and tried to concentrate upon the dance.

The evening wore on. They danced together several times, and then Beatrice danced with her brother and her uncle, and Remy danced with her aunt and her cousin Joanna. More toasts were drunk and the wine barrels depleted steadily. Beatrice and Remy began to lose their sobriety as they were plied with drink and delicious food and the laughing, happy company of all their guests could not help but make an impression.

Her cheeks were flushed and her hair dishevelled by the time Aunt Margaret called together some of her favoured ladies and Beatrice realised, with a jolt, that it was time for the bedding ceremony. There was some banter as Remy watched her go, with narrowed eyes and grim mouth, but in light of the fact of last night's dreadful joke-gone-wrong and Beatrice's recent loss of her father, her age and her quiet dignity, the usual coarse ribaldry was restrained.

She was led upstairs to her bedchamber, that now Remy, as her husband, would share with her. Elwyn's pallet had been removed and this familiar, comfortable room, that she had known all the days of her life, suddenly seemed very different.

The flowers were removed from her hair, now sadly

wilted. Her bridal gown was unlaced and set carefully aside. Beatrice slipped off her shoes and Elwyn rolled down her hose and set these aside too. Then she brushed Beatrice's hair out and dabbed rosewater between her breasts. Standing in her muslin shift, Beatrice waited nervously while a noisy throng escorted the bridegroom along the stairwell and into her chamber.

As the men burst in the door, Beatrice avoided Remy's eyes. Her glance slid to the four-poster bed, the covers turned down and strewn with rose petals. Her glance quickly slid away and remained firmly fixed upon the canopy of the bed.

Father Thomas came then and made the sign of the cross upon her forehead with his thumb. 'May this union be blessed,' he murmured, moving away to the far side of the room, where stood Remy.

He had been stripped of his belt and tunic, but he refused to remove his shirt and there were none brave nor large enough to argue the point. Father Thomas gave him the same blessing as he had given to Beatrice and then the guests were ushered away by Aunt Margaret. Being the last to leave, she turned to Beatrice and Remy, smiled at them across the width of the room and said softly, 'Goodnight, dear children. Be good to each other.'

Then the door closed and there was silence. The candles ringed about the room on ornate wrought iron stands flickered and Beatrice could hear her own breath as it passed from nose to throat to lungs. Her heart was hammering very hard and she started when Remy spoke from the far side of the bed.

'Beatrice?'

She tried to speak and then had to clear her throat of a nervous obstruction. 'Aye?'

'Will you not get into the bed?'

She felt frozen to the spot upon which she stood.

'Are you afraid of me?'

'Nay, of course not,' she croaked in a husky voice and took a tentative step forwards, only to halt at the sound of his voice.

'I have not forgotten our agreement,' he said, his voice bleak of emotion, however much it cost him. 'I will do nothing that you do not want me to.'

Beatrice shivered, partly cold from standing for so long barefoot and in just her shift, partly intrigued, alarmed and excited all at once. Stepping closer to the bed, she dusted off the rose petals and climbed beneath the covers, lying down quickly upon her back, her hands folded over her chest. She closed her eyes. She felt the mattress sag as Remy sat down upon its edge and pulled off his boots and his hose.

He shrugged off his shirt, looked with chagrin upon his hairless chest, and turned to slide beneath the covers. He lay on his side, his head propped on one hand, and surveyed the profile of Beatrice as she lay beside him, as though doomed and about to meet her fate. He smiled, and then stretched out a hand and stroked back a stray tendril of hair from her cheek.

At his touch Beatrice started. Her eyes flew open and she turned to stare at him. A cold shiver caused her to shudder and Remy exclaimed, as his fingers felt her arm and her clasped hands, 'Why, you are freezing!'

His arms slipped about her and gathered her close against his cosy warmth. Still she quivered and remained stiff as a board. He knew then how very nervous she was and his heart contracted painfully. For nothing on earth would he have his Beatrice frightened, especially not of him. He kissed her temple chastely.

'Goodnight, sweet little wife,' he murmured. 'I am tired, and I guess you must be too. For me it is a great pleasure just to sleep in a soft bed, as I have spent most of my nights rolled in a blanket upon the floor. I ask for no more than that. Tomorrow, when we have had a good night's sleep and our minds are clear for proper thought, we will consider whether this marriage is to be, or not. Do you agree?'

Relief flooded through her and Beatrice nodded her head eagerly, her eyes lifting then to his in grateful acknowledgement.

Again a smile touched the curve of his mouth. 'You look surprised, as well as relieved. Hardly flattering to a bridegroom on his wedding night. What did you expect I would do? Throw you down and force myself on you?'

She eyed him warily, 'Is that not your right?'

'I have no right to hurt or abuse you.'

As trust began to seep its way slowly with his warmth throughout her body she relaxed and snuggled against him, her cheek pillowed on his bicep. Her glance strayed to his bald chest and she raised her hand, gently touching the two little nicks here and there with her fingertips. 'It will itch when it grows back.'

'I must look a sight. I am sorry. The horror upon your face as you approached the chapel, I thought you were about to turn around and run away.'

'It is not your fault. But it was a shock…' her gaze moved to his head '…and it did cross my mind to run.'

'But you did not.'

'Hal had such a tight grip on my arm I could not,' she confessed, with a rueful smile.

He sobered. 'But would you have, if he had let go?'

She hesitated to answer him, and hedged. 'I do not know.' Her eyelashes fluttered down then, a wave of exhaustion passing over her. 'Let us sleep.'

He murmured an agreement, but while she fell into slumber he remained awake for a long while, just watching her. His eyes roamed over her face, indulging himself in the uninterrupted luxury of minutely examining her nose, her cheeks, her eyebrows, her chin, her lips. Her full, lovely pink lips. Quickly he moved his glance away, tenderly giving attention to her ears and the way her hair grew at her temples. Then he went on to examine her throat and the pulse that beat at its base, the delicate bones of her clavicle. His gaze strayed further, to the soft mounds of her breasts, the dusky rose peaks just visible beneath the thin muslin of her shift.

He sighed and slid his arm from beneath her cheek, climbing out of the bed and moving around the chamber as he snuffed out the candles; many a fire had been caused by unattended candles. Besides, if he could not see Beatrice in the dark, then mayhap he too would be able to sleep. He climbed back into bed and noticed that she had turned over on to her side. He lay against her back, fitting himself to curve about her small, slender form. As he lay awake in the dark he thought there was much to be said for the teachings of Father Thomas. He mused that there was something pure and perfect about the way he felt for Beatrice and he reasoned that her innocence was part of that attraction. How would it be when he destroyed her virtue? There was nothing pure, innocent or perfect about his male body. He was a warrior who bulged with hard muscle and had scars from wounds inflicted on the battlefield; he had killed men and his hands were stained with blood. Since growing to manhood, he had bedded many women in many different ways. If there was no bed then it had been in a field, against a wall, or on a tabletop. He cringed now to think of all the things he had done with women. Slowly, inch by inch, he moved away from Beatrice. He was not worthy. He must not dare to ever blemish her with the rudeness of his carnal male lust.

It was hardly surprising, given the past few weeks of trials and journeys and anxieties, that they both slept deeply and soundly. Beatrice awoke first, the unfamiliar and heavy weight of a male arm around her waist drawing her out of the depths of slumber. For a moment she enjoyed the warmth that surrounded her, her senses attuned to the feel of the hard male contours pressed against her body. She stirred then, with a little sigh, and the arm tightened about her waist. A hand cupped her breast and one thumb idly stroked her nipple. Beatrice gasped, surprised and delighted by the stab of sensation that shot through her, her nipple hardening like a pebble.

She turned over then and faced Remy. He still had his eyes closed and appeared to be asleep. But a groan came from the strong column of his throat and she looked up at him for direction, her hands laid flat against his chest. Every inch of her could feel the weight of his body and the smooth skin of his chest was a marvel beneath her exploring fingertips. Instinctively, she pressed herself against him. His head moved on the pillow and came down towards her, his hand sliding up her back and into her tumbled hair, urging her closer still as he bent his head and kissed her.

Beatrice was startled by the ferocity of that kiss. His mouth pressed down hard on hers while his jaw worked with determination, forcing her mouth to open and give access to his questing tongue. As his teeth pressed into her tender lips she gave a little whimper, pushing him back. At once his eyes snapped open, with a soft cry of self-disgust, and he pushed her away. In his befuddled state of half-sleep he had known that he held a woman in his arms, but he had forgotten that it was Beatrice!

'Oh, God!' he exclaimed.

'What is it?' She was now genuinely alarmed.

'I hurt you! I am sorry!'

'No,' she lied, trying to soothe him, 'I was merely startled. I have never been kissed like that before.'

He groaned and remembered his vow from during the night. He realised that with one glance from her brown eyes and one touch from her gentle fingers he could easily forget every vow he had ever made. With a sigh of regret, he fought valiantly to be the honourable knight, and murmured, ''Tis daylight. We should get up and dress.'

Beatrice blushed and lowered her eyes, yet finding the courage to murmur, 'Do you not wish to begin the day as we would begin each day for the rest of our lives, by having… relations… with your wife?'

He frowned and his mouth tightened grimly. It was a serious question lightly cloaked, but he was fully aware of the implications of his answer. He suspected that she was still uncertain of her feelings for him, and thus he could not consummate their marriage and force her to submit herself to a lifetime spent with a man that mayhap she did not want. Now he sought to avoid the final denouement, hoping against hope for more time, a chance to coax her heart. Hating himself for hurting her with his palter, Remy prevaricated, 'We should wait until the darkness of night.'

Beatrice eyed him warily, a little confused by the sudden change from hot passion to reluctance.

Remy met her puzzled gaze. 'Besides, we have not yet been married for the prescribed three days.'

'Other couples consummate their marriages straight away. Why shouldn't we?'

He cleared his throat and tried again. 'Is it not a saint's day?'

At that Beatrice shrugged and pushed away from him to sit up. 'If you do not want me, then say so. I will understand.'

'You know well enough,' he said softly, 'how much

I want you. Have wanted to possess you for these many months.'

She looked at him over her shoulder. 'There is nothing stopping you. Is there?'

Remy swallowed. He noted the pleading in her eyes, and then he too sat up and leaned closer. His fingers swept aside the long swathe of her honey-brown silky hair and he kissed the nape of her neck, murmuring, 'You are right, Beatrice. There is nothing that could or should stop me from making love to you.'

'Then we had better hurry, for the daylight is bright and Aunt Margaret will not tarry in her eagerness to inspect the sheets. And we have nothing to show them.'

He shook his head, 'Nay. The door is barred. We have no need for haste.'

He pulled Beatrice into his arms and laid her back against the pillows. Her world was blocked out by a pair of very broad male shoulders. She felt the weight of his heavy body against her own slenderness. He gazed at her for a long moment, and then said softly, 'You understand that if we do this there is no going back? We are wed for life.'

She lowered her eyes, and nodded. Silently she begged that he would ask no further questions, for she could not bear to consider her own thoughts and feelings for a moment longer. She wanted only to feel his body against hers, and to feel the passion and power of being made love to by a man. Nothing else, at this moment, mattered. At her nod of consent she felt his fingers pull at the drawstring of her shift. Suddenly she remembered why she had chosen this particular shift for her wedding night—it had long sleeves and hid her scars well. As Remy undid the ribbon bow and made to shrug aside the thin fabric covering her body, a small flicker of doubt fanned the warm and unfamiliar flames that were glowing deep within her. Oh, what a fool she had been not to agree to wait for the concealing shadows of night!

'Wait!' She clutched at his wrist, pulling his hand away. 'It is not necessary to remove my shift, is it?'

He looked at her then, with a quizzical frown and a perplexed smile upon his warmly sensual lips. Then he answered slowly, 'Nay, it is not necessary. I could just lift up the hem. If that is your wish.'

'Oh.' Beatrice sighed with heartfelt relief, and smiled up at him. 'Aye, that is my wish.'

He shook his head then, his smile broadening as he shook off her fingers clasped about his wrist and returned to his task of removing her shift, 'But it is not *my* wish, Beatrice. I want to see you. I have dreamed and ached and longed to see every inch of your lovely body for so long now.'

'Nay!' With a cry Beatrice again stopped him, this time using both hands about his broad wrist, 'I am not lovely, Remy. My body is a sight you surely do not wish to see. Have you forgotten already my scars?'

For a long moment they stared at each other, engaged in a battle of wills. Gently he stroked his forefinger against the soft skin at the base of her throat and whispered, 'I too have scars, Beatrice. In fact, many more and many that are more ugly than yours. Do you find my body repulsive because of them?'

'Nay!' She was swift to make a heated denial. 'Of course I do not!'

'Then neither do I find,' here he bared her shoulder in one swift movement, and kissed the pink, puckered skin '—this tiny emblem of your courage repulsive to me. Your scars are part of you and I find no part of you repulsive.'

He slid the sleeve of her shift from her shoulder and kissed the velvet skin beneath it, while his other hand moved to her opposite shoulder and removed that sleeve too. Her shift fell down to her waist and his lips trailed kisses down along her chest and the valley between her breasts, until with a small groan of pleasure he found her nipple and covered it with his mouth.

Beatrice tipped back her head, baring her throat, gasping for breath and feeling a vivid heat prickle across her skin. She murmured her delight and closed her eyes, her heart picking up its beat as his fingers kneaded the weight of her breasts in both hands, his tongue circling hot and wet over one nipple.

Then he reluctantly abandoned the pleasures of her breasts and tugged her shift down past her hips, tossing it aside to the floor. Remy let his eyes wander at leisure over her naked body, resting for a long moment on the dark curls at the juncture of her thighs.

'Remy.' Beatrice blushed and squirmed uncomfortably beneath his examination and turned towards him, lifting her hands to his neck to pull him over her.

But he held her off and growled, 'I want to look at you. You are so beautiful, like a goddess, that I fear to touch you.'

She gasped at that. 'But I am only a woman.'

'Nay.' He shook his head. 'You are more than that. You are my Beatrice. My wife.'

Then he lay down beside her and bent his head. Gently he kissed her, his lips moving sensually and drinking with reverence of her mouth. He felt her skin glow with warmth and her heartbeat drum against his chest, and he smiled. His fingers moved softly over her, exploring and arousing all at the same time. He leaned over her and pressed soft, delicious kisses to the scar upon her hip, hoping that with his touch she would be freed from all hurt and inhibition.

Beatrice sighed with pleasure, languorous under his gentle touch, awed by the sensations he was arousing through her skin. When he moved his lips from her hip and began to kiss her breasts again, his tongue sliding with magical effect around her hardened nipples, she gave a soft little cry, 'Oh, Remy, this must be heaven.'

He smiled then at her sweet innocence. 'Wait. There is more.'

'More? I don't think I can bear more pleasure than this.'

'You can. You will.'

His hand slid down over the curve of her ribs, down past her waist and her flat belly, down even further and her eyes snapped open as he pressed his palm to the crisp curls of her female mound. 'This is where,' he whispered in a husky voice, 'all the best pleasure is to be had.' He tenderly brushed his fingertips over her, until she relaxed again, and then he searched with his finger and found her tiny bud hidden away, smiling as she gasped at his careful stroking. 'My lady likes that?'

She felt faint as waves of acute pleasure rose from between her thighs and she groaned, turning towards him and pressing her aching breasts to his chest. With such a sensation pulsating from within her she instinctively reached out to him, her hand on the back of his neck drawing his head down to her. She pressed her lips to his and he responded with a deep and delving kiss.

Now it was he that groaned and his hand slid behind her knee, pulling it away from the other so that he could slide the bulk of his thigh between her legs. He noticed how she tensed, how her virtue caused her to hold him at bay. He intended to accustom her to his presence between her thighs gradually, moving slowly and gradually forwards, but wondered whether he had the strength to hold himself in check.

Beatrice trembled at his weight, feeling the hot hard length of his manhood against her inner thigh. She quelled the *frisson* of fear, comforting herself with the knowledge that Remy would not intentionally hurt her. She felt him moving against her, kissing her, his fingers stroking her tenderly and she tried to match him in his eagerness, but her uncertainty and her ignorance restrained her.

His lips kissed her neck and he murmured, 'Do not be afraid, Beatrice.' Gently his hand slid between her thighs, and eased them further apart. 'I will not take you until you say I may.'

Beatrice gasped, her back arching at his skilful

touch. 'And how will I know, Remy? When should I tell you?'

He smiled at that, his eyes warm and dark with desire as he watched her body undulate beneath his touch, her hips lifting and her nipples hard and rosy. Her lips were dark and swollen and he returned again to them, kissing her again and again. At last he lifted his head and murmured, 'You will know, and if you don't then the fault is mine.'

She felt his hand warm and heavy between her legs and then the soft touch of his finger, delving deeper, sliding inside her and she gave a small cry as pleasure swelled within her. His mouth covered her nipple and his tongue sucked gently as his finger stroked her, exploring the tight confines of her womanhood, now slick and hot with the honey of her passion. Beatrice closed her eyes and instinctively shifted her legs wider apart, lifting her hips to the rhythm of his caress. Her breath came in small gasps, quickening as a heated flush spread over her skin and he answered her urgency with his own.

'Beatrice.' His murmur was a plea as he lowered himself between her thighs, the feel of her small hands clasping his back a torment he could hardly bear.

'Oh, Remy, I want you!' Beatrice exclaimed.

He smiled as her hands slid down his back and grasped his buttocks, urging him closer, and he cautioned her gently, 'Easy, my lady. I would not hurt you with my haste.'

'You could not hurt me, Remy...' but her words were lost in a cry of delight as his manhood touched against her.

Carefully he eased himself inside her and Beatrice felt a stab of pain, quickly overcome by the sweetest of pleasure she had ever known as he moved slowly but surely within her. There was no awareness of thought in her mind, only her body that consumed all within its sight and senses. Beatrice opened her eyes to look up at Remy, as he removed her hands from his buttocks and linked his fingers between hers. He pulled their clasped hands above her head as he leaned over her and drove more deeply inside her body. His thrusting gathered momentum and Beatrice was lost upon a sea of such pleasure that she floated upon its rolling waves, buffeted and yet secure within his clasp. His broad chest rubbed against her breasts and his jaw scraped her chin as he claimed her mouth in a tender kiss. His body moved with hers, guiding, exciting, rocking her with his male strength. Her cry of fulfilment was lost between their entwined tongues and she clung to him as he thrust harder and deeper, until at last he too gave a muffled shout, and poured himself and his pleasure within her.

It was some long moments before they could both take control of their breathing and beating hearts, and then they quickly found each other's tender gaze. He kissed her brow, her cheeks, and gently, so carefully, her aching lips. He whispered endearments and carefully eased himself from between her thighs, gathering her close in his arms as they lay side by side in happy silence.

After a few moments he murmured, 'Beatrice?'

'Mmm?' She moved her head languidly, to look at him.

'I did not hurt you too much?'

'Nay.'

'And…' he hesitated, uncertain, bashful at his need to know her answer '…it was not repugnant for you?'

'Nay!' She looked at him strangely. 'Should it be?'

'I have heard men complain that their wives do not enjoy the act.'

'Then it is the husbands who are at fault. Fortunately…' she sighed and snuggled closer, pressing against him '…there is no fault with mine.'

He laughed then and grinned at her, 'How would you know?'

Beatrice shook her head, gazing down at her delicate and supine body curled against his vast male frame, aware of the delicious languor that spread throughout her limbs in the aftermath of the most astonishing joy that had gripped her from within. 'I just know. My body and my heart tells me so.'

He kissed the top of her head. 'Then I am glad.'

'Remy?'

'Hmm?' His voice was lazy, content.

'Will it always be like that?'

'Nay, my love.'

'Oh.' Her disappointment was acute.

'It will be better.'

She lifted her head from his chest and smiled up at him, digging her finger into his ribs. 'How could it be any better than that?'

His smile was mischievous and full of promise. 'There are many ways in which to make love.'

'Indeed? And you will teach me all of them?'

'If it is my lady's wish.'

Beatrice opened her mouth to speak, but was interrupted by a thunderous knocking upon the barred door of their bedchamber.

'St Leger!'

They both started, and Remy lifted his head from the pillow. They stared at each other, and then at the door, and Beatrice tightened her arms about Remy's waist.

Hammering erupted on the door, accompanied by a bellowed shout. 'Lift your arse, St Leger! Now!'

Remy sighed and cursed, shaking his head. 'What ails your brother?' he demanded in annoyance. 'I swear he is the most ill-mannered lout I have ever come across.'

Beatrice cleared her throat and shouted back, 'Go away, Hal!'

'Tell your husband to get off you and get dressed. I have need of him.'

'Well, I have more need of him, and I was here first, so go away!' Beatrice stared up at Remy wide-eyed and aghast at daring to speak so to her brother. When Remy grinned in support, she relaxed, with a mischievous smile of her own.

'St Leger, if you are not out by the time I count to ten, I will call the guard to break down this door.'

'Don't you dare!' shrieked Beatrice.

'What,' demanded Remy, in a deep, clear, calm voice, 'is the problem?'

'I have had word from Hepple Hill. The steward has been killed by a large band of Gascon mercenaries and they are now looting.'

Remy hung his head, muttering an oath in a pained

voice, and then he disengaged her hold upon his midriff and said with regret, 'I will have to go. Your brother is my liege lord and I cannot say him nay.'

Beatrice sat up, watching him as he rose from the bed and strode naked across the floor. The cold hand of fear, already, reached out to grip her. He stooped and picked up her shift from the floor.

'Cover yourself,' he said curtly, reaching for his everyday linen tunic and leather chausses, already the soldier returning to his duties.

Beatrice raised her eyes to Remy as he pulled on his clothes. 'You are leaving me?'

'Aye.' He dressed swiftly, then turned to her with hands on hips, shrugging his broad shoulders. 'I am sorry, but I have no choice.' Then he stooped, gently grasping a fistful of hair at the nape of her neck and pressing a tender kiss upon her swollen lips. 'Do not look at me with that fear in your eyes.' He kissed her again, quickly, promising, 'I will be back.'

Beatrice felt the blood in her veins turning to ice. Her hands trembled as she lifted them to his neck, stroking his firm skin with her thumb. She murmured, with eyes lowered, 'Do not of me a widow make.' Uttering those words made it all too real that Remy was going into battle. She raised her eyes to his and said desperately, 'Let me come with you.'

'Nay!' His reply was swift and definite.

But she would not be so easily set aside. 'Are we not to make our home at Hepple Hill? We would have journeyed there on the morrow anyway.' She turned away from him then and hurried to her coffer, to reach for her maroon kirtle.

His fingers closed about her wrists and jerked her to a halt as she tried to hurry on her clothes, 'You will not come with me,' he said firmly, a hard glint of challenge in his eyes.

Beatrice stood her ground. She tipped back her head and looked up at him. 'If you do not let me come with you, then I shall follow. Later. On my own. The choice is yours, my lord.'

He gnashed his teeth and groaned.

'St Leger!'

'I'm coming!' Remy replied with a furious shout, frowning at Beatrice and then at the door. 'Your sister is proving to be stubborn, as usual.'

'Then show her the back of your hand, if she will not listen to your voice.'

'Advice I am greatly tempted to take,' muttered Remy, shaking his head grimly at the look of outrage on Beatrice's face. He lifted his hand and made a sharp movement through the air with it, but he halted the motion well short of her face and stretched out his lean fingers to tenderly cup her chin. He stooped over her as with his other hand he curved it about her waist and pressed her slender length against him. 'You will not come with me, Beatrice,' he repeated, hushing her as she made to protest. 'I cannot take you into danger. These Gascons are vicious bastards, 'tis why Edward employs them against the Welsh. I cannot do my duty if I must worry over your safety.' He leaned closer, and whispered in her ear, 'You will stay here.' He repeated each of the words slowly and with unyielding firmness.

Beatrice subsided. She had no wish to put Remy in

danger by imposing her presence. She hung her head, her kirtle falling from her hands. 'I will miss you,' she whispered.

'And I you.' He chucked her under the chin, coaxing from her a watery smile. 'I will be back in a day or two—'

'Come on, man,' drawled Hal impatiently. 'For the love of God, save your sweet talk for later.'

Remy sighed heavily, whispering, 'One of these days I am going to break your brother's neck.' He bent his vast shoulders over her again and kissed her, once, twice, until at last he gave her up. '*Adieu*, my little wife.'

'*Adieu*...' she reached up on tiptoe and stroked his cheek with her palm '...my giant husband.'

He laughed, and then hurried away, unbarring the door, greeting a disgruntled Lord Henry. She heard him quietly ask her brother, 'How strong are they?'

And Hal's reply, 'Between twenty and thirty.'

Their voices faded with their footsteps running down the stairs, already men of war.

In the armoury Nogood helped Remy to don his mail armour and latch on his sword. When they rode out of the gates they were forty knights, most garnered from the wedding guests, and a hundred men-at-arms. They streamed out across the drawbridge, intent on delivering to the Gascons swift and merciless English justice.

Beatrice spent a disconsolate day, listening to her aunt and Joanna chatter, admiring her many wedding gifts, and missing Remy so much that she ached from head to toe. She blushed to think at how he had touched her, and wondered with great impatience when she would again hold him in her arms. And always there was the terror that clutched at her insides and her mind and her soul, so that she felt she could hardly breathe, and barely think, of anything except Remy. Though he was miles away, she felt his presence, and knew that she was within his thoughts, as he was within hers, cherished and, she hoped and prayed, protected.

That evening, as she rose from the supper table, she spotted Nogood and beckoned Remy's squire to her side. She smiled reassuringly at him as he bowed and eyed her warily, asking him, 'You do not ride with Sir Remy?'

'Nay, my lady, he says I am not yet ready to join in the fight.' He blushed in agony at his inadequacy.

Beatrice frowned, curious and troubled about this young boy who worked so hard and with such loyal diligence for her husband; he would be an important part of her household, and yet she knew nothing about him. 'How old are you, Nogood?'

'I am sixteen, my lady.'

So young! 'And what is your real name? It vexes me greatly to hear you called Nogood, for truthfully I think you are everything that is good.'

His blush deepened and he shifted uneasily from foot to foot. 'My real name is Gounoud, but my lord Sir Remy sometimes...um...er...became confused in the beginning, when I was first sent to serve him as squire, and called me Nogood.' Here he stammered and quailed at this obvious criticism of his lord. 'In all truth I do not mind and sometimes my lord calls me by my first name, which is easier for him to remember.'

'And what is that?' She persisted gently, resisting the urge to hug him as she would a child.

He bit his lip, eager to escape her inquisition. 'Kit. Short for Christopher.'

'Kit?' Beatrice tried it out and then smiled. 'Aye, it suits you. I can understand how that would be easier for Sir Remy to bellow when he is in a hurry.'

At that they both laughed and then she offered him her hand and he kissed it quickly, before hurrying away, glancing back with a smile of such adoration that Beatrice was in no doubt that she had won his loyalty for all the days of her life.

That night she had much to think about and refused the offer from Joanna to sleep with her, preferring to have her privacy and to lie against the pillow that Remy had slept on, still aromatic with his male scent. She fell asleep praying for his safety, and awoke early with the hopeful thought that by evening he would be back.

But he did not return that day, nor the next, and the waiting became an agony. Late in the afternoon a trumpet blast from the highest watchtower warned them of approaching riders and Beatrice made herself tidy and hurried downstairs. It was Hal who strode briskly into the hall, looking weary, dirty and yet triumphant. Beatrice approached him cautiously as he stood with arms upraised while his squire unlatched his armour.

'Ah, Beatrice,' he said, noticing her then, 'pack your things and be ready to go at first light. I have left your husband to hold Hepple Hill and you will join him there.'

Stunned by this casual command, she ventured to ask, 'He is well?'

Hal observed the wide-eyed fear of her countenance, and smiled with reassurance. 'He is well. Fought like a devil in his haste to deal with the Gascons, and no doubt I know why.'

'Indeed?'

Hal chuckled and suggested that her husband feared she was missing his company in bed which earned him a slap, brother or no brother, lord or no lord. With the peal of his laughter ringing in her ears, Beatrice gathered up her skirts and ran across the hall. She trotted swiftly up the stairs to her chamber and there breathlessly, smiling and suddenly light-headed with relief, informed Elwyn that they were to make ready for their removal to Hepple Hill.

## Chapter Thirteen

It was but a morning's ride to her new home in Wessex, and Beatrice rode under heavily armed escort led by Sir Hugh Montgomery. She was accompanied by several female attendants, including her own dear Elwyn, her wedding gifts and the good wishes of her family and guests as they waved her goodbye.

The countryside they rode through was pretty enough, with rolling green fields and dense woodland, but Beatrice had little appreciation for it as she barely contained her impatience to reach Hepple Hill and see Remy. It had only been three days, but felt more like a lifetime she had endured without him. She wondered if he felt the same and urged her horse into a swift trot.

As they neared Hepple Hill towards midday, there were signs of devastation and conflict—burnt-out cottages that still smouldered, dead animals lying in the fields, and the earthy mounds of freshly dug graves behind the small stone church.

'My lady,' cried Elwyn, 'avert your eyes!'

Her maid tried to protect Beatrice from seeing the

bodies that hung from several trees beside the track, but it was too late. She had already seen them, and she gasped, turning away in horror. Quickly she spurred on her horse and they cantered up to the wide moat that ringed the castle known as Hepple Hill. Her escort called to the guard on duty, and the drawbridge was let down after their identities had been established.

Beatrice swept into the courtyard, which was too small to be rightly named a bailey, and dismounted. She looked about her, noting the fearful and watchful eyes of the serfs, the general air of disrepair and neglect evident in the weeds growing about and the piles of refuse left to rot when they should have been carted away and dumped elsewhere. She wrinkled her nose in distaste, and exchanged a glance with her serving women.

'We'll have our work cut out for us here, my lady,' muttered Elwyn.

Beatrice nodded, with a wry smile, and then turned towards the steps of the keep. 'Come, mayhap it is better within.'

Her women did not share her optimism, and followed Beatrice with glum expressions. Once inside the double doors of the hall, Beatrice glanced about, relieved that at least here it was cleaner. There were several servants busy putting up trestle tables for the noon meal, and the reassuring smell of roasted meat and baked bread wafted from the direction of the kitchen at the rear of the hall.

She wondered where Remy might be, and then, as her eyes accustomed themselves to the gloom, she saw him. He was seated on the dais, listening with a perplexed expression upon his handsome face to a vassal, who appeared to be making a complaint about a neighbour who had crossed his land and taken his pig. The moment he saw Beatrice he held up his hand to silence the man, and leapt to his feet.

She hurried across the hall to greet him, her eyes devouring him from head to toe to make sure that he had not incurred any injury. His cheek and brow were bruised and there was a cut on his chin, but apart from that, and grazed knuckles, he appeared to be whole and healthy.

'Beatrice!' He swept her into his arms, whispering by her ear, 'Thank God you are here.' And then he moved his head and kissed her with hot and greedy need upon the mouth.

With a blush, noting the chuckles of her women and the sniggers of the handful of knights lounging about the hall, taking their ease from their bout of hard fighting, she struggled out of his arms and made a formal curtsy to him.

'My lord,' she murmured, impressing upon him with her eyes that he should behave in a more judicious manner.

Remy sighed, bowed, and said, 'Your timing is well done, my lady. We are about to sit down for the noon meal.' Then he noticed that she was wearing a wimple, the pale linen folded about her head and neck and hiding her hair. He flicked his fingers at it disparagingly. 'Take this thing off. I do not care for it. I prefer to see your hair loose.'

Beatrice felt herself redden with embarrassment and

anger at his words and his manner. 'I am a married woman now, my lord. I am obliged to wear it.'

He snorted in disgust. 'Not in your own home and not when your husband orders you to remove it. Do it now!'

She jumped at his bark and eyed him charily, awakening to the unpleasant awareness that this was not the same Remy who had left her. When she had removed the offensive wimple he offered her his arm and escorted her to the table. Remy employed every ounce of his self-discipline to behave in the manner that her flashing brown eyes indicated that he was sorely in danger of lacking. He enquired politely how she had fared and how was her journey, while his instinctive reaction was far more basic. He longed to throw her over his shoulder and carry her off to the solar chamber above, there indulging himself in the sweet nectar and solace of her love. But he reasoned that she had had a long journey, and must be tired and hungry.

Somehow he managed to contain himself, but it was no easy task. Sitting next to Beatrice, listening to her voice, admiring her lovely face, her bosom brushing his arm as she leaned towards him to tell him of something—he knew not what, for his brain was in a dizzy whirl—was slow torture. Throughout the meal his eyes strayed again and again to her lips, as she placed tiny morsels of food in her mouth, to her graceful white hands, his skin burning with the memory of their touch upon him. His gaze strayed to her small breasts, his loins hardening as he remembered the feel of their delicious weight in his hands and a rosy, hard nipple in his mouth.

Beatrice frowned at Remy. She had the distinct feeling he was not listening to a word she was saying. He had a rather strange, glazed look to his eyes. She began to worry that he might have taken a blow to the head during his skirmish with the Gascons. He had certainly forgotten his manners and had neither introduced her to the knights who would be part of their household, nor to any of the servants that she would rule. Just when she was about to ask him whether he was feeling well, he suddenly set aside the apple he had been peeling and stabbed the sharp point of his dagger into the table top. He scraped back his chair and stood up. Her words died on her lips, and she craned her neck back to stare up at him.

Remy fastened his hand around her elbow and he drew her from her chair, announcing to the company at large in a loud voice, 'I am going to take my wife to her solar.' He looked around the hall with great significance. 'There will be no interruptions.'

To this bold statement different reactions were evinced. The knights cheered and applauded him with envy, whilst Beatrice flushed bright scarlet and was mortified. Her waiting women tittered in sympathy, and then she had no choice but to follow Remy as he stepped down from the dais and hustled her across the hall towards the stairs, that spiralled up to the floor above and their private apartments.

'My lord!' protested Beatrice, stumbling upon the steep stone steps. 'I beg your pardon!'

He paused and turned back towards her, muttering, 'So formal, Beatrice?'

He grasped her hand and she nimbly leapt up the

steps in his rapid wake. When he reached their solar he shut the door firmly, and rammed home the bar.

Beatrice looked about. It was a pleasant enough room, although rather small, but there were two windows, with shutters thrown wide open on the warm summer day, and a four-poster bed made up with clean linens and a brocade coverlet, hung with dark green curtains. There was a table against one wall and two chairs beside the hearth, several tapestries on the walls and a large, ornately carved coffer at the foot of the bed. Before she could inspect her new quarters further, Remy spun her into his embrace.

Without a word he stooped his head and kissed her. Beatrice laid her hands flat on his chest, gasping for breath as his tongue invaded her mouth and his lips crushed hers. Against her hip she felt the bulk of his arousal, his hands moulding her buttocks and pulling her hard against him.

'God, I have missed you,' he murmured savagely, his lips travelling down her neck.

'So I see,' she replied, now seriously concerned at this change in her husband, and she placed her cool palms either side of his jaw and raised his face up. Gently she asked, 'What is amiss, my lord?'

For an answer his arms circled about her waist and he held her tightly against him, his face buried against the curve of her neck. 'Hold me, Beatrice. Wash me clean with your purity and make me brave again, for I fear all my courage has deserted me.'

With a wide-eyed and startled expression upon her face, she stroked the back of his neck, her voice a soft whisper. 'What is it that you fear, Remy?'

At that he shook his head, unable to reveal further his weakness and his torment. 'Do not ask, for you would not want to love the man that trembles with fear inside of me. A knight must be strong and bold, and here I stand before you, whimpering like a child.'

Her heart ached painfully for him and tears burned at the back of her eyes. 'There's a frightened child within all of us, sometimes. It takes only a little comfort and patience and rest to make us full-grown again.' Tenderly she caressed her fingertips against the smooth tanned skin at the back of his neck. 'Do not be so harsh on yourself, Remy.' She raised her eyes to the rafters and for a moment tried hard to think what could be amiss, seeking divine inspiration. Then it came to her. 'Was the fighting against the Gascons very bad?'

'It was bloody and fierce.' His voice was muffled against her neck. 'They put up a determined fight and were intent that they would not be taken prisoners. It sickens me to have to slaughter men like that, but I am accustomed to battle and well trained for it.'

'But still it is not pleasant, and I would not have married you if you were a brutal man who had a lust for slaying.' She had a feeling that this was not all that was troubling him. 'I know you do not fear battle, yet earlier you spoke of trembling with fear. What is it, my husband? Tell me all.'

With a sigh he straightened up and turned away from her, hardly able to admit what he had only today realised. He went to the narrow window embrasure and stood gazing out at the green fields and the softly blue sky dappled with clouds. Then, with great reluctance, he told her, 'I am inadequate, Beatrice. I am a failure. An illiterate, battle-scarred and battle-weary knight who knows little about anything except a sword and a horse and killing.' He sighed heavily again, his broad shoulders stooped as though a great weight bore down upon him, and he spread his hands in defeat. 'Your father gifted me this estate, Hepple Hill, and yet I have no idea, no notion at all, of how to run it or look after it, or how to hold it or make it prosper. I fear we shall lose all.'

For a long moment Beatrice stared at him, and then she smiled and would have laughed out loud if she had not feared he would misunderstand and take offence. But it was relief that made her want to laugh, not contempt, and quickly she hurried across the intervening space and took his large hands in hers, exclaiming, 'How lucky it is then that you have a wife, Sir Remy!' She reached up on tip-toe and kissed his cheek. 'No doubt you think a wife is only for the pleasure of bedding, but we have other uses too.'

He turned then and looked down at her with a frown. 'And what is that supposed to mean?'

'Do not look at me with thunder upon your brow.' Beatrice softened her words with a wide smile. 'It means that I have been well taught to be chatelaine of a great estate like Castle Ashton, having learned at my mother's knee, and since her death some months ago I have put to good use the knowledge she gave me.' Then she giggled mischievously and pressed closer to him. 'I will make you a deal, Sir Knight—a trade.'

Remy leaned back against the wall, the darkness in his eyes lifting and a smile, for the first time in days, touching his lips. 'Indeed? And what might that be?' His hands on her waist drew Beatrice closer, and she stood between the arch of his powerful thighs and leaning against his broad chest. His fingers reached up and toyed with several silky strands of long, honey-brown hair.

'It means that we can learn from each other. You can teach me all there is to know about...' here she blushed scarlet and lowered her eyes '...about bed-sport. And I can teach you all I know about running an estate.' She raised her eyes to him, with a shy smile, 'Is it a deal?'

For a long moment he gazed at her, and then he glanced out of the window, thoughtfully. 'Aye, my lady,' he agreed at long last. 'But these lessons, I give you fair warning, are to be held in private. Never try to, shall we say, *instruct* me in front of others. I do not care for the whole world to know that I am a fool and that my wife is wearing my breeches.'

For a moment a *frisson* of anger flashed through her, and then she considered his words from his point of view, which was male and so different from her own. Pride was so tender and valuable to a man, she decided, and she smiled gently and slid her hand around his shoulder. 'Of course, my lord. Providing that you do not intend to instruct me in public places either.'

He laughed then. 'My lady is growing bold now that she is wed.' His eyes grew warm and lazy as they ventured over her slim form. 'Shall we begin your first lesson now?'

'But 'tis daylight, my lord.' Beatrice lowered her

eyes demurely, hiding her delighted smile, 'We should wait until nightfall.'

'I cannot wait.'

Beatrice gave a small cry as suddenly his arms went around her and swept her feet off the floor. Carrying her across the room, he placed her on the mattress and was shrugging off his tunic before she even had time to glance up. Then he sat down on the edge of the bed to unwind his cross-garters and pull off his boots, throwing them with a thump upon the floor.

Beatrice observed his broad sun-tanned back as he leaned down to remove his chausses, muscles rippling with his every move, and she was astonished at how quickly he had made himself naked. He turned to her then, and his eyes roamed over her, ending on her boots, which he pulled off and tossed to the floor over his shoulder. His hand slid beneath her skirt and she shivered as she felt his fingers pull down her hose, withdrawing them one by one with a sensual smile and dropping them to one side. She watched his lean brown fingers as he began unlacing her kirtle and she made no protest as he stripped it off and threw it in the direction of her hose, but she did make a little murmur as he made to remove her shift.

'It is cold in here,' she whispered shyly.

He grunted, and pulled back the bedcovers, manoeuvring her beneath them and himself beside her. She quivered as his hand boldly covered her breast.

'Kiss me,' whispered Beatrice, tilting back her head and looking up at him. Battle lust warred with the tenderness that was part of his nature, the killing spree of the past few days bringing out the hard warrior in him. He bent his head and kissed her with passion, rolling her over on to her back and pulling down her shift. He groaned at the feel of her breasts crushed beneath his chest. Her shift tangled between them, hindering his access to her soft body. With a throaty growl he tugged at it, the fragile muslin shredding in his hands and he hurled it out of the bed.

Beatrice felt heat flush across her skin and she was awed by his power and his strength. He had taken command of her body and she was helpless to resist. She lay back and let his fingers move where they would, little gasps and shudders escaping from her. His mouth closed over her breast and she arched her back, seared by the sweet agony of his hot, wet tongue sucking on her nipple. She started when his fingers delved between her thighs, dipping and stroking, and she felt herself melt, felt moisture seep from within her, and she whimpered in embarrassment.

'Do not,' he admonished roughly, his voice a harsh whisper by her ear, 'there is naught to be ashamed of. Indeed, it pleases me to feel your dew. It tells me that you are ready to take me inside you.' Yet he reined in his urgency, wary of hurting her with his eager need, and gently he guided her hand to find the hot, hard length of his arousal.

Beatrice was startled by the feel of his manhood, rigid and smooth like a silk-covered lance. She blushed hotly as he closed her hand about him, whispering by her ear, 'My lady holds me in her grasp, and may do with me as she wishes, when she wishes.'

Her breath escaped from her in ragged gasps, as her heart drummed a tattoo and a sheen of sweat glowed upon her skin. She felt dizzy with the heady whirl of sensual need, and while he kissed her she guided him to her with one hand. She shuddered with pleasure at the feel of him, and raised her eyes uncertainly to his. He took back the control then, and entered her. Her hips rose in response to the sweet joy of his maleness. It was a tight fit and he thrust again, deeper, harder. She cried out with desperate pleasure and clung to him, her legs wrapping around his waist as he growled and groaned, and dug his elbows into the bed to keep his weight off her, while his hips strained and bucked. She said his name and clasped her hands around his muscular shoulders, holding on to him, adrift on a sea of ecstasy and seeking his anchor. He kept on with a steady impetus, lost to the bliss of being inside her and yet also waiting for her, his fingers sliding between them and helping her reach the goal he knew so well and she did not. At last she shuddered and wept his name out loud. At that he surrendered and knew it must all end, exchanging long moments of pleasure for a brief burst of sheer ecstasy. With one final powerful lunge he released his seed within her. Panting, he came to a halt and lowered his forehead to the curve of her neck, spent and satisfied.

Aware of his great weight and her slender frame, he withdrew with reluctance from the warmth of her silken sheath and rolled away. He lay upon his back and released a long, gratified sigh, yet tenderly connected to her still as he held her hand, his fingers laced intimately one between each of hers.

They dozed in the warm afternoon sunshine, murmuring softly to one another, and all the while Remy pondered if he dared make love to her again, or whether she would be too tender. Beatrice had other thoughts, and speculated when he would speak the words she longed to hear.

Remy was not a man to lie about idle for long and he soon suggested they get up and dress. He wanted to take a walk around their new home and when she agreed he rose from the bed and dressed. He discreetly turned his back and went to stand at the window, gazing out, allowing Beatrice some privacy while she rose, washed from a pitcher of water standing on a coffer, and dressed. Beatrice slipped on her hose and her shoes and followed him when he turned about and headed for the door, yet when she reached the threshold a sudden thought struck her. Thanks to Remy's audacious statement earlier everyone would know what they had been doing! Her cheeks flamed, and she retreated, taking several steps backwards, and then moved to sit down on the edge of a chair beside the hearth.

'Beatrice?' Remy turned towards her, his voice gentle with concern, noting the flood of colour to her cheeks that drained rapidly away, leaving her pale. 'Is aught amiss?'

'I—I…' She hesitated, unwilling to slight him with her shame. 'You go on ahead, I am more tired than I thought and I think I will rest this afternoon.'

He groaned and dropped to one knee beside her chair, taking her hand in his palm and cursing himself soundly. 'I knew it! You did not complain, but I knew

I must have hurt you. It will not always be so, Beatrice, I swear.'

She smiled at him, her eyes exploring his anxious face, and while she was sore in that place where he had possessed her it was not greatly so, and in a way pleasant, the burning ache reminding her that she was now truly a woman. She stretched out her fingers and stroked his cheek whispering, 'I thank you for your concern, but 'tis what others think that troubles me more than any pain I may feel.'

He looked at her with a puzzled frown.

She sighed and patiently explained, 'You more or less told everyone you were going to bed your wife. What will they think when we go downstairs now?'

He grinned wolfishly. 'That I am a lucky devil.'

'And of me? That I am brazen and without holy reverence to allow you to do such a thing in broad daylight, and on a saint's day.'

He growled deep in his throat, his frown ferocious. 'They will show you no disrespect nor utter a word, for if any did they know well enough that I would kick their backsides till their noses bleed!'

'Remy!' she admonished. 'Violence is not the solution to every problem.'

He snorted. 'You talk like a woman.'

'I am a woman!'

He smiled, dazzling her with his blue eyes and his charm, as he murmured, 'So I have discovered.'

'Go you on,' she urged him, 'and see to your duties this afternoon. I will stay here, and Elwyn can bring me my things. I will set about unpacking them and later when you are free, we can look at them together.'

His eyes narrowed as he surveyed her in silence, and then he said quietly, 'It seems to me that it would be ungallant to leave you alone on your first day in your new home and—' here he gently stroked her cheek '—after such a sweet lesson in your…wifely duties.'

'I do not mind. Indeed, I have hardly had a moment to myself these few days past and would welcome a little time alone. Go you on. I know well how you hate to be confined.'

As he held her hand, his eyes flitted briefly to the rumpled bed. 'I am sorry if I have caused you embarrassment. It will not happen again.'

'Indeed?' She gazed upon him with speculation, suddenly gravely aware of his youthful impulsiveness. 'What if, in the future, I should say you nay when with rough impatience you wish to drag me from the dinner table and take me to our chamber?'

'I did not drag you from the dinner table! Besides, it will not be so. I have given you my word. It is only that we are newly married and I have missed you so these few days past that I could not wait a moment longer to have you alone.'

'But what if it is so again, Remy?' she persisted. 'What will you do if I say you nay?'

'Why would you? Did you not enjoy my lovemaking?'

She shrugged, aware of an elusive yet vital answer that he must give her. 'Mayhap I have a cold. Or a headache. Or we have quarrelled, or I am merely contrary.'

He floundered then. He hung his head and shrugged

helplessly. 'I have given you my word.' He rose to his feet and gave her a short bow. 'You must trust me, my lady. That is all I can say.'

He left her then and Beatrice watched as he closed the door quietly behind him, and listened to the sound of his footsteps fading away down the stairs. A great wave of aching doubt washed over her, and seemed to threaten any vestige of happiness she had struggled to find. The years had been long and hard and lonely, and it seemed to her not easily forgotten. Was she so accustomed to loss that now she actively sought to achieve it? Did she deliberately seek arguments when happiness seemed too good to be true?

When Elwyn came to find her she glanced at the bed and the tear-stained face of her mistress and rushed to embrace her. She patted her and murmured, 'There, there, my pet! All will be well. I feared waiting so long to become a wife might be hard on you.'

Beatrice laughed at that, wiping away the tears that threatened all too easily. 'Do not think so badly of Sir Remy. That is not why I weep, Elwyn.'

'My lady?'

'We have quarrelled.'

Elwyn sighed. 'Why?'

Beatrice shrugged. 'Well, not exactly quarrelled. It is I who is at fault. I find it too hard to believe that so much happiness could be mine.'

'What!' Elwyn expostulated. 'My lady, there you are vastly mistaken. If anyone on this earth deserves happiness it is you. Accept it, my lady, and find no reason to doubt.'

'You think so?' Beatrice looked up, sniffing, with a tiny glimmer of hope in her spiky-lashed eyes. 'My husband has not yet said he loves me. Mayhap it is only lust that binds us together.'

Elwyn patted her shoulder. 'Give him time. Some men are not wont to speak soft words. They fear it will undo their manhood.'

Her maid winked and Beatrice sighed, only slightly mollified. At Elwyn's urging she set about unpacking her chests, as they were delivered one by one by several groaning serfs. On the table she set out the wedding gifts, and stood back to admire the silver plates and candlesticks, a jewelled mirror, several filigreed goblets, two bolts of silk, one in lilac and the other pale blue, a chest filled with tiny wooden bottles of spices. She wondered if Remy would join her, but the afternoon faded to dusk and he did not.

Piqued, Beatrice decided that she would not hide in her chamber and briskly tidied her hair and straightened her kirtle before running lightly down the stairs to the hall. Here she found Sir Hugh Montgomery, who had been the captain of her escort and would be the most senior of their hearth knights. He bowed to her politely and offered her refreshments and while they seated themselves beside the cosy fire burning brightly in the great hearth, sipped wine and nibbled on honey cakes, she looked about and wondered where Remy might be.

Sir Hugh cleared his throat uncomfortably at her enquiry and admitted, 'He has gone out with a party of men to cut down the Gascons that were hanged, and to make sure that there are no other sights that would offend my lady should she choose to ride about the estate on the morrow.'

Beatrice fell silent, chewing on her lip. Then, with thoughtful quietness, she asked Sir Hugh, 'How do you feel having Sir Remy for your overlord? He is by far the youngest man here and yet you and all the other knights must take his orders.'

'And proud we are to do that. There is no finer knight and we bear him no disrespect because of his age. Why, there are many men twice his years and yet half his valour.'

It pleased her to learn that her husband was so highly esteemed. And yet, could a man so well venerated by other men be capable of loving a woman? Was it mere lust that attracted him so greatly to her? Would he ever declare what she so longed to hear? And if he did, would she have the courage to bear it? These questions plagued her. Then having inspected the kitchens and met with the cook and butler and several of the servants, and approved the meal to be offered for supper, she ordered hot water for her bath and returned to her chamber.

A wooden tub was brought up, smaller than the one at Ashton; she would have to sit with knees tucked well under her chin, Beatrice observed as it was placed before the warmth of a fire in the hearth. The serfs struggled up with bucket after bucket of steaming water, pouring these in until the tub was halfway full. Then, wishing to clear the confusion from her mind with solace, she dismissed all the servants, even Elwyn.

Beatrice stripped off her gown and shift and stepped into the hot water, fragrant with her favourite rose and lavender oil that Elwyn had sprinkled in for her. She sat down and the hot water lapped about her hips. She bent up her knees and rested one cheek upon them, hugging them to her with her arms. In this comfort position she sighed, again and again, letting go of all the hurts and angers and worries that plagued her. And yet they would not leave her, swirling about her like the water in which she bathed.

The ends of her hair floated in the water and she watched it idly bobbing about, her eyes half-closed as she stared into the fire flames. She felt so much love for Remy welling up inside of her that she thought she might drown in it. How great and wonderful it was to love someone so much, and yet how vast and violent the fear of losing him! This was the knowledge that caused tears to drip slowly down her cheeks, splashing into the water one by one. This was the painful reality that she had sought to avoid when she had refused to marry him many months ago. Now she feared that a terrible mistake had been made! And if she should be made a widow she had a lifetime in which to repent it, in this strange place, amongst strangers. At that she began to sob in earnest, hiding her face against her knees.

She did not hear the door open, nor the soft footsteps that crossed the wooden floorboards. But she started when a hand settled on her naked shoulder.

'Beatrice?' Remy's voice was infinitely gentle. 'What is it?'

'Nothing!' She sniffed loudly and turned her face away from him.

Remy squatted down on his heels beside the bathing tub, brushing back the wet strands of hair that clung to her cheek and obscured her face from him. 'Come now,' he coaxed, 'tell me what is wrong and I will make it right.'

She shook her head and croaked in a watery voice, 'You can't.'

'Has someone caused you offence? If so, I will have them flogged.'

Her head jerked up and she glared at him, her voice sharp. 'Is that the only way you can deal with anything, by force of arms! Mayhap it is you that has caused me offence. Will you flog yourself?'

'If that is your wish.'

'Don't be foolish!'

He sighed then. 'Tell me what is troubling you. You gave me comfort and encouragement earlier, will you not allow me to do the same for you?'

She bit her lip, and her tongue. She would not let him see her weakness!

At her stubborn silence he said firmly, 'I will not grovel to you, Beatrice. There is not one man in this keep who does not trust me. Why should my wife be any different?'

'Is that all you want from me, Remy?' she asked in a small, smothered voice, 'My trust?'

As her shoulders shuddered with a fresh bout of weeping, Remy surveyed the smooth curve of her gleaming white back and the gentle slope of her half-submerged legs. Suddenly all became clear to him. And he smiled.

'No, Beatrice—' his voice was very soft '—that is not all I want from you.'

He reached out then and slid his arms around her, lifting her out of the water, ignoring her small cry of surprise and protest, ignoring the water that splashed all about and dampened his tunic. He carried her to the bed and laid her down, and himself beside her. He wrapped her in a coverlet and dried her hair and her face and Beatrice stared up at him with huge, tear-streaked eyes. He kissed the tip of her nose.

'I want all of you. Without your smile, and your laugh, and your gentle spirit, my life would be cold, dark winter all the year round. You are my spring, and my summer, my light and my warmth. Without you I am only half a man, and with you I am everything a man must be.'

'Remy.' Her arms struggled out of the coverlet and her hands slid to his powerful shoulders and around his neck.

'I am not one for clever speeches but even I can offer three of the sweetest words God ever made. I love you.'

At that she began to cry again, and then to laugh as he nuzzled her neck with tender lips, the rough stubble of his jaw scraping her skin and sending shivers all over her. His hands roamed over her slim back, holding her gently, then one large palm travelled over her shoulder and slid to cup her jaw, and he whispered, his eyes gleaming with bright desire, 'If it is only possession of your body that you say me nay, then I will wait. Whenever you want, how long you want, for whatever reason, but…' his voice lowered to a husky whisper '…if it is your love that you deny me then I will do what I have never done for anyone in my lifetime. I will beg. I will beseech and plead for your love, if that is your wish.'

'Never,' she answered, 'you have no need to.' She wriggled closer to him and reached up to touch his face with her fingers, her lips kissing the corner of his mouth. 'It is the same for me too. Since the day you so roughly pulled me off my horse and carried me across a muddy yard. Since the first moment our lips touched in a forbidden kiss.' Her fingers slid to the nape of his neck, the new growth of blond hair short and prickly to her skin, and she urged his head down to her. Their lips were only a breath away when she whispered, 'I love you, Remy St Leger, and I am yours always.' Here she shuddered, and hid her face against his neck. 'I love you so much, Remy, that it frightens me. If I were to lose you in battle, as I did before with my betrothed, I think the pain of it would kill me. I could not bear it. That is why I am so afraid to love again.'

'Oh, Beatrice, my Beatrice.' He wrapped his thick arms around her slender body and held her tightly to him, understanding her pain and her fear and yet wondering what he could do to vanquish them. Then he told her, 'Is it not better to love and be loved, and bear the burden of loss *if* it comes, than to spend the whole of your life alone and lonely?'

She sniffed and gulped, raising her face to his, nodding slowly. 'You are right, my love. Of course you are right, it is just so very hard to do.'

'You have a very deep scar, Beatrice, and you have not allowed it to heal properly. Let me love you, and heal that scar. And if I should die in battle, I know that you will always hold me in your heart. More than that no human being can ask for.'

'And,' she spoke slowly, 'will you hold me in your heart, Remy?'

'Always, and forever.' He bent his head, and kissed her with such deep passion that she knew she would never be alone again.

\* \* \* \* \*

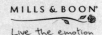

**Published 17th December 2004**

# SusanWiggs

# THE CHARM SCHOOL

From wallflower to belle of the ball...

"...an irresistible blend of *The Ugly Duckling* and *My Fair Lady*. Jump right in and enjoy yourself."—*Catherine Coulter*

*A*
# Regency
*Invitation*

## to the House Party of the Season

*Nicola Cornick, Joanna Maitland,*
*Elizabeth Rolls*

## On sale 3rd December 2004

*Available at most branches of WHSmith, Tesco, ASDA, Martins,*
*Borders, Eason, Sainsbury's and all good paperback bookshops.*

# 2 FREE

## BOOKS AND A SURPRISE GIFT!

We would like to take this opportunity to thank you for reading this Mill Boon® book by offering you the chance to take TWO more specia selected titles from the Historical Romance™ series absolutely FRE We're also making this offer to introduce you to the benefits of t Reader Service™—

- ★ **FREE home delivery**
- ★ **FREE gifts and competitions**
- ★ **FREE monthly Newsletter**
- ★ **Exclusive Reader Service offers**
- ★ **Books available before they're in the shops**

Accepting these FREE books and gift places you under no obligation buy, you may cancel at any time, even after receiving your free shipme Simply complete your details below and return the entire page to t address below. You don't even need a stamp!

**YES!** Please send me 2 free Historical Romance books and a surpri gift. I understand that unless you hear from me, I will receive superb new titles every month for just £3.59 each, postage and packi free. I am under no obligation to purchase any books and may cancel subscription at any time. The free books and gift will be mine to keep any case.

H5ZI

Ms/Mrs/Miss/Mr ................................Initials ......................

BLOCK CAPITALS PLEA

Surname ................................................................................

Address ................................................................................

................................................................................

................................................Postcode.........................

**Send this whole page to:**
**UK: FREEPOST CN81, Croydon, CR9 3WZ**

Offer valid in UK only and is not available to current Reader service subscribers to this series. Overseas an Eire please write for details. We reserve the right to refuse an application and applicants must be aged 18 years or over. Only one application per household. Terms and prices subject to change without notice. O expires 29th April 2005. As a result of this application, you may receive offers from Harlequin Mills & Boor and other carefully selected companies. If you would prefer not to share in this opportunity please write to The Data Manager, PO Box 676, Richmond, TW9 1WU.

Mills & Boon® is a registered trademark owned by Harlequin Mills & Boon Limited.
Historical Romance™ is being used as a trademark. The Reader Service™ is being used as a trademark.